Valour

Book 1

A. Calibre

Copyright © 2024 by A. Calibre

All rights reserved. No part of this book may be used or reproduced without the written consent of the copyright owner.

Valour Book 1-Paperback 1st edition

Book design by A. Calibre

Book ISBN-9798884102552

This book is dedicated to friends and family.

I won't name names in case this turns out awful and they think I'm insulting them or something.

1. Solitude

Upon its founding some hundred years ago, there was a little village in the middle of nowhere, affectionately named Solitude.

It was called this as it embodied the name perfectly. Whilst the rest of the world toiled and fought, Solitude had no problems in its isolation. Lords of the Light burned and roared, Lords of the Dark cut and whispered.

The population of 150 or so knew nothing of the clashes, barely even qualifying as a village. Their biggest problem was all the empty houses and wasted land.

Just under a third of this village was a park and inside one of the entrances to this park was a river. Hopping over this river was a young girl.

Fiery red hair flew out as she ran, leaping over upturned roots; she could not contain her joy as she danced through the air. Ruby eyes, sparkling bright, glistened in anticipation.

Little Valour had been told of a new castle being built within their woodland domain, a great building that held all the books anyone could ever read. And even though she knew to wait a while, she could not contain herself.

It did not matter that the few things her grandmother told her usually had yet to come to pass.

Through the trees she moved, over streams she jumped and into the clearing she burst with an eager smile. She gasped, smacking her cheeks with her palms, as all her expectations were surpassed.

To many, the building in the cleared-out square would be a sore sight. A half-finished wreck, even when completed it would appear as a simple obelisk, rather than a sanctuary of knowledge.

But little Valour didn't care one bit. Appearances were usually dulled, to hide the treasures within. Her grandmother had tried that trick with the cookies one too many times and she was now much wiser to her trickery.

She ran past the sign, 'DO NOT ENTER', and grinned when the only thing decorating the door was a basic book beneath a circle, all painted in silver. Nothing that said don't come in, no words she could claim ignorance of.

Pushing the wooden door open with a tiny squeal of effort, she traipsed in and spun about with stars in her eyes.

Whilst the outside was an unfinished mess, a mere skeleton, the inside—in her opinion—was absolutely glorious. The openings in the walls that had yet to hold windows shone light upon the bookcases.

Fantasy, adventure, wisdom, all symbols of these beautiful dreams were carved flamboyantly into the wood.

And in the dark corner, where lies a great cage of dark oak, two more bookcases were locked behind a chained door. Above the gleaming silver, the word 'FORBIDDEN' was darkly stamped in red paint.

She could already imagine herself sneaking in, like a spy! Or a great and dashing rogue! She giggled and swore to herself, to make it real.

And then, she ran. Not to the books where great heroes slew deadly beasts and not to the shapes wizards used to cast their spells, no. She had no interest in either of these things.

This 10-year-old child ran straight for the history books.

The books that told in vague detail the history of the war that eclipsed the world. A battle between two gods that trickled down to the mortal races.

She looked across the shelves with a furrowed brow, biting her lip to concentrate harder. She pulled a book from the shelf—the title was somewhat familiar—and started flipping the pages with a smug grin.

So enraptured, she did not hear the footsteps. She did not hear the annoyed groan. She had no choice when the man started coughing pointedly a few feet away from her.

He rolled his eyes as she yelped, jumping back and clutching at her chest.

The old man narrowed dark-blue eyes at her. He was dressed in simple clothes and wore a leather vest, held closed by silver studs. His black hair was greying, but not quite completely silver yet.

"If you're a thief, you're not a very bright one," he grumbled, further narrowing his eyes at her. "Then again, you'd have to be an idiot if you chose this place to steal from."

"U-uhm, s-sorry mister," she whimpered, her eyes tearing up from the sudden fright. "I-I just..." She weakly held up the book, showing him the cover.

"Bugger," he sighed, softening at her distress. Then, he scowled at the title she held up. "Well. What do you know about that?"

She looked confused and he winced with regret as she fidgeted nervously.

"The book," he muttered gruffly, looking away.

"L-light and the Dark. Humans picking up a flag," she said, and he hummed as her voice gained strength.

"Indeed," he murmured. Looking down at the girl, he couldn't stop the forming words from flowing. "In the beginning, there was one. And then, split down the middle, there were two. Their first clash brought forth everything else."

Little Valour just nodded along, not understanding at all. She heard his words, she was following the story, but she didn't know why he was still talking to her. Oh well, at least she wasn't being asked to leave.

"Light and Dark. The powers that exist beyond the universe, and the broken pieces that fell to our plane. Manifesting in specific aspects, taking advantage of the mortal races' most prominent traits. Unable to directly act on this world, they chose certain mortals to wage war in their name. And so, the Chosen did battle, calling upon mighty armies. Then when the Chosen fell and it became time for the next to pick up their sword, leaders became subordinates and the fight was no longer between them but the armies they once led."

He shook his head solemnly, staring through the books around them. "And thus, thousands of years' worth of battle, blood and death."

"The Ring and the Promise." He blinked, brought back to the present by her voice, and nodded.

"The Ring and the *Premise*," he corrected. "But, over thousands of years and countless victories, the Premise has grown complacent. Protected in their homeland, soldiers became scholars, the magic of battle stagnate and decline. The Silver Premise had power, but as the conflict grew easier, that power waned."

He waved his hand and a small drawing on the back of his palm lit up. Valour jumped in shock as a chair dragged across the ground for him to sit on. "H-how?"

"Magic," he grumbled. "You know their names. What do you know of them personally, little one?"

She flapped her jaw, staring at the chair in shock, looking between it and his hand. He sighed and she snapped up with a flush. "U-uhm, not much? A-all I could find before were brief spotting and some words 'they live by.'" She furrowed her brow in such an intense look of confusion, he had to chuckle.

"Ah yes," he muttered. "The words they live by. The oath. Serve the Light, destroy the Dark. Obey the Council, abandon all earthly connections to better serve the Light. When the Chosen call, you must answer the summon." He shook his head.

"But that doesn't make sense." He glanced down, surprised to see the girl looking upset. "Abandon? That's not a good word. Why would they make you leave your conn-eck-shones?"

"Connections," he murmured again for the girl, ignoring her as she moved her jaw, parroting the word with determination. "And yes. The oath is flawed, but it came from the mouth of an idiot."

"So why don't they change it?"

He furrowed his brow, glancing at her strangely. "Because no one cares, little one. And the ones that do are told not to. That's the reality. Those with power keep the rules the same, because with change always comes the possibility of losing that power."

"Oh," she murmured. "That's sad."

"Devastating," he agreed dryly. "As for those who lose faith, well. They get sent to the middle of nowhere, ordered to build a place of learning, in a village where no one can read."

"I read!"

"That you do. The majority, however, do not. I checked."

"What's a majority?"

"A large group."

"Oh."

"Since you do read, might I suggest a dictionary?"

"What's that?"

"... Never mind, I just remembered how annoying it is to mock children. Especially when they don't realise they're being mocked."

"What's mocked?"

He narrowed his eyes at her again, but aside from a nervous shift, she remained curious. "Also the fact that I can never tell if they're screwing with me."

"What's—"

"Never mind. Just..." He sighed irritably, struggling for the right words. "It all comes down to pretty words. Don't be fooled, the world isn't black and white. Nothing is purely good, just as nothing is purely evil. Everyone has their own agenda, and so long as it leads to victory, no one really cares. Even the Premise," he muttered bitterly.

"Well, I don't care about them then," she said matter-of-factly. "If they're not nice to nice people, then they're not nice."

"Again, it's a matter of agenda. Just because someone does a mean thing to nice people doesn't mean that they are mean. Maybe they are misguided, maybe they have no other choice, just keep an open mind." He sighed and leaned forwards, feeling all his years press down on his back. "On the other hand, they could most definitely be mean."

"So nice people can do mean things and mean people can do nice things?"

"Precisely." He ran a hand through his grey-striped brown hair. "Your actions do not have to define your nature, just as your nature does not have to define your actions." He glanced at her to see if she understood, and her blank face produced a laugh from him.

"By the Light, how far I have fallen," he mocked himself with a grim smile. "Debating with a child. A far cry from the scholars and warriors, but how long has it been since I spoke with someone who cared?"

He stood up suddenly, startling her. "I'll leave you with this," he told her. "There are vampires in this world. Predators. Hunters of humanity. They are spoken of as beasts of the night, animals that care for nothing but blood and the thrill of the hunt. Remorseless, merciless. And yet, I once witnessed a vampire save a man's life. I once met a vampire, a woman who cared not on who she fed, butcher another vampire because he was a merciless cretin."

He walked away, then threw over his shoulder, "In men, you will find monsters. But in monsters, you may find the noblest of men."

2. Heroes and Visions

The doors opened but the librarian didn't so much as twitch. There was only one young woman who visited outside of the regular schedule.

That's right, people who willingly enter the library are so few and far between that he was able to write up an almost completely accurate schedule.

And she proved him right; the 16-year-old woman strolled through the door. She hadn't changed much, a few inches to her height, faint definition on her arms, presumably from her job, and her attitude.

She was still annoying, but far bolder, to his dismay.

"You've already read most of these books, and know they're nothing special," he grumbled. "So why do you insist on charging through my door like this?"

"Oh come on, Bastian," Valour chuckled and then whined a little, a mocking reminder of the 10-year-old that waltzed into his library all those years ago. "Besides, it's that time of the month!"

"Ah, yes," he mused. "The new arrivals. You know where they are. With all the others the temple keeps sending me, ignoring my requests to stop."

She chuckled at his frustration. 'The temple' is the part of the Silver Premise in charge of providing resources to the various libraries and other knowledge-based facilities that bear their symbol.

"You know, if you send a request for an expansion fund, they might help you out! Who knows, they might even send you an assistant."

He threw her a sceptical glare. "Of course they won't. They sent me here because they didn't want me talking to others in the Order, that's the whole point of banishment. And I did send a request, but the reply was from Auracious Crow."

"Ooph," she hissed. She'd heard him complain about this 'Auracious' person more than enough over the years and learned a *lot* of new words to describe... not nice people.

"So, why don't we do it then?"

"Excuse me?"

"The expansion. Come on, it'll be fun! Break out a toolkit, we'll get a new wing attached in no time," she grinned.

"Are you out of your forsaken mind?" he said, staring at her in disapproval. "I am 65 years old, and you are no carpenter. Where, in the blazes, did you even get this idea?"

"From granny."

"Ah yes," he said, darkly. "I should have known. Let me guess, she had a 'vision' that you had a great time swinging a hammer around like a lunatic?"

"Pretty much. And you shouldn't doubt—"

"Oh, I don't doubt. I am well aware of that woman's ability. I am also aware of Lydia's fondness for jokes and annoying the ever-loving hell out of me." He narrowed his eyes, staring judgementally at her, "And also your fondness for going along with it."

"Good," she grinned, flashing her canines, which was another new thing, but no less annoying. "Oh, I almost forgot, she wanted me to boast on her behalf—"

Valour paused, and scowled. Tilting her head, she sniffed the air and bit back a look of disgust.

Once again, Bastian chuckled, the early-warning system prevails. Valour was a marvel, and just like him in this instance as well. She hated people, and when they approached, she reacted like this and gave him enough time to bolster himself for the unpleasantness that was interaction.

The door flung open and a man he didn't care to remember breathed in deep. "There are heroes approaching the village! One may even be a Chosen!"

"Stop!" The man's jaw clicked shut. "Why do you think I care? Why do you even think, this was important enough to come running all the way out here to tell me?"

Valour hid a smirk, and he could not blame her. Most people tended to laugh when he was annoyed, well, except for those who barge in like they own the place.

"D-Donna told me to tell everyone..."

His eye twitched. "I see. Unfortunately, I do not give a rat's arse who 'Donna' is. There are rules, you do not break. Don't run in the halls, and don't shout in the bloody library! Now take your pasty, illiterate face out the door, and only come back to tell me the world is ending, or you've finally learned how to read a word that isn't the letter 'a.'"

He paused, then glared at him. "On second thought, don't come if the world is ending. I don't want my last sight to be your waxy features. For the sake of the Light, you're not a ghoul. The sun won't set you on fire if you try to tan."

The messenger ran out, almost reduced to tears, and Valour laughed.

"You didn't have to be so mean," she half-heartedly chided. "But a Chosen? What do you think about that?"

"Foolish gossip. A fantasy. The Chosen do not come to this island; they know better. Probably just the next in line to beat some villain or beast."

"Fair enough, but why would they come *here*?"

He sighed. "Yes, I wonder. There is nothing special about this place. Your only claim to fame would be how clean your river is, the particularly pretty shades of leaves or!" He stared at her like she was dumb. "One of the eldest seers alive, that we know of."

"Granny?" She frowned.

"Indeed. Last I heard from the merchants, the Royal City's last seer just fell into madness." He scratched his chin as he thought, "I think that makes her the eldest known right now…"

Valour spun around to leave, "Sorry for the quick exit, but if some strangers are coming for granny, I need to be there to back her up."

He waited until she was at the door before he shouted, "Be careful! If they are indeed heroes, then keep one eye on the door. People like that only come for terrible things, and don't always leave peace in their wake."

She threw a thumbs up over her shoulder and sprinted through the door. He shook his head in disbelief, "Not even a thank you. Kids, really bloody disrespectful, especially that one," he muttered.

***

"Huh," Valour mumbled as she cut through an alley off the main street. "So everyone just turned up? That's annoying," she sighed.

The street was completely blocked, with a small wave through the crowd as they let the newcomers through.

Valour just shook her head and felt the weight drop off her shoulders the closer she got to home. She lived in a comfortable neighbourhood; her house was small and away from pretty much everything.

There was no one living within a ten-house radius and it was amazing.

The house itself was pretty plain. It had never been painted or decorated, except for a strange pretty rope that was saved for that one festival. Of course, it was only done under duress, peer pressure and because Bastian wanted to annoy her grandmother.

She hopped over the first stone, barely visible from the overgrown grass, and strode down the path.

She sniffed the air, cocked her head, but there were no new scents or sounds. She sighed in relief and then opened the door with a smile. She opened her mouth to yell a greeting and got beaned in the head by a sack filled with metal cutlery.

"Ouch."

"Oh, oops! Sorry dear, thought you might be Derry!" her grandmother smiled bashfully, hurrying to pick up the sack. "Were you doing your bloodhound thing again? If you're not careful, you might sniff something up one of these days!"

"Please don't change the subject like that," Valour grimaced, scratching her nose. "Why would you... wait, what are you wearing?"

"Who knows. I had to dig through the attic to find it though. What do you think?"

She spun in a slow circle, billowing the bottom of the brown robe. A lock of silver hair fell from her tight bun and into her eye, and she started blowing it away.

Valour shook her head and glanced at her outfit again. A dark-brown robe, a necklace of pearls that looked expensive but was really painted pebbles and no shoes. The last bit was, surprisingly, the only part that didn't make sense.

"Uh, do you have a date or something?" she cringed sympathetically as her granny hissed, grabbed the hair and *yanked*. When her sight was clear, the woman beamed.

"Of course not, don't be silly," she chided. "I had a vision, and if I didn't wear something like this, I wasn't going to be taken seriously. That or I was gonna fall over and brain myself on the door, and I didn't want that, obviously."

"Obviously," Valour agreed with a wry smile. "You look nice."

"Oh, really?" she sighed despairingly. "I was going for pretentious prick, that's why I copied Bastian."

"Bastian wears shoes, granny."

"Does he? Oh, I just assumed he had poor hygiene." She glanced around and then leaned in close to whisper, "You know, because of his face?" She shot back, cackling madly.

Valour bit back a laugh. "So, what are you going to say to these 'heroes' when they get here?"

"All depends on them, dear, and the questions they ask." She frowned, looking off to the side, "And who actually shows up of course."

"Well, the moment is coming." Valour frowned. There were footsteps coming through the open window. They were still a way off but were approaching quickly.

"Go on, dear, we still have five minutes. If the bald one doesn't have tea, he'll open his mouth and annoy the girl. If that happens, they'll wreck the house." Valour's eyes flickered. "But we can avoid hostilities with some tea. Hurry along now, dear!"

She frowned and pouted as she walked into the kitchen. She swiped her granny's weapon from her and emptied the knives and forks back into the drawer. There was a distinct lack of shiny objects, of shiny anything.

Granted, it was her fault, she had a... *thing* for the shiny stuff. Like a cat with that one plant, she was happy and blissful, and then when someone tried to take it, she bit them.

Needless to say, what cutlery they had was dulled and jewellery was hidden away.

The door swung open and her granny greeted the five people standing at the door. "People's footsteps should *not* be capable of driving me to murder," she sighed.

She set the cups on a tray and put one of their water bottles under her arm and held a wine bottle between her fingers.

"Are you here about Hardam?" her granny asked, speaking in her 'mysterious voice,' the one she used when spouting off random nonsense.

Being a seer, and having people know about it, could get very annoying very quickly. And so the 'apocalypse solution' was born. Basically, if you don't bugger off, you'll die. Or some variation of.

"Fear not! You have two winters, and then the traitor shall tear down the Royal City, and the scarred lady shall drown the fields of Hardam in a sea of black dragon fire!"

Not the funniest, but it would normally do. Unfortunately, this was neither the place nor the time.

"Granny, the battle at Hardam already happened." She walked in with a regretful sigh that fooled everyone somehow. She put the tray on the little table in front of her chair, gave the wine to her granny and filled up the cups with water.

"It has?" The woman stared at her, eyes fogging up in genuine disappointment.

"Yeah, 500 years ago." She smiled, sitting in her chair by the unlit fireplace. "But for curiosity's sake, was the fire black or were the dragons?"

The 60-year-old woman huffed like a child and fell back in her chair. "The fire was black; the dragons were made of dark magic. It looked bloody awesome. Damn it, it's always the cool ones that'll never happen."

One of the heroes grumbled beneath his breath and Valour bit back the urge to snarl. Granny just smiled at her gently, easily ignoring him.

For so-called heroes, she thought they'd at least be memorable. Bright and noble clothing, golden swords and the like, but no. They were dressed in simple leather armour. Granted, it smelled nice, like lavender soap, but it was hardly a striking image.

The grumbly man, tall and bald, didn't like being ignored. "If you were a real seer, why didn't you have chairs set out, ready for the rest of us?" he demanded, acting as though it were a really well thought out question.

"Why in the hell would I do that?" granny asked him, baffled. "You're all here for less than half an hour, then *we're* stuck with five chairs we've wasted money on and will never use again."

The black-haired woman subtly stepped on his toes, "What my companion means, is that it's hard to believe in a power as great as yours. We know it's hard to provide proof of such a gift, but we must ask anyway."

Granny sighed deeply, sat back and locked her fingers together. "Fine, fine. What do you want to know?"

"Why did we come here?"

"Well, if you don't know the answer to that question, the world is quite screwed," she chuckled.

The two cloaked teenagers behind the group giggled to each other, then the one on the left spoke out. "We know, we know. But do you? Our journey is a secret. Only someone who knew before we did would know."

"Ah yes." She lazily scratched her chin. "Unfortunately, there are over a thousand different reasons you could be here, not limited to one of you falling in a toilet and needing new trousers. Why you came here? Well, you'd know that better than I."

Their leader, a blond man with icy brown eyes, leaned forwards. "Thousands? I had heard that time is infinite. Surely there would be more than that?"

She blinked and only Valour noticed the flicker of irritation that passed for a second over her face.

"Timelines die and are born every second, this is true, and is what makes people think like you. But time is not everlasting. Every action, every thought, every month, year and day, all leads to the end. The moment when every vision ends. Is that proof enough?"

"It is indeed," he nodded, smiling with satisfaction. "I request knowledge about the Dark Lord."

"Which one?" There were shocked murmurs and uneasy looks, but granny just chuckled. "Come now, what did I say not even a minute ago? Multiple timelines. I need a bit more to go on than 'Dark Lord.'"

"He is stealing human souls and preparing a great ritual of some kind," the black-haired woman explained.

Granny snapped her fingers, "Aha! I recognise this one, Gregory. Give me just a moment dears, I'll need to focus this next part." Her body relaxed as her gaze narrowed, the colour in her eyes darkening.

At the back of the group, the twins were trying not to choke on their laughter. "The Dark Lord Malfeasance's real name is *Gregory*?" they snickered.

"I don't know." The woman smiled, "Gregory the Soul Snatcher has a ring to it." Her smile turned into a smirk as they broke, collapsing with giggles.

Granny gasped loudly and Valour was at her side with one of the cups of water. She waved her off with a grateful smile. "He is in an ocean base, guarded by a hydra. To defeat him, you will need a gold dagger with a blue stone on it. To get past the sea beast, you'll want a big blue ship with a hawk figurehead. Understand?"

The group started chattering excitedly amongst themselves, ignorant to the dread on the blond man's face. "Ah, yes. We are familiar with these things." He stood abruptly. "Thank you for your assistance. We must hurry if we are to stop him." He bowed his head and marched out of the door.

His companions looked after him, confused, but thanked her and quickly followed him.

"That dagger. It isn't good, is it?"

"No," she sighed deeply, anguish bleeding out of her. "Gregory did something to himself. Spat in the face of magic, bound his soul. The dagger uses the soul of the wielder to break the chains. The tall gentleman will die getting them past the hydra. The young lady will free the captured souls, but end up in despair and blame the King, who gave them their quest. She will kill him and then go into hiding. The twins will be hired to find her, but when they do, they will tell no one. They will not be seen again."

Valour said nothing, kneeling down beside her and holding her hand as she stared into space.

"If I didn't tell them this, they all survived," she said, eerily detached. "But Gregory finished his plan, corrupting a lot of people. Then, a force from across the ocean arrives to extinguish the darkness. I sent two people to their deaths and ensured the death of a third, to save the lives of 300,000 others. It was the lesser evil."

"It was the right thing to do," Valour murmured, then grimaced at the lack of conviction she felt in herself and her voice.

"It wasn't," granny whispered.

"No. But when you're given two terrible choices and trying to do more would just end up hurting everyone, you have to accept it and resign yourself to whatever comes next."

Granny squeezed her hand and Valour bowed her head, ashamed she could do nothing else, as her grandmother mourned the lives she changed and ended.

3. The End of the World

Two men walked into a bar on a Monday.

The owner of the building was the thin reedy man, with the windswept brown hair. Everything about him was soft, subtle, unassuming. And yet, he was betrayed by the hatred that turned his grey eyes to stone whenever another person crossed his sight.

The other man was the opposite to the man dressed as a bartender. Long black hair tied back, he had a warm smile and his blue eyes twinkled with amusement when his companion glared at him. He wore a crimson half robe and baggy black trousers, dressed like a holy man when he was anything but.

"Five years and the first thing you do is demand to come inside." The owner grinned sharply, shaking his head. "How unlike you."

The blue-eyed man just smiled, staring into space wistfully.

"Seren? You alright there?" He waved his hand in front of the man's eyes. "So, the meditation's finally bleached your brain? Such a shame, always hoped I'd be the one to 'mess you up,' but the magic got there first."

"Your tongue runs quicker than your mind, though I can't say this is dissimilar." He rolled his eyes. "My mind is fine, I am merely reminiscing."

Savage strutted over to the bar and hopped up. "Reminiscing about what? All the pretty grey stone? I know prison's supposed to be boring, but really, I didn't think you'd be broken enough to actually *miss* the dull and bland."

"As I have told you many times before," he sighed as the other man flicked his legs up to roll over the bar and land on the other side smoothly with a small hiss of victory. "That place, it is one of the strongest places of power upon neutral ground. My visions have never been clearer."

Savage hummed, eyeing him disdainfully as he practically radiated joy. He picked up a clean glass and started scrubbing it with the towel by the cleaning bowl. "A place like that, in a land where the Ring and Premise hold little sway," he snorted. "Ironic."

"My friend." Savage paused his cleaning to stare at him in bafflement. Friend? News to him. "I need your help."

"Obviously," he murmured, cautiously replacing the glass with a knife. "I'll hear your words."

"The last vision I ever had, alas, my strongest, I saw it. The end of the world."

Savage hummed. From anyone else, he'd laugh and call it lunacy, then kick them out deeming them not sane enough for him to *interact* with. "So, you want me to help you, what... stop it?"

"Of course not!" he denied vehemently. "Imagine. A world cleansed of all the taint. No more Light, no more Dark, no more magic." He paused and smiled at him knowingly. "No more living."

Savage licked his suddenly very dry lips. "That does sound..."

"Exquisite?"

"Tempting."

"Indeed. I saw this only once and knew that I must do anything I could to see it one more time."

"So what do you need from me?"

Savage smirked as the first scowl darkened the usually calm man's face. "My power was damaged. Cursed place blessed me, and then stole most of my 'sight.' Now I must work blind. I have an idea, to set the Light against the Dark."

Savage huffed, disappointed. The idea was good and yet far overdone. So far, that many actually found it tedious, rather than threatening.

"It took me all of five seconds to come up with my own plan. You ready?" he chuckled. "Start a rumour. They'll take any reason to have a go at each other."

"Nothing quite that inelegant," he scolded. "I have other plans of course, but they have yet to bear fruit. For example, my efforts to break the Treaty of Resolute."

Savage placed the glass carefully on the side and braced both hands against the wood. "I was about to ask if you were insane, trying to get everyone killed." His breath quickened, his eyes started turning bloodshot and his grin tore at his cheeks. "And then I remembered..."

Seren raised his hand in a mock toast.

"That is precisely the point."

4. The Fire

Valour released her breath as the tree fell. She placed her axe in the holster on her back and stepped away as it hit the ground with a thump.

It had been three days since the 'heroes' had left and things quickly returned to normal. Her neighbours were still annoying, no matter how far away they were, and her job was still interesting enough to get her through the day, until she could go to the library.

She patted the tree with a silly smirk. The thing was twice her height and width; the carpenters would have no reason to complain.

She bent her knees, gripped it and, with her fingers breaking through the bark like paper, she swung it off the ground and over her shoulder.

Without a pause to breathe, she started the five-minute trek back to the village, where she'd drop this one off and either go looking for another or some stone for the stonemasons.

She had always been stronger than normal. People had claimed it to be magic, but she wasn't so sure. She'd never been able to throw light at something nor was she able to "invoke the runic languages," as Bastian once taught her.

Of course, once people learned she couldn't do any of the special sparkly stuff, they quickly lost interest. Any potential friends turned their backs, and she grew a little bitter towards it honestly.

She put the tree down in the little storage garden behind the carpenter's office and a man came out to talk to her. As she was collecting payment for the tree, the wind carried in a strange smell.

"Smoke?" She glanced up at the sky, the clouds were covering the sun and the day was quite chilly. The man coughed lightly and she glanced quickly back down at him.

"Sorry." Her apologetic smile was more of a grimace. "Just wondering who would cook outside on a day like this."

He looked at her weirdly after sniffing the air. "Can't smell anything," he said gruffly. He tossed her a small sack and went back inside without a word of farewell.

"How polite," she muttered.

She sniffed the air again, curious. "Smoke, but no food?" She shook her head and started walking back out to the forest.

She stepped to the side early, barely two minutes on her walk back, and a group of people soon came screaming past. The smoke smell was faint on them and they didn't look like arsonists. She glanced the way they came, spotting the smoke now rising in the air, and her heart dropped.

"Home." She started sprinting.

She bit back a growl. It wasn't just her home that was burning but the two houses surrounding it as well. She charged the charred mess that used to be the door, which splintered beneath her shoulder, and she ran in.

Her vision was wavy and filled with tears and smoke and ash. The floor creaked ominously beneath a timid step and, with a crash, something near the back of the house collapsed.

"Granny?!" she screamed.

No response.

She crept to the door to the kitchen but, as she opened it, the ceiling fell down with a groan. She coughed on the billowing smoke and backed off. She didn't hear any sounds of pain or something being crushed, so thankfully she wasn't there.

She closed her eyes and inhaled deeply, her face twisting in pain as the ash and smoke filled her lungs. But so did the smells. She blinked her eyes open, the sharp glow cutting through the haze, and felt her perspective shift as she searched the room.

The chair, her grandmother's favourite chair, was burned and smashed. She glared at it, smashed and *then* burned, she corrected. There were five scents she was able to separate. Five that shouldn't be there, five that she'd never come across before.

They left a trail.

She ran out of the house, ignoring the crash behind, ignoring the gathering crowds, and sprinted through the streets.

Down the main street, past the turning into the park and out through the village gate. She skidded to a stop; a new group of scents hit her all at once. Her grandmother's scent met the newcomers for a moment and then split off to the side while the new scents doubled back on themselves.

Off to the side, through a small patch of trees, she ran through and burst into a clearing, scaring everyone into action.

"I am truly sorry," her grandmother sighed mournfully. "But visions can only truly be changed if people are willing to change their actions." She spoke to the man holding the end of the rope that bound her wrists.

She patted his shoulder comfortingly. "Fear not, you won't die. It's just going to hurt a fair bit."

There were five of them. Three in plain sight, two were up in the trees, hiding their bodies but not their scents or sounds.

"Be careful!" one of them yelled back as he advanced. "This thing's not human."

Her smile cut her lip. Her teeth sharpened as her eyes glowed. How rude.

She snatched an arrow out of the air, her arm blurring without thought, and the branch exploded beneath the archer. He yelped, hitting the ground with a cry.

Her body twisted as a sword swung for her. She caught his shoulder and kicked out at his leg, but he threw himself into a roll. His shirt's shoulder ripped and she was left with a scrap of cloth as his two friends leapt at her with swords drawn.

Her grandmother winced, covering her eyes as Valour jumped forwards, swinging wide haymakers with both arms. Her strikes were ducked but she ignored them as she ran for the grounded archer.

She barely had to move, the hasty arrow whipped over her shoulder, and she slammed into him. Another arrow sprouted from her shoulder and she growled in pain. She tore the archer from the floor and spun them both around in time for another arrow to pierce his back.

She gripped his shoulder and his leg, *lifted* him off the ground and threw him at the archer's tree. He crashed *through* it and the archer screamed as his perch tumbled down.

Her success made her grin, then she hissed as a sword cut her hip. She lashed out, punching at the aggressor, a blond man. She barely clipped him with her knuckles but he howled as his arm dislocated with a loud crack and he dropped his sword.

The other two, both brown-haired men, came at her and she caught their wrists as they both swung high downward slashes at her. The air shifted behind her but all she could do was grit her teeth as the arrow in her shoulder was harshly torn out.

She pushed forwards and overpowered both, knocking them away and kicking backwards with her left foot, smacking the blond man across the clearing. He landed with a cry, gasping for air.

"Valour!" her grandmother called out, still covering her eyes. "This must end soon! The others are on their way and if you're still fighting when they get here, they'll join in!"

She gritted her teeth. Enhanced strength and speed could only compensate for so much, a swarm when she barely knows how to fight?

As the two men stepped forwards, she stepped in. They swung their blades and she fell to her knees. Their blades collided above her head and she swung out with both fists, slamming into their guts.

Her ear twitched and she grabbed the attacker on her left, swinging him around and shielding herself from the two flying arrows. She advanced quickly, holding him out before her, then threw him forwards.

He knocked the two archers down and she lunged forwards, punching them both in the face and knocking them out.

She stood up and scanned the clearing. All the kidnappers were down, but one of them stirred and she growled.

"They're done, Valour." Her Grandmother stepped in front of her, hands raised and a pleasant smile on her face. "You won. It's over."

She wasn't so sure, but as she looked around again, all of them were down and didn't look to be getting back up, she had to concede. Her eyes lost their glow and she gasped.

"Granny!" She picked up one of the swords and cut through her bonds, pulling her into a hug. "Are you okay?! I was so worried when I saw the house!" She blinked away the tears.

"Yes dear, and I'm glad you're safe too." She wiped the blood away from Valour's shoulder, frowning sadly at the wound. "But we do need to go. Just as soon as I..." She hurried over to the blond man.

"Uh, granny?" She shuffled nervously, and in no small amount of pain, as the woman rifled through the unconscious man's pockets, pulling out a folded piece of paper with a grin.

"Not now dear, we really must be going."

"But what about..." She gestured to the bodies lying around the ground.

"Oh, they're quite dead, don't worry about that."

"Wait, what?! I didn't hit them that hard, what's...?!"

Granny watched her freak out, smiling sympathetically, then chuckling in amusement as her granddaughter ran over to check the pulse of the man she kicked.

"You didn't kill them dear, have no fear. Their employer will, once he finds out they failed. We need to go."

She took off towards the village, leaving Valour to follow, after a short, mournful glance at the others.

"Granny, the house is... where are we going to go?"

"Three times," she simply muttered. "Three visions, not a single change in dialogue. Sometimes, I believe the visions are just there to irritate me. If you must know, we're heading to the Pretentious Palace."

Valour almost felt the urge to chuckle, but the fallen bodies behind were a killer of joy. "You know, you could just call it the library."

"I could, but then it would be lying. As if any place *he* resides could be an institute of learning."

***

The door clicked open. They took only three steps in before there was a loud thud and they heard a deep, tortured sigh. Bastian rounded the corner with a bitter scowl.

"I thought there was a hint of sulphur on the air," he said. "Why are you here? Shouldn't you be out robbing some innocent fool of their soul?"

"Delightful," granny drawled. "The former Silver Premise soldier accusing an innocent woman of consorting with demons. Will the hypocrisy never end?"

"The outer realms are not demonic, and I was, and am, a medical practitioner. Also, innocent? Far be it for one to accuse the cheater of being irreproachable."

"For the last time, I did not cheat. You and those other witless dolts are just terrible at poker."

Valour dragged the chair by the door, not even having to look for it any more. She had brought it a couple of years back, after she noticed a pattern developing. The insults would start flying, comments would be made about skill or lack thereof and she'd just stand there staring awkwardly.

Now she could sit and stare. Far less awkward.

"Not that you darkening my doors is *anything* but the utmost pleasure," Bastian blatantly lied, "but what the hell are you doing here?"

"Delightful," she sniffed. "As always, your hospitality is unrivalled. Earlier, I was kidnapped by five unknown gentlemen and interacted with five more outside the village.

He paused and looked over to Valour, who was absentmindedly picking at the dried blood on her shoulder. Beneath, a pink mark was all that remained where the arrow had pierced her skin.

"Oh. Very well then." He turned away.

"Seriously? That's *all* you have to say?"

He shrugged, "What else is there? You were kidnapped, you're here, so you obviously got rescued. You're here, so you obviously didn't need a hospital." He shrugged again. "What does the great seer need from me, that her visions could not show her how to accomplish herself?"

"You know it doesn't work that way. The visions are random. Sometimes they aren't even about *this* time. I could force one, but that'll leave me with a blinding headache, and at my age? Might actually kill me. Earlier today, I had three different visions of the same conversation, and the only difference was Valour twitched her thumb instead of her pinkie."

"I can confirm," Valour added. "She talked about this earlier."

"Alright, fine." He slumped. "What do you want from me?"

She smirked victoriously and handed him the folded paper she took from the blond man. "I don't know what that is, only that it's important."

He frowned. After a single glance, he started mumbling. "Obviously coded. Never seen this type of cipher, but… oh." He showed them a wax seal at the bottom, the word 'Sage' beneath a bear face.

"That looks familiar." Valour frowned. "Where have I… wait, didn't you tell me about this once?"

"Well remembered," he smiled encouragingly. "This sigil was used exclusively by a mercenary guild, started 15 years ago. Five years after, they hit a rough patch and were decimated by a rival. They became a small-time gang in Senway."

"So why would a gang want to kidnap granny?"

"Wrong question." Bastian leaned back, staring thoughtfully at them. "Why do they want a seer?"

"What everyone wants," granny huffed. "To see the future. What is the group called?"

"The Wise Bears company." Granny's breath hitched and Valour caught her as she flinched back like she was struck.

"That sounds ridiculous!" she chuckled, guiding granny into her chair. "Wise Bears? Come on!"

"Indeed," Bastian smirked. He walked back around the corner, speaking loudly over his shoulder. "Quite formidable they may have been, but now they are a shadow of their former selves. Small jobs, quite unlike this one."

Valour frowned, her granny glaring at the air, the colour in her eyes starting to blur. Her face was turning a deep shade of red and a vein was starting to pulse on her forehead.

Bastian returned with a cup of water cradled in both hands. "Oh dear," he grimaced. He gripped her chin and tilted her head back, and she didn't react.

Normally, if anyone entered her personal space like Bastian just did, she would have swung for them and had a few choice words to say about their upbringing. That she did neither worried them both far more than they already were.

"Not much choice," Bastian sighed. And then, in a brief moment of levity, he grinned and threw the cold water in her face.

Granny flailed back with a startled scream, tilting the chair back into Valour, who caught it with an "Oomph!"

"What the hell is the matter with you?!"

"You're welcome," he smirked. "Now, what was so important, that you did the one thing that you quite literally just warned us about?"

"Don't patronise me, troglodyte." She wiped some water from her face and flicked it at him. "I saw Valour in a warehouse in Senway." She bit her tongue, frustrated.

His humour faded, "Oh dear. But why would she…" He paused and raised a brow at Valour. "Why would you go there? I never took you for the vengeful type."

She shrugged helplessly. "I have no idea what possible future me is thinking."

He stared her down and shook his head. "You're a terrible liar."

Valour shrugged, long having accepted this fact. She did have an idea. These people came after her grandmother, attacked her family and trespassed in her home. And more might be sent soon.

"If the seer sees you in that place, our efforts to keep you away clearly fail." She didn't blink and just like she thought, "so instead, we shall tell you all of the reasons why this is a terrible idea."

Joy.

***

After the dressing down of a century, she left.

It's hard to explain, especially when you think differently from the person you were speaking with. But someone walking into your village, breaking into your territory and assaulting your family?

Some things are universal.

Valour was not one for travelling. She had never been further than where she rescued her granny. But when something stronger than instinct was screaming at you? Sacrifices are made.

And she gave gladly. An attack would not go unanswered and her retaliation would be swift and brutal. There would be no room for a second strike to pass through their minds.

She was angry. And when the fire consumed her, she was not the only thing that burned.

***

She recalled everything Bastian told her as she approached the city.

Senway, the 'Throw Away City.' A prototype, a test run for something greater. And when it was abandoned? The 'rabble' moved in.

At first, many years ago, the Ring occupied it as a foothold in the island of Brinia. The two armies weren't actually present on the island today but in continents and other islands to the west.

Back then, Senway was apparently the Dark's attempt at a subtle invasion, but the Light informed the King and he sent his army to kick them out. 'Unfortunately,' the Silver Premise declared Senway 'tainted' and so the King washed his hands of it.

Eventually, people migrated there, set up shops and made it a fully functional city. It also became a hub for mercenary groups and a networker's greatest dream.

There were no walls and no guards to keep anyone out. The mercenaries themselves dealt with anyone wanting to start problems, declaring the city a safe zone. Anyone wanting to cause trouble was quickly taught their place.

Valour walked straight in and headed east. Bastian's map wasn't the clearest. He was mostly going off of memory and rumour, but hopefully this was still the safest route to the warehouses.

As her granny had once told her, visions are not absolute. She could have one, then another that contradicted it right away, simply because someone decided to do something else. The web of fate, unspun by a human's flight of fancy.

And then Bastian thankfully simplified it for her. Basically, she may not even make it to the warehouse if someone else decides to... knock her off course a bit. And even if she does, she may be injured if someone decides to attack her, even though her granny had seen her unharmed.

In her granny's own words, "It's an unreliable gift, depending on circumstances. But it's better to have information than not."

The street where the buildings were located was as clean as it could be. She didn't think a bunch of sell swords would care all that much about hygiene, but she was pleasantly surprised.

However, she became confused, both irritating and worrying her, as she looked both ways and discovered that all the buildings looked the same.

And then, her saving grace. A familiar scent caught her attention, familiar, in a place no one she knows has been recently.

She followed the trail to the sixth building on her right and tried the door. It was locked, but she just smirked. She held out her arm and poked the lock. With a pop and a screech, a hole replaced the metal.

She chuckled. Walking casually inside, she blew imaginary smoke off her finger and froze.

The scene before her was captivating, a fight so vicious she was appalled and confused that she wasn't able to hear it from outside, and then distantly realised she still couldn't. But that wasn't important right now.

She was... magnificent, to say the least. The way she moved, she practically danced around the room.

Blood flew, the seven men and women that fought her stood no chance. She spun around their blows, feinting towards one only to slip past the guard of another.

It was... enthralling.

***

Bastian hid his face behind his cards. Whenever Lydia started cackling for no apparent reason, it was always to the detriment of someone else. Usually him. He peeked at her as she started scribbling on a scrap of paper. So maybe not him then?

When she was done, she read back over what she had written, then threw it into the centre of the table, on top of the green and red cardboard coins.

"That right there is worth fifty."

"No way in hell," he snarked, but his curiosity was piqued.

She grinned as he kept pulling his gaze away from it. "And. It's about Valour."

Called it. He grimaced, weighing the idea in his mind. "How funny?"

She laughed so hard it came out as a bark. "Oh, you sod. It keeps getting better and better."

5. A Dance of Blades

Fifteen minutes earlier...

Vivian El Lock, heiress of the noble house of El Lock, was angry. Vivian was also mourning. Her dear friend Lucas had told her of a 'gig' in Senway that would, in his own words, "Set me up for life!"

She had tried to sway his mind, explained the dangers both within and in the surrounding areas of the city. But he was stubborn and always so foolish when it came to his plots.

She had always said it would be his death, but always in jest. Always prayed it would remain a joke. But the caravan he travelled with returned without him. Bandits, they had claimed. Lies, she had spat in their faces.

They were unharmed and retained all of their possessions. Eventually, the group had admitted that another had accosted them, claiming one unknown to be a seer.

Lucas had taken the fall for a terrified 10-year-old boy, stepped forwards and boldly declared himself the seer. It was foolish, brave and kind-hearted. The group questioned him but he refused to tell them anything unless they let the others go.

One of them had looked back and he told her of the confusion, the frustration and the moment when one of them had drawn his sword and struck Lucas down.

Upon hearing this, in a fit of grief and rage, she took up her armour and sword, saddled her horse and left her father and stepmother behind, ignoring their pleas and worries.

She arrived at Senway two days later. The trek was long from her countryside complex and when she arrived her temper had cooled. But she sharpened herself, stabled her horse and entered the city proper.

Her first instinct was to go to a bar and ask around, but she had heard stories of this place and knew better than to ask direct questions.

So she spoke to the tender and asked about hiring opportunities. The gruff man looked at her, this golden-haired woman, glaring at him with steel-grey eyes, noted her light armour and rapier-like sword and immediately told her about the so called 'Wise Bears.'

He said they were looking for extra hands to pull off a huge job. A few minutes and a few drinks later, he told her about the warehouse they owned where they planned out all their jobs.

She thanked him and, after one last drink, left. She didn't know if they were the ones who killed her friend, but mercenary groups always had an ear to the ground about competition.

She broke in through the back door, sliding her blade through the lock. There were filing cabinets lining the walls, drawers had names on them, too ridiculous to be anything except operation names. And then, dead centre in the room, there was a large board twice her size with multiple pieces of paper pinned to it.

They were drawings of different people, vague outlines, you could barely tell if they were even human let alone identify them by eye. However, there were dates and locations written on the bottom of each page.

Frosthelm, the Broken Horse, seventh day of the third season.

Silvy, the red-brick house, twentieth day of the third season.

Solitude, the lone house, thirtieth day of the third season.

And the one that choked her up.

Senway, the main road, thirty-first day of the third season.

Glancing around, she was the only one inside. No one there to take her anger. She picked up a folder off the floor in front of the board, but there was nothing of value to her. She tossed it aside, the crossed-out pictures fluttering to the floor.

There were sounds coming from the door she came in, warnings and panic, and she smiled. Perfect.

They ran in with weapons drawn and she turned to greet them with a smile. Four female, four male. All wearing leather armour, uniformed, fashion over function. Three of them gripped their hilts too tight and in the wrong place.

One of them, the leader she assumed, was the only one on guard. He had no chest piece, just a sleeveless shirt. She spotted some scars on his off-hand, a strong offense and a weak defence?

"You picked the wrong party to crash, lady," one of them called out with a smirk. Her sword wavered and she shifted her grip. A bead of sweat rolled down the hilt, her body betraying her nerves.

Vivian ignored her, staring only at the leader. "Two days ago, you or your people attacked a caravan. You murdered an innocent man. What do you have to say for yourselves?"

"Do you have any proof?" he snarked. His minions chuckled and grinned, as if watching some basic comedy. The leader glanced past her for a moment and she smiled coldly when she next caught his eye.

"You sent a group of armed thugs to attack innocent civilians. You were looking for a seer, but by the courage of a merchant, you lost him." The laughter stopped almost immediately. They traded nervous glances and the leader scowled.

"I see," he grimaced. "Unfortunately, that means I must inform my employer. He will not be too happy about that. Handle her." He ordered his group and turned away, sheathing his sword.

"Running away?" Vivian hissed, stepping after him. "What's the hurry? Your boss isn't going anywhere, but if you'd like to see him, I'd be happy to escort you." She drew her blade slowly, looking each of them in the eye. "After I'm done with them, anyway."

One of the men, blue-haired and the smallest limp in his left leg, stepped in front of him, blocking her view. "Sorry girly, but boss said he's busy. You get to deal with us."

"And what an intellectually stimulating fight this shall be," she flung instinctively.

"What, you think this'll be a fight?" he laughed, the insult flying a mile over his head. "Seven on one and you expect us to fight you?" he cackled.

"I expect you to try," she drawled out. "I expect you all to fail." She turned to the leader, who was annoyingly one foot out of the door.

"Come on, you were man enough to order your gang to kill a child and his civilian companions, so why not come face me?"

He glanced over his shoulder, a wide smirk on his face. "Nice try." The door slammed shut behind him and she ground her teeth.

"Well, well, boss is gone. So how about you pay attention to the real danger in the room?" he cawed, swaggering forwards with his blade pointed towards her.

"As you wish." In a drilled instinct, she raised her blade in a fencer's salute. "I'm in a hurry, so if you will. Match your blade with mine, and let us see who stands in the end."

He paused, looking very taken aback. "Was... was that a catchphrase?"

He yelped as Vivian's sword was parried an inch away from his face and one of his friends shouted at him angrily.

"Pay attention!" before launching herself at the armoured woman, swinging her sword.

They were sloppy. Uncoordinated, unskilled, their blows lacked strength and they worked together as well as a herd of blind antelopes in a stampede. It was drilled into her head early on that, when in a fight with multiple foes, you must keep moving. Never allow yourself to be surrounded.

And so she began the dance.

She spun as she caught a blade on her own, throwing it at another. Completing her spin, she knocked away another blade and twirled again as another lunged for her.

She spun circles around her opponents and so allowed her pride to flare, showmanship not usually allowed by her strict teachers.

She flourished her blade, catching the tip of a sword and spinning it in a wide arc, for no reason at all. Two of them rushed her and bumped into each other. They hesitated and she slammed into them. A cut and a punch, and they both fell down.

She spun once more, avoiding a blow and smacking the throat of someone to her left. As she thought, none of the group cared when their own were knocked out. She smirked as the blue-haired man with the limp leapt at her.

She stepped forwards, aiming her blade so that, when she thrust, his own would be knocked aside and she'd be safe to spin again. Only, something inconceivable happened. Something she did not see coming, though she really should have, something her teachers had yelled about time and again.

She lost track of her surroundings. She stepped in a puddle of blood and slipped.

She did not stumble more than a fraction of an inch but her arm trembled. The blue-haired man's sword pierced through her armour and slotted into her heart. She gasped flecks of blood and spittle, staring numbly at the sword.

She dragged her gaze up with the last of her strength and glared at him, embarrassment and shame the last things on her mind.

"Ha… haha!" The blue-haired man pounded the air in triumph, both fists raised. "I think that there deserves a promotion!"

One of the others whacked him upside the head, ignoring his whine, "You think you get a promotion because you killed someone? Buddy, if that was the only requirement, the Wise Bears would be all bosses and no plebs like you."

They laughed and jeered, slapping shoulders and walking away, ignorant in their victory. Ignorant of two frightening facts. One, the body was still standing. Two, a golden light was searing the wound shut.

Too busy with their laughs and cheers, they didn't see her pale skin regaining colour. They didn't see her pulse beating in her neck as her heart restarted. They didn't see the shame and fury in her eyes as the fog lifted and her teeth bared.

Her sword ripped through them like paper, all twirls and flourishes abandoned as she ploughed through them, a wild bull seen red. The blue-haired man was the last standing and he trembled at her approach.

"You killed me once. Care to test your luck once more?"

He jumped forwards again, desperate, and with her feet planted on solid, dry ground, she thrust ahead. His blade pinged off to the side and her own stabbed into his chest, poking a hole in his heart.

"The debt is repaid. A heart for a heart, a life for a life." He slid off her sword and she swiped it through the air, flinging the loose blood and wiping the remnants on his shirt.

She set off towards the door purposefully and, as she was sheathing her blade, *sreee!* She slipped again. She squealed and resigned herself to another death by cracked skull.

But someone caught her.

She hissed, shock knocking the breath from her body, staring up into red eyes, a strand of crimson tickled her cheek.

"H—*ahem* Hello there." The woman grinned lopsidedly, cringing at her own stutter.

"... Hi" was all she could say back.

6. A Wishful Man

Twentieth day of Fall.

Two days south of Senway, there was a trading village by the name of Silvy. It was a pleasant little area, but known for being quite average. The houses, the people, even the visitors, they were all content with the label.

The only reason anyone took note of a place like this was the items brought along. Of course, there were the usual things, foods, bits of jewellery, but occasionally there were the odd shiny and interesting little knick-knacks.

And yet, in this stellar example of human normalcy, two would-be kidnappers gathered before a burning building.

There were screams of terror as people ran away, shouts of encouragement and orders as others ran towards the fire with buckets of water and awed whispers as even more just watched in simple contentment.

"Why... on the name of the planet, did you do this?" a man with a forest-green bandanna asked of the bald man.

"I didn't do anything," the bald man denied harshly. When the bandanna wearer merely glanced down at the lit torch and half-empty bottle of oil in his hands, he just shrugged and moved them behind his back.

"... Stealthy, quiet, secretive, covert. Have you any idea what these words mean? When our mission was given, I was assured of your professionalism. And yet, not even five minutes since we stepped foot here, a building gets blown up."

"Hey, it's only on fire, it hasn't actually—" A glass smashed inside the building and the fire roared. "Ha! See? No explosion. Just a bit more fire." And with a groan, the building collapsed. "Oh. Well, that's a let-down."

Bandanna man groaned, rubbing his face with both hands. "Alright, we need to get out of here before someone starts asking questions, or worse, the local guard decide to get off their arses and do their jobs."

"That's alright mate, you're covered there."

"Thank the Light and Dark." He groaned happily. "*Something* is going my... way." He frowned and followed the voice.

Approaching the duo was a brown-haired man in a long duster coat. He had light stubble across his face and dull green eyes with a dark black ring around the irises.

"The guards done nothin' but kick up their feet, so you won't have to deal with them. But unfortunately for you, you made a mistake."

The bald man threw his incriminating evidence away and withdrew a small dagger from his belt.

The man in the long coat tilted his head and then let out a little sigh. "I'm sorry." He waved a hand placatingly, even as he shook his head in abject disappointment. "I'm so, so sorry, but come on. I thought you'd have an axe or something, but this? You have to realise how ridiculous you look."

The bald man gritted his teeth, pointing his dagger threateningly, and the whole picture made him chuckle.

"Alright, alright, I'm done." The chuckles faded and he straightened up. He turned serious so quickly, it was unnerving. "Where was I? Oh yeah, your mistake. See, it was unfortunate you chose today of all days, to act out. See that pile of burning wreckage right there?" He pointed at said wreckage, believing they needed the extra help.

"That, was the only bar in this town. For some odd reason, it's also the only place that sells booze for two days in any direction. And you burned it down. Gentleman, it was unfortunate you chose today, for the worst thing to possibly happen, is currently happening. Your plans have gone up in smoke. Your dreams are broken. Your ambitions are futile, and why? Because I am sober. And I, am going to break every bone in your arms."

The bald man rushed him, every advantage was in his grasp. Height, muscle, a weapon, all of it. He was going to stab the man, then make a run for it. The rest of the group was only a few—*BAM!*

"... Why is the sky red?"

The man in the coat strolled past him, brushing his knuckles across his collar. "There's blood in your eyes," he pointed out.

The bandanna man drew his own knife and charged. His wrist was caught mid stab, a blow caught his ribs and an armlock forced him to his knees, wrist high above his head and his back bowed forwards.

"Gah, what the hell?!"

"I heard you talkin' about a secret mission. Call me curious, but I'd like to know what's goin' on."

He spat on the floor and flailed his free arm, but with a sharp jerk, he howled in pain as his arm was almost tugged out of its socket.

"Ah, come on, cat got your tongue? I know your type. Loyalty to the employer only gets you so far, trust me. But silence isn't healthy, especially for you right now."

He stayed silent, glaring at the ground, but with another sharp movement, he caved in. "Alright, alright! Some guy paid us to ask a kid some questions!"

"Okay, now tell me the whole truth. What's the kid's deal, why is whoever after them?"

"I-I-I don't really know; he just wants to know what she knows! Kid's a seer, a weak one, but he told us that even a weak seer can see the Big One!"

"The Big One," he echoed softly. "Well, that makes no sense. There are thousands of possible 'Big Ones,' how are you supposed to know which one to ask about?"

"Hell if I know!"

"Where's the kid?"

"At a house made of red bricks! That's all we were told!"

"The apex of precision. Lovely. I'm sure that's where I'd find the rest of your group as well."

"W-wait, how did you?!"

"No one would leave an important mission solely to two chuckleheads like you. And no one would openly attack a village unless they had backup waiting in the wings. Well, unless they were stupid." He paused and then glanced uncertainly at the bald man. "Uhm-oh, wait, never mind. He already confirmed it. Phew. Now then, one last order of business before I split."

"What's tha—" *CRACK!* "AAAHHH?!"

"That's for the cheap, horrible beer I'll have to walk all that way for, you prick."

"B-but I didn't do it!" he whined, falling and curling around his broken limb.

"Oh. Oh yeah, it was the other guy wasn't it?" He scratched his nose, wincing. "Uh... sorry?" Bandanna man glared at him with tearful eyes.

He just nodded, and whilst he was walking away, stepped on the bald man's forearm and *CRACK* yanked it back.

"AAAGHHH?!"

"Who-who the hell are you?!"

He grinned over his shoulder, "Just a bird flappin' around."

"That makes no sense?!"

"Course not. It wasn't supposed to. Why the hell would I tell a mercenary I'm leaving alive my name? Good luck tracking down some brown-haired guy in a coat, jackass."

The man's name is Raven Spectre. These days, he was all about justice and the like. Helping the weak, doing favours for good people, no matter how menial. He volunteered where he was needed, and when he wasn't, he drank to honour countless ghosts.

This wasn't the first time he'd saved someone; he couldn't begin to count the number of times he'd leaned against buildings, watching idiots break in. He'd asked around, the would-be kidnappers weren't even discreet.

Anyone could tell him there were four, and everyone could see them outside the door, scowling at anything that moved.

Obviously they weren't professionals, they relaxed seconds after they crossed the doorway, seconds after the first man kicked the door down.

So relaxed that none of them noticed when the last man to enter was yanked out, one arm around his mouth, the other around his throat.

A minute later, an unconscious body hit the floor and Raven crept into the house.

The voices of the home invaders were coming from a room further in the house. Something about tea?

He stalked slowly through the hall, treading lightly on the red wooden floor, past the green-painted walls. There was a single mounted lamp above a closed door. He swerved around the edges of the light and closed in on the man in the doorway at the end of this poorly lit tunnel.

"I don't think you understand the situation."

"I disagree. You know what I am, that is the whole reason you are here, is it not? Unfortunately, my gift is weak. My visions are not as clear, not as frequent. Fortunately, I managed to see this unpleasantness in its entirety."

"Oh, you saw us coming, did you? But you didn't run. So much for planning ahead, and for someone so confident, your hands are shaking an awful lot."

"You broke into my house, and are now accosting me in my safe place. It wouldn't matter how prepared I was, this would unnerve anyone," she said, the faintest tremor in her voice.

"Well, you don't need to be afraid, so long as you're helpful. So if you've seen this as you so claim, I don't need to ask, you already know what I want, don't you?"

"Actually, no. You never manage to get that far."

"What the hell is that supposed to mean?"

THUMP!

Before the man in the doorway hit the floor, Raven snapped his fist across the closer man's temple. As he fell, the man in the coat moved past, kicked the back of the speaker's leg and smacked him across the back of his neck.

He spun around, placing himself between the girl and the fallen men with his fists up, for no reason. There was only a light groan, all of them down and unconscious.

"Oh. Okay. Bit of a let-down."

"Don't worry." The girl breathed a sigh of relief. "I thought it was quite dashing."

"That's adrenaline." He snarked a grin at her, "Give it a minute, you'll be properly disappointed, trust me. I know I am."

The seer girl grinned at him, looking at him closely. It was enough to make him shiver. "Please stop that. It's very creepy."

"Sorry," she chuckled, flushing, embarrassed. "It's just that, you look more like a drifter than you did in my hallucination."

"That's... fascinating," he lied. "You unharmed?"

"Yeah, you got here just in time. Thank you Mr. Spectre."

"No problem. If I were you, I'd get out of this place, or at least change houses or something."

"Seriously?" she chuckled. "How many buildings do you think I own?"

"I meant find an inn or somethin', but also, you're a 16-year-old livin' alone in a house. Either you're resourceful, or you're squattin'."

"Does it matter which?"

"The mystic tone doesn't work with either that sentence, or your age. Just get ready to leave, these guys may have friends, and I'll be skippin' town tomorrow, so you won't have me there with ya."

"I will be fine, but thank you for the concern," she smiled reassuringly.

"Alright. I'm gonna dump these idiots with the guard and book it. Be seein' ya. Take care of yourself and always keep an eye over your shoulder."

He picked one up and threw him over his shoulder. He carried the second under his opposite arm. The third? Well, he ran out of both arms and care, and just used his foot to start rolling him across the floor.

7. A Trail

"I'm sorry, who are you?"

Vivian was in shock, her head swimming in circles. A few short seconds ago, she was positive that an old battle would be waged once more and her life would be taken by her greatest, unbeatable enemy. Gravity.

But then, in the blink of an eye, she had been saved by this... speedy vision.

The red-eyed woman gasped, "Oh, s-sorry, my name is Valour. It's nice to meet you!" she smiled, her face turning red.

"I-I see. I apologise, but it would be proper to introduce myself standing."

"Oh! Of course!"

Vivian choked as she was physically lifted up and planted both feet on the ground. To do that to a person wearing armour and a sword would mean she's... quite strong.

"E-er, *ahem* I am Vivian, heiress of the noble house of El Lock. I thank you for saving my life." And she bowed her head.

"O-oh! There's no need for that! I was just passing through and I saw you needed help, so I gave it!" she grinned.

Vivian frowned, glancing past her. She saw the door swinging back and forth, the lock clearly broken. "You were passing through a warehouse."

She flushed, but nodded. "Yep. I was on my way to, uh..." She stuttered, eyes darting around in a panic.

Her hand tightened around her hilt. Her movement was slow, the grip quiet, but the other woman's eyes still flickered down to her weapon. Only one of them was obvious with their alarm.

"Wait! I'm after the guys you were fighting! They tried to kidnap my grandmother!"

Vivian narrowed her eyes. Valour was pleading, her expression was sincere and she gave no sign of deception. If anything, she was quite bad at lying.

Almost too bad. So terrible, it may even be a trick.

"I see. So what brought you *here*?"

"Well, my granny's a seer and she had a vision that showed me standing in a warehouse. When I got here, I just followed the scents."

"Scents?"

"Oh yeah, I caught the smells when I was rescuing her. I picked up the same trail and it led me to this place." She sniffed the air again. "I also got the smell of honey, and really nice dust?"

"That's useful," she murmured. "How far can you follow a scent?"

"Eh, usually until it ends at the source. Even a scent that someone's tried to wipe away has a trace. Hunting dogs couldn't pick up what I can. My sniffer's greater than any old mutt," she claimed proudly.

Vivian just smiled, not showing how disturbed she was. "That is a powerful nose," she murmured, trying not to imagine all the smells she could pick up.

"Yup! So, where's the trail you want me to follow?"

"Over by the door."

Valour walked over to start sniffing the air by the door. "Oh, I recognise this guy alright. He was at Solitude with those ones on the floor."

Solitude. Vivian sighed unhappily. The board mentioned that isolated village two days away. This lot couldn't have been there on the thirtieth day and murdered Lucas here the day after. It must have been a different group.

The door flung open and Valour strolled out. Vivian cursed and ran after her. Thankfully, for subtlety's sake, the redhead only took soft sniffs of the air as she walked. Hopefully, if anyone cared enough to ask, they could pass it off as a mild cold or something.

"So…" Vivian twitched, surprised that Valour was talking to her, walking with her nose up in the air like a high-born. "Uhm, noble house? What's that all about?"

A safe topic, at least, she smiled. "My ancestor did a great favour for a previous King. In return, he granted us a fiefdom and noble title. We eventually surrendered our lands when we could afford our own, and though our allegiance is to the King, our loyalties are our own to grant." A soft glow of pride warmed her stomach.

"Oh. Cool. Last question, I promise. But you kind of died back there," she said with all the grace of a war hammer. "And then you glowed and lived. Uh, how?"

Her walls slammed up and she glared forwards, her eyes hardening to chips of ice. "That is a family secret. I apologise, but it is not something I can share with outsiders."

She flinched and then snapped to the road to hide her blush. "Oh, yeah, totally get it. Cool. Cool, cool, cool."

Vivian frowned in bemusement as the girl nodded to herself in time with the last three words.

***

"This is it?"

"Yep."

The building was small, much smaller than all the others around it. In an attempt to be subtle, it stood out among the bright, graffiti-covered monuments to art surrounding it. Hidden on the side, in the alley between it and its neighbour, was a poster of a bear head wearing a glass disc over one eye.

"Not well hidden, but a respectable effort. Onwards."

She marched for the door, then yelped as an iron hand clamped her shoulder and yanked her back.

"Woah, woah, what are you doing?!" Valour whispered loudly at her. "Don't we need a plan before we go in, swords blazing?!"

Vivian looked at her weirdly, "Of course. I already have a plan. I go in, and I kill him."

"That's, what? That's not a plan!"

"It worked back at the warehouse."

"You died."

"I got better."

"That's hot but irresponsible. We need to come up with something better."

"What was that?"

"Okay, I have something better. He'd recognise you, but not me. He's never seen me before. I go in first, you hide behind me. We go in like we belong, find the guy, wait for him to leave, then follow him. Agreed?"

She gritted her teeth, but nodded, sighing. "If it will keep peace between us, then so be it."

For some reason, Valour gave her a strange look after her words were spoken, but she shook her head and entered the building.

***

It was a bar. Not a headquarters or secret base as she'd expected, but a bar. Valour winced as she breathed in, the smoke scratched at her lungs and the foul smell of rot and hidden vermin made her want to puke, but she had to focus.

Her eyes sharpened, the nausea was pushed down and she zoned in on her prey. He was at the bar, speaking with the tender. The beautiful, murder-happy blonde shadowed her steps over to an empty table off to the side.

There were groups of people around, who gave curious looks, but nothing more. As Vivian went to speak, Valour lifted a finger to her own lips and closed her eyes.

"Look, I don't know what you were expecting, but all our vets are out on more important missions. Not snatching old people and teenagers. You get the people you pay for; you pay garbage, you get garbage."

"Three failures in a row is not garbage. Three failures is an insult. You do know who you're insulting, right? You mess up like this again, my boss will come for you."

"Great! Perfect! We can renegotiate. First, my scouts get kicked around by some superpowered monster, and now we've even got blondey mcwannabe hero cutting in."

The tender growled, a guttural feral sound that perked her ears. "Enemies are to be dealt with. We cannot afford to be known, especially so early."

"We don't even know who they are. I mean, we did rough up the first one's gran and apparently we killed the lass' friend. If not them, then others are gonna catch on eventually."

"I don't care if you spat on their house and danced naked at a family reunion, even just one move against us is enemy action. You get rid of them, or I'll kill the lot of you."

"And the Street Hound bares his fangs once more. You threaten my people again and you'll have the whole of the Wise Bears coming for your tail."

"I'm terrified," he grunted. "You know that name? Then you know damn well I don't need an army to deal with you."

"No, but you'll need a pretty strong shield for all the silver we'll toss at your head."

A low growl vibrated the floors. There was a lot of anger in that noise, but also a shred of fear. Valour filed that information away as something cracked in his grasp.

"Here's the next list." The tender threw a scrunched up bit of paper onto the bar. "Don't screw this up."

The other man coughed pointedly and the tender rolled his eyes. Reaching under the bar, he grabbed a small brown sack to toss at him.

"Pleasure doing business, lieutenant," he smirked sardonically.

"Get the hell out of my bar."

Valour's eyes snapped open and she grabbed Vivian by the face, tilting her away from the Wise Bears leader. "He's leaving," she hissed, stopping the other woman from moving.

The leader glanced at them as he passed, smirked and left the building. Valour nodded to Vivian and they got up and left quickly, neither noticing the curious look the 'lieutenant' gave them.

***

"So what's with the bear?" Valour mused to herself as they lagged behind. "Does it symbolise protection? No, he didn't seem like he needed it. The job's taken? Eh, maybe," she scowled.

"Why does it matter?" Vivian asked. "It was not their base, therefore it is not a part of our mission."

"True," Valour agreed.

They had been following him for what seemed like a half hour, but they had yet to stop anywhere. Valour frowned. She had a bad feeling about something and it was getting worse as the seconds passed.

She sped up to catch a glimpse of him as he turned a corner and he blurred a bit, like he was passing behind a waterfall or something.

Vivian lightly touched her arm, peering around her at an alleyway on their left. "An illusion," she announced.

"Pardon?"

"A moment ago, I assumed he was onto us. We have been going in circles for a few minutes now. However, from that alley, a black cat with two white rings around its tail has walked out three—" A low meow announced the cat's arrival as it strutted into view. "Excuse me, four times."

"Damn it," she grimaced. "So it's a trap, or just a defence of his base? Either way, I don't smell anything bad."

"There's that at least. But I do not know how to break it," she admitted reluctantly.

Valour swore quietly, ignoring Vivian's confusion. She closed her eyes, then snapped them open, her irises glowing. The town around her shivered, then collapsed in on itself, blowing away like a cloud of ashes and revealing a tunnel.

She growled. The space was tight and she couldn't fully extend both arms in any direction. The lack of light was no issue, but the space was far too restrictive for her liking. An open area with access to the grand blue sky was much better.

She held her hand out behind her, *SNAP!* and Vivian flinched back, her body jolting in place as her mind realigned itself with the real world. She shook her head, "I hate illusions." She grabbed her head, wincing, "especially powerful ones."

Valour glanced back to ensure she was alright, then scented the air. The trail had gotten older, maybe an hour? They were down here at least that long. She growled again, irritated at her lack of memory.

Well, nothing to it. She rolled her shoulders and marched down the tunnel.

The ground was dry and cracked beneath her feet, like they were in a desert. The tunnel itself was cylindrical, made of bricks. There were random damp patches on her right, but no water dribbled down.

After a few more minutes, she saw the end, an archway. They walked straight through and it was like escaping a fog. Silence and darkness was slaughtered by the light and music, bright flashes and hollering. They froze in shock as they entered what seemed to be a large party.

8. Interest and Summons

Is there anything better than the indulgence of one's own pleasure? Happiness is a rather addicting feeling after all, and when one has fallen into a well, what else can you do but spread your arms and enjoy the feeling?

Happiness is like lightning. Surging through your body, igniting your nerves, boiling your blood and scraping your bones.

For many people, happiness is hugging a loved one, stroking a pet or an activity that makes them shiver with joy.

For Savage, the latter is his own guilty pleasure, without the guilty part of course. He had... a certain tick. There was a reason he was so eager to follow Seren's plan. The end of the world.

All that death.

It made him *shiver*. He positively squeaked with joy. Just the thought made him hum happily.

Leaving behind a soaked and stained room, he tossed a bloodied rag over his shoulder. A guard marched past and his eyes were dragged to the pulse that thrummed in his neck. With every beat, he imagined the blood that would spill forth, like a child playing with a faucet. With every beat, a new geyser erupted from his flesh.

He grinned, his face tightening as he pictured every moment in his mind. The blade that caressed his skin, and then it hit him. He was recalling the memory of mere moments ago, and he lost all interest with a pout.

He shoved open the door to Seren's room and sat down across from the man. Seren was meditating. Was he ignorant to Savage's thoughts? Maybe not. He never truly hid his feelings from the other man.

How he longed to peel his veins from his body like he was skinning a grape.

Seren opened his eyes slowly but glared at him quickly. Annoyance, it seemed, was the default emotion when it came to their talks.

"We have problems."

Savage rolled his eyes, "We're trying to kill the planet and everyone on it. I think we've long since surpassed 'problems.'"

"Not like that you idiot," he sighed. "Three of our operations have been interfered with."

Savage was confused. Operations? This was the first time he'd heard of them. Then again, the other times he likely wasn't paying attention.

"How many did we have?"

"Four. We were only able to question a single seer, but she knew nothing of value."

"Are you sure there's even a point to talking with them?"

"There isn't. I am just investigating all possible angles. It was a long shot to begin with, but it seems doomed to failure, like the Treaty of Resolute."

"Damn non-humans," Savage sighed mockingly. "You want me to call off the Bears?"

"No. I admit, I'm curious about the reports we received. Mr. Adam believes his group killed a blonde armoured woman, and yet, your lieutenant claims he witnessed the same girl in the presence of a red-haired girl."

"Any connection?"

"None. The red-haired one interfered at Solitude and there seems to be an alliance of sorts. But Mr. Plato claims something very interesting. I want you to capture the red-haired one and have Mr. Plato see if she knows about the temples."

"Got it. Is that all?"

"It is."

"Then if you don't mind, all this talk's sparked me up a bit." He grinned, pulled the rag from his shoulder and ran a gentle thumb across the bloody stains.

9. A Rose Unlike Any Other

Valour grimaced, rubbing her ears gently. The music was an interesting choice. An acquired taste maybe?

Unfortunately, she just didn't get it, and she didn't think she ever would. Hopefully.

She flinched with each bang on steel drums, the sharp screeching of knives and sword hilts, plain slapping metal against metal and the screaming! They weren't even words.

A man dressed sharply in uniformed clothing walked up to them. She barely bit back a warning growl and his red eyes flickered to her. He offered them a glass of wine each, then walked briskly back into the crowd.

"He was being nice," she murmured to herself, sniffing the contents. "Oh. Never mind." She grabbed Vivian's glass before she could have a test sip and put them both on the floor.

"What's wrong?"

"He just gave us glasses filled with blood."

And what a sharp perspective twist that was.

Red 'wine' flowed like water. Some people drank it straight, others flung it into the air above the dance floor. It rained down and the dancers grew more manic in their movements.

"I don't think this is a mercenary base," she mumbled.

They turned to leave but the door had disappeared. "Damnit."

Someone stomped their foot. The music cut off. The people on the dance floor grinned and spread out into a circle. A man walked out into the centre, pale and with a mouth full of sharp teeth.

"We have some special guests for tonight's main event!"

"Oh, this is a trap."

She felt something sharp poke her in the back and her spine straightened. "Correct, missy." A low growl filled her ear.

Valour turned a nervous eye, looking to Vivian, who just appeared bored. The dagger in her back failed to even make her twitch. Oh, right. Can't die. Hooray?

The speaker gestured towards them and Valour was pushed up front. "Hailing from parts unknown! This woman personally tore apart a pack of Serpent Hounds barehanded!"

What the hell is a Serpent Hound?

The crowd went wild, screaming and hollering. "You all know the deal! Beat the champion, they go free! Lose, and we feast!"

Valour stiffened and glanced at the crowd. Suddenly, it all seemed a thousand times more oppressive than before. A woman close to her snapped her teeth in her face, the sharp daggers were tainted red and her pitch-black eyes made her look like some sort of demon from a horror story.

She grimaced and tugged her jacket off, baring her arms in her sleeveless top. It wouldn't do much for intimidation, but she was stronger than her wiry frame suggested. Hopefully this champion only looked and thought skin-deep.

There were screams of disappointment and bets were flying from every mouth. There really was no other choice, she mourned.

Her eyes glowed. The doorway was missing, she and Vivian were surrounded by a hall full of enemies and the room was much more than what first appeared.

The illusion slid away and she saw another exit! She tensed, her arm twitched, she had only a second to grab Vivian and—it moved! She only blinked and it had turned into a wall. She glanced around and saw it on the opposite side of the room. She blinked again and it appeared up by a VIP box.

Only one choice remained.

The air shifted and she dipped her right shoulder, a massive fist flew by her left ear. She staggered and another fist clipped her shoulder. It hurt, was likely to leave a bruise, but nothing she couldn't handle.

She hopped back and matched the taller, muscled man's pose. Head down, fists up, she blocked jabs and threw her own.

The noise of the crowd faded away as she flowed into a rhythm. She didn't think, of course, instinct was all she ever used.

The punches came so quick she was surprised his blurred force didn't break the air. But what she couldn't dodge, she blocked, wincing as the bruises built up.

The tide of the crowd was turning, many of them cheering for her rather than against, surprisingly, but she paid them no mind.

She couldn't afford to. With half of her attention on the fight, the other half was tracking the door.

It was sequenced, not random like she first thought. There were about ten seconds between each shift and five places it cycled between. If these people reneged on the rewards of her fight, she would only have mere seconds to act.

She fully focused and caught a punch on her forearm. She hissed; a little harder and it might have actually broken. The man grinned, victory in his sights as he pulled back his other fist, and her own caught his jaw, knocking out one of his teeth.

The crowd went silent as he landed face first on the floor. She glanced around, tense and wary. When the first of them stepped forwards, she'd grab Vivian, wait three seconds and run for the door. She had to be confident she'd outrun them, but she wasn't sure if she could.

The crowd was staring, her nerves were firing, did they hate her? Fear her? She could never tell. Just as the atmosphere was getting to her, someone burst into applause. They started screaming, cheering and the music slammed back on.

Valour was frozen in place; the sudden change had thrown her off. Were they guards? Hostage takers? Whatever they were, they walked away with beaming smiles, nodding to her with respect.

"That, was incredible," Vivian whispered, struck with awe. And then they locked eyes and she faltered. "Humans wouldn't be able to move that fast without magical enhancements," she said. "I'm surprised you know such a useful thing."

Valour shrugged, the glow faded and embarrassment flooded her, leaving her shy and meek. She tugged at her hair, "It's the only thing I'm good at." She winced after she said it. Confidence, it seemed, was not her strong point in recent hours.

Luckily, Vivian just nodded, eyes softening, but before she could say anything else, the speaker bounced over.

"Ladies, that was amazing!" he beamed. "I think I speak for everyone when I say that was a *huge* upset! You have certainly earned your prize. Follow me for your audience with the leader of the Senway coven!"

Valour blinked. Her what with the what?

***

The second they stepped into the VIP box, Vivian had to resist the powerful urge to draw her sword and back away. There were four of them in each corner of the room, but they weren't what frightened her.

It was the creature in the middle of the room, the one sitting in a chair so black it looked to be made of shadows. She flowed to her feet and sashayed over to them. Her grace was so perfect, it was unnerving.

Her wavy black hair glistened in the darkness, her eyes a beautiful shade of ruby and her skin was pale, though not as unhealthily as some of her fellows.

"I congratulate you on your victory, little one." She smiled pleasantly, but honeyed words could not hide the malice that radiated from behind curled lips. "In accordance with my fledglings' little game, I ask of you your boon."

"Game?" Valour repeated. The girl was frowning and keeping an eye on the others in the room, to Vivian's silent approval. "Games aren't usually life and death, ma'am."

She tilted her head and hummed in agreement. "No, indeed they are not. Do not worry, little one. I have an accord with the city above. We take no blood from them and they do not try to hunt us."

"Hunt you?" Valour asked. "What, like animals?" She looked disgusted by the very notion.

"Indeed. Those with magical blood and lineage are often hunted for sport or honour." She waved a hand dismissively. "Think not, it has been like this since I care to wonder. And *that* was a long time ago."

"And how long would that be?" Vivian cautiously murmured. "You make it sound as if you are older than you appear."

The woman huffed. "Please, dear, try not to ask my age, directly or otherwise. It could make our interactions," she peeled back her lips and licked a sharp tooth, "unpleasant."

"Ah, yeah, that makes sense," Valour interjected. "Last time I asked my granny how old she was, she broke a chair on my head," she pouted. "I just wanted to know for her birthday, but no. Instead, I had to put up a banner that had an 'ieth on it with no number."

They both stared at her for a moment and Vivian was stuck in an awful moment, debating whether to applaud her for breaking the tension or slap her own face at how awkward it had become.

"It infuriates me to realise." Vivian flinched, but the look on her face was far from murderous. "But, I have yet to introduce myself. I, am Rosalia Skewered. May I ask for the names you go by?"

It was like a molten rod had been fixed to her spine. The knowing look she was given wasn't much better.

"Sure. My name is Valour. Nice to meet you, ma'am."

Rosalia beamed at her and then turned to Vivian with an expectant look.

"What gave me away?"

"Nothing you need to worry about, dear."

"I beg to differ."

"Allow me to rephrase. Nothing that anyone else would be able to see."

She shifted her weight. Rosalia's knowledge, and the ease with which she shared it, honestly had her contemplating a fight. But even without the guards around the room, straightening as they perceived a threat, she had a bad feeling that trying anything would be a losing battle.

Rosalia just smiled.

"I am Vivian El Lock."

"Ah, Jonathon's daughter! I knew I recognised you." Her smile became less neutral and more happy. "He brought you to one of the parties I hosted while visiting the glades. You are far from home, dear. What brings you all the way out to a scum-infested cesspool like Senway?"

"… My friend was murdered," she admitted, "saving a young seer from a kidnapping attempt."

"I see," she frowned. "But then, why are you here?"

"We were following the boss of the Wise Bears. Members of his mercenary band were the ones, but he noticed we were following him and led us to this place. We were trapped in an illusion and had no choice but to follow the tunnel here."

Rosalia hummed, "He used our defences to trick you. How… despicable." She sighed in disappointment and waved over one of the guards in the corner.

He moved with the same inhuman grace she did, kneeling at her side.

"Spread the word. The Wise Bears are evicted. Their leader, Adam, has violated terms and tried to lure us into breaking the Treaty. Should he or any of his show their faces within our territory, they are fair game to all."

"As you say," the guard mumbled, and left the box through the door behind the two.

"I thank you for this information. You have provided quite the service for us, and brought an unseen enemy to my attention."

"You claimed to owe us a boon," Vivian said, shivering. The underground, the presence of this woman and her 'coven,' it was all starting to get to her. "Tell us where the headquarters for the Wise Bears is."

"If you take the exit over there," Rosalia pointed at the wall to her left and a doorway appeared, "and follow that tunnel to the surface, you shall enter a shed. Across from it shall be where they rest their heads. I wish you luck and give thanks for your words." She bowed her head.

Vivian nodded stiffly and marched towards the doorway. Valour bowed her head towards Rosalia, "Thank you for the help, ma'am." The woman gave a faint smile and a small wave, and Valour ran after Vivian.

Rosalia snapped her fingers and the door vanished. She chewed her nail thoughtfully and allowed one of the guards to approach with a nod of her head.

"Madam? Should we not hunt after them? They could be allied to the ones after all…"

"No," she denied instantly. "Put a tail on them, but do not engage. They don't have him, but I have a feeling they shall engage our true enemy. And when the time comes, I shall emerge myself."

The guards in the room held their breaths, staring in shock, before bowing in reverence. Rosalia stared at the wall, deep in thought and smiled.

10. A Coincidence

Raven pushed the mug away with a disgusted sigh. Was it mocking him? This nasty smelling dirt water, full of strange berries and *something* foul that actually fogged up the air.

"... No. This makes sense. However many days of good, it's only natural that it ends so horribly," he uttered mournfully. The waiter just smiled sympathetically; seems he was under no pretences of quality.

"Can I take it away, get you a different one?"

"Don't worry about it, kid." He pinched his nose and drained the glass, slamming it down when he was finished. "But you can bet your arse I won't be having another."

He passed him a few silver coins and walked out with a polite nod at the busy man behind the bar. He was wiping a glass in front of his face, the towel hiding his features.

"Why do I get the feelin' that I just got scammed," he muttered. The bartender moved the cloth and Raven felt his eye twitch at the not-so-small smirk.

He'd made the mistake of accepting the challenge written on the wall. The sign said "Outdrink any of our staff and win a free week! If not, pay for the lot!" It was a challenge he couldn't resist.

Only the kid had set the line by drinking a barrel the height of his shin and the width of his torso. Raven was impressed, but he had a fair bit of experience. There was this one time when he challenged a group who practically lived—not important.

With full confidence, he took the first mouthful of his own keg, spat it out and instantly called it quits.

He'd had a lot of alcohol in his time, many different brands from all over! But he had *never* had anything as foul tasting as this... *liquid*. He didn't even have the heart to call it beer.

And when he told the tender, who also happened to be the owner, the smug git just shrugged, smirked and offered a mug of their best to wash the taste out of his mouth. As you could probably guess, their best was worse than their worst.

He sighed unhappily and pulled a metal flask from the inner pocket of his coat. He popped the cork and checked how much he had left.

"Maybe a few mouthfuls," he mused. "If I'm lucky. Let's hope this washes that dirt out," and swigged some of the sweet nectar. He instantly corked it and replaced it in his coat, closing his eyes as his hands shook.

He grinned as the warmth hit him and he felt the buzz coming on. And then he saw stars and the dirt as his face hit the ground.

"Only a single hit? Either that was some booze or you have a weaker will than anticipated. I look forward to seeing which is true, Mr. Spectre."

***

There was pain in his head. The front burned as the hangover seared him like meat on a pan and the back prickled, like he'd just been hit on the back of the head.

"... At least this is one of the nicer cells." He bit his thumb until it bled and painted a small flower-like sigil on the back of his hand. "Oh A'oria," he mumbled, and winced as what felt like needles pierced the inside of his skin.

He glanced around, the pain in his head fading to a buzz. The area was surprisingly clean, with a mattress on the floor, lit by a source outside his 'room.'

He tilted his head, straining his ears, then yelped as his body kept tilting. He fell off the chair in an awkward mound of loose rope. Was he bound to the chair?

He jumped up. "No one else saw that, no one knows it happened, let's move on. In a cage, no coat." He wiggled his feet. "No shoes. Little strange, but okay."

As he wandered over to the bars, he did a slow spin, "Hm. Not too bad honestly. If they hadn't taken my flask, I might even have stayed a few nights. Beats payin' an inn."

He rolled his shoulders as he approached the bars and fell forwards. There was always a moment when the irritation almost felt too much. But the fur is too useful to give up and being a cat is just plain awesome.

The little brown cat easily slipped between the bars. He looked back and forth, before trotting over to a table. Until he passed the second cell. There was something familiar in the air. No, not something, some*one*.

He slipped into the third cage and exploded outwards. Raven stretched his human hands out a bit awkwardly and gently lifted the girl's face. "Wrong," he grimaced. Not her, but it didn't really matter. Anyone here was likely as innocent as he was.

He untied her arms, untied her legs and caught her as she fell forwards. He brushed her red hair from her face and gently patted her cheek.

"Oi, wake up! We might be about to die soon and no one wants to die peacefully in their sleep," he drawled with a chuckle.

Her eyes slowly opened, red irises fogged over focused on him and a strange series of emotions flashed through them. Her hand clamped his throat and an unmanly squeak left him as he was *lifted* up off the floor, all before she *snarled* at him.

"Who are you?! Where am I?! And where is Vivian?!"

11. Beware the Night

Yesterday.

As they walked, Valour chanced a look at the other girl. Damn, she grimaced, even angry the girl walked with grace and still managed to look distinguished.

"So… you wanna talk about it?" she winced. Clear thought was still evading her.

"Thank you, but this is a delicate secret. I cannot tell anyone."

Valour shrugged, "Okay. So long as you're doing alright."

"Thank you," she murmured, with a small smile.

At the end of the tunnel was the promised room. On a coat hanger hung a key that presumably opened the large silver lock chaining the door shut. Valour hissed as the descending sun hit her eyes.

Vivian passed her, "There," she growled.

Valour blinked the spots out, "Oh not this again, wait up!"

Vivian slammed her boot into the door and it burst open. There was a mad scramble as the dust settled, but Vivian didn't care. All her attention was on him, Adam, the leader. He stood up from the table, fetching his blade from the floor.

A man rushed her with a wood-chopping axe held high and a red blur hit him like a charging horse. As the other mercenaries of the Wise Bears scrambled, Vivian stormed forwards.

Valour hissed as she caught a sword by the edge. It bit into her skin, but she twisted her hand and snapped the metal like a twig. She grabbed the man by the collar and spun him, throwing him into another and chucking the broken blade in her hand.

It spiralled through the air and slammed into the leg of a woman who was approaching Vivian's back with a dagger.

A man from Adam's table rushed her and she faked a one-handed parry. As both blades were slapped off to the side, she punched him across the jaw with her left fist.

Her metal knuckles knocked him down and Adam waved his hand.

"Leave. As soon as we kill this one, that one," he nodded at Valour, who just punched someone so hard they hit the ceiling, "will kill us in return. I'll handle this."

They cleared out and, on seeing this, the rest of the room abandoned the fight and fled as well.

"Well, that's disappointing," he deadpanned. "I was at least expecting one of them to refuse. I remember when this band had loyalty."

"You murdered my friend," Vivian cut in, glaring at him. "Or you know who did, at least."

"I do," he admitted. "And it wasn't me. The one who killed your friend is dead. He died about an hour after the failed raid. Our employer doesn't like failure. And as much as I'd like to set you on his trail for what he did, I still have professional pride."

"... You sent that man on his mission. You ordered him to kill his target if he didn't get any answers."

"Not true. I specifically said to bring him in alive."

"If it weren't for you, he'd still be alive."

Adam smiled at her piteously. "If you're done trying to convince yourself, I'll save you the trouble. I am going to kill you, for intervening with my job."

He lunged forwards and she parried his thrust, moving out of the way of a thrown punch. She raised her arm and thrust down at his leg, but he moved it out of the way. She kicked out and knocked his other leg, sending him to the floor in an awkward split.

She stabbed at him and he threw himself aside.

"Damn, you are good," he idly complemented her. She said nothing and slashed at his face. He blocked her blow and chuckled. "If only Lucas were this skilled, he wouldn't have died so quickly."

Her arm wavered. He knocked her blade away and cut her shoulder.

"See, that's the way the world works. The skilled, like us, live to see old age. The weak? Well, they end up face first in the dirt and fertilising the grass with their blood."

She saw red.

She rushed him and swung her blade, aiming for his neck, his head, his arms, anything she could reach she tried to cut. He avoided her blows and countered often with little cuts, satisfied with watching the sweat fall across her bared teeth and feral scowl.

And then she made a mistake. She overextended a lunge, stumbled and he slid his sword straight through the hole in her armour, right into her chest.

"Next time, try not to get so angry," he whispered mockingly in her ear. He pushed her off and she hit the floor. He turned to Valour warily; this woman was the true threat. Her speed and strength was ridiculous. He'd never—"Aaargh!"

A burning pain stabbed through his leg like a metal poker fresh from a fire. He stumbled forwards, dragging his leg in a limp and collapsed as the blood spurted from the gaping hole in his calf.

His face started paling, and not just from blood loss. Vivian was scowling, still just as angry, fresh blood dripping from her blade. *His* blood.

"Next time, try not to turn your back," she mocked, and stabbed him through the chest. She watched him die, detached and on edge.

She stared at his body, expecting something. Him to come back and start insulting her again, for something to blow up, anything but the disappointing nothing that followed.

Valour cautiously edged around the body, a little green, and hesitantly put a hand on her shoulder. "Are you alright?"

"Yes." And she was. She was feeling perfectly fine, back to the pinnacle of her strength and in perfect health.

"Are you satisfied?"

"No."

She killed him. She made it hurt. He was the leader of a mercenary band. He was with the one who killed her friend, probably killed a lot of innocent people himself. She avenged them.

Lucas was still dead. Her heart still hurt more than a sword ripping it in half. She stared down at him blankly and felt... nothing. She didn't know what to do. There was no next step, no one else to fight for, nothing to plan.

"You wanna go grab a drink?" Vivian startled, as Valour smiled at her hopefully. The woman had blood on her shirt and her shoes were a lost cause, but there was something about that friendly smile that made her nod.

"We should probably change first though."

"Into what?"

***

There were plenty of clothes upstairs. Turns out the base had living quarters with clothes, small knick-knacks and some coins in little jars.

They took as much as they could carry. The mercenaries couldn't complain about someone stealing from them, seeing as they'd most likely stolen everything in the first place.

They were five glasses and a new bartender in when the buzz started to warm their bones. They'd gone to the bar Vivian somewhat knew and, now that she was paying attention, she could properly laugh at the name.

"Who names a bar the 'Easy Exit'?"

Valour giggled, blowing bubbles in her drink. "Who names everything anything?"

"Good point!" She giggled as well.

Valour waited until she drank another mouthful and put her glass down to hiccup a delightful little noise.

"Tell me about him. Lucas. What was he like?"

Vivian gasped, her lip wobbled and her eyes teared up. "Wha?"

"Tell me what you remember. All the good things. I know he's got a heart of gold, but what else?"

"He did," she murmured, "have a good heart. I remember one time, we went fishing with my dad. The ol' man was in a 'try something new every day' phase. That was over in a week, thank the gods. I caught a fish, but my line was weak and it snapped. I was devastated. Little 8-year-old me started crying and he jumped into the river. Dad and I just stared, didn't even think to go in after him. Couple of seconds later, he was uphauling the thing by the line. No idea how he did it. Every time I asked, he just wiggled his fingers obnoxiously and called it magic."

"Ha!" Valour cackled. "Not too bad, not too bad at all. So, he was your best friend?"

"He was. Actually, my only friend," she sheepishly admitted. "Because of my, ah, condition, I was heavily isolated."

"Your 'condition'? You mean the deathless thing?" Valour's eye twitched as she said that out loud. She may have agreed not to talk about it, but the whole thing was… weird, to say the least.

"Indeed. We met at a party my father hosted. He'd gotten an invite by doing a favour for one of the so-called high-born and snuck off to explore. We met in the gardens. I broke his arm when he startled me, and, through tears of pain and laughter, he declared us 'besties.'"

"You broke his arm...?"

"I was on a tree branch spying on the party. He climbed up to try and scare me, and I freaked out. Also, first time I ever landed a perfect spin kick."

"Of course," she deadpanned. "So, is this whole deathless thing, natural?" She waved her arms about when Vivian hesitated, "You don't have to tell me! I was just kinda curious..."

Vivian sighed. "Don't worry, the secrecy was more my father's fears. My birth mother cast a spell on me when I was younger. She had eight coins, did something to my soul and now here I am. Or so my father said."

"Ah," Valour mused in a sage-like tone, as if she had any idea what any of that meant. Spoiler, she didn't. "Sorry, birth mother?"

"Yes," she nodded reluctantly. "My mother left us shortly after the spell was cast, a few years after my birth. Alura is every bit my mother bar blood, but she still has a place in my heart. Even if she did leave us."

"Ah, mothers," Valour smiled bitterly, raising her glass. "You're not alone there. My own mom left me with my granny a few weeks after I was born. And though she's not my blood, granny is as much my granny as any other I may or may not have."

Vivian smirked and raised her glass. "To wayward mothers. To whatever they left behind."

"May we surpass what they saw and make them know regret," Valour smirked back, and clinked their glasses together.

They passed the hour with two more drinks and a nice long chat. Valour paled as the world blurred.

"Ah, think ah'm two sheets to the wind 'ere."

Vivian wheezed, turning green and feeling her limbs go numb. Valour grimaced and grabbed her glass to pour the rest of the poor woman's drink into her own and quickly drained it.

"Think tha's us. Where ya sleepin tonigh?"

Vivian pulled herself together enough to give her a confused shrug and Valour tried to slam her hand into her forehead, only to miss and cuff herself around the ear.

"Ah new ah was forgettin' somein… Yah don' suppose tha dead body cares if we nick a bed or two, doo yah?"

She stood up and the world blurred again. Her head burned and she stumbled. "S-somethin… wrong…" she murmured.

Her vision blurred and she saw the bartender walk over. He was joined by three men, one of them pale and scarred and holding a serrated dagger.

"Why… scentless…? Adam… boss… interrogation."

She caught every other word, but they slipped out of her head as the sweat in her eyes blinded her. She was picked up off the floor and slung over someone's shoulder. Her eyes rolled up and she watched the scarred man drag his knife across Vivian's neck and then bark orders at the others.

***

Vivian gasped awake; her hand clutched at her throat. It wasn't a fun experience, choking on her blood. But for every second of discomfort, fear and pain, she was going to pay him back tenfold.

Her sight came back just as he finished slitting the throats of everyone else in the bar, everyone he had poisoned.

He turned around and violently flinched as the dead woman studied him with gleaming eyes. The blood around her throat and dripping onto her woollen shirt was still fresh and he very clearly remembered the feeling of his knife slicing through her trachea. He remembered hearing her wet gasps and gurgles as the blood invaded her lungs.

Vivian smirked. It was always amusing, those rare moments when a new person saw her die and rise again. The confusion, fright, curiosity. And on the faces of her enemies, the slow realisation of a fight that cannot be won.

The fog muddling up her mind vanished and, as the rest of her mental faculties returned, she noticed someone important missing.

"Where is Valour?" she asked calmly.

The assassin glared at her and held his dagger out before him. He was pale and bald-headed. He had scars, like someone had dug a knife into his mouth and *ripped*. He had no armour that she could see, which was good. She had abandoned her own broken chest plate back at the Bears' base, only wearing her gauntlets and greaves.

She picked her sword up from the floor. "I have no time to play. Tell me where she is, or I shall simply kill you and go after her myself. The first lets you live. The second, does not."

He ran at her and she rolled her eyes. He stabbed at her and she whipped her blade around, but he ducked. She lashed her knee out at him, but he blocked it with his palm and stabbed her in the stomach.

She stumbled back with a gasp and cut down as she clutched her stomach. He caught her wrist and grabbed her arm. Slamming his hip into her wounded stomach, he flipped her over his shoulder.

She hit the ground back first and he stabbed down into her chest. He tugged it out and wiped her blood on her shirt. He surveyed the room, looking for any others he might have missed, growling angrily.

He turned and stomped towards the exit, and froze at the annoyed gasp. Vivian pushed herself up, grumbling. "Why is it always the heart? I'm going to develop actual heart problems at this rate."

The assassin stared at her as she sheathed her sword and settled into a loose boxing stance. "Come on," she grimaced. "A good fighter you may be, but I have traded blows with the best. So come, match your fists with mine. Let us see which one of us stands at the end."

She lashed out with two right jabs and hooked a blow with her left. He ducked and dodged all three punches and slashed with his dagger. He cut her once and she grabbed his arm and slammed her hip into his stomach, copying his earlier move and flipping him, but he bent himself and landed on his feet.

He fell forwards, dragging her over him and slamming her into the floor. She hissed and rolled to her feet. Jumping forwards, she kicked him in the chest and knocked him back towards the door.

He glanced between her and it, "Don't you even—" He almost knocked the door off its hinges as he fled, and she cursed and raced after him.

He was quick, but she was gaining on him. It was going so well, until a familiar instinct forced her gaze upward and she watched as the clouds covered the moon.

The last thing she felt was horror and regret. Sympathy for the assassin filled her and was then quickly quashed by the rising tide of motion in her body.

She choked as her heartbeat intensified, a pulse shot through her bones, vibrating her blood. Her eyes burned and she felt her body thrum, as though she were dying once more. The little hairs on her skin burned away and her body *strengthened*.

Two loping strides brought her alongside him. He looked at her without a hint of shock. Did he not feel anything at all, she wondered. His fist raised and she smiled in amusement as it moved towards her face in slow motion.

She looked him over. The assassin was wearing plain black clothes, he wasn't uniformed. Slightly worrying, for even hardcore professionals liked to have something that spread their name.

Reputation is especially important to people like him, one who didn't care? It brought up a few questions and a good deal of worry. The air brushed her cheek and her eyes widened in surprise. She had ignored him for so long; his fist was a hair's breadth from marring her skin.

Before the other could even register her movement, she grabbed his wrist with her left hand, tugged him towards her and kicked out his legs. Then, she let him fall. His momentum, and a little shove from her, carried him head over heels and she winced in fake sympathy as he left small blood trails across the stone.

She stopped her sprint and sashayed towards him with a cold smirk. She felt like a lion stalking a wounded, quivering, pathetic little animal. The only thing that could make this better was if the little prey could muster up a few tears for her.

Instead, he looked up at her with barely hidden rage behind his eyes. She could *feel* his hatred for her, as though it were a campfire she was standing mere feet away from.

"… Werewolf…"

She felt her brow raise. "Excuse me?"

"You're a werewolf. A mongrel of the moon."

She felt a twitch. Comparing her magnificence to the flea-bitten mutts that shed their humanity, losing themselves to the madness and hysteria of the curse? Why, she could feel her rage as it flowed through her veins.

"Look up, hated fool. The moon is full, and I," she waved over herself with a demeaning smirk, "am beautiful."

And she was. Her skin had a faint glow to it and her body had turned ethereal. Blemishes and scars, little marks that branded her form had perished. Her features had sharpened, perfection had forced itself upon her.

"Werewolf," he growled, adamant in his insult, though he probably did not see it that way.

But she was not the result of a curse. So, as a display of benevolence, she decided to enlighten rather than punish. To teach, rather than to slight. She cupped his cheek and gave him her most patient smile.

"I am no dog. Please desist from referring to me in such a manner. I am bound by no curse but gifted by the night. When the dark has stolen the moon's light, and when the sky is nothing but stars and shadow, the blood of my mother shines through."

He stared at her, uncomprehending, so she decided to give him a little nudge. She kicked his leg and he howled as his shin bone shattered on impact.

"Fear the world as it ripples, my will made manifest. Beware my power, and the laws that sunder before my stride." She paused and grinned at him, her perfect white teeth sharpened into subtle points. "Behold, the presence that graces you, upon this moonless night."

His eyes lit up in understanding, and at last she saw that fear she longed for. She also saw the hatred, the anger. She felt the Dark within the city laying in wait, felt the shadows surge and hunger.

And an idea struck her. She giggled. "Well, well, looks like it's *someone's* lucky day." She ignored his confusion and reached out to wrap her hand around his face, covering his eyes.

She closed her own and focused. Images flashed through her mind and she smirked as a prison came into view, together with a long road. A few landmarks appeared around it and she frowned as a man rose through the stone.

An actual werewolf, he possessed all the features, and she felt a hint of disgust as she remembered Kythe comparing her to such a monstrous figure. She glared down at him, though he could not see her displeasure.

She was happy now that her plan allowed him some suffering, as she reached out to the darkness around them and laid a curse upon him. He started screaming in agony and she smiled.

She tossed him aside. It would take a while, but he would eventually succumb. The pain would end when he acknowledged his failures and faults. She glanced up at the sky and waved her hand. The clouds vanished and the moonlight struck her.

Her perfect form slid away and Vivian hit the ground with a gasp and threw up. She stared at the screaming assassin in morbid curiosity, even as the horror-fuelled urge to be sick again bubbled up. She thought about helping him, but something inside *violently* fought against it.

She shook her head and gritted her teeth. Valour needed her help. The woman was her friend and she refused to allow her to die. Not again. Not while she still stood.

12. The Lieutenant

Plato cursed as he made a careless reach for something on a shelf, and the armpit of his bar uniform tore. He growled, gripped the shoulders with clawed hands and *ripped* them off.

"Much better." He grabbed a scalpel off the top shelf. "Now, where were we?"

He turned back to Valour, hanging from the ceiling by iron chains. Her clothes were ripped and she was covered in blood, glaring at him with tired, angry eyes.

"No werewolf blood." He checked her arm. "Silver wounds healed without a scratch left. Not a vampire." He glanced at the soaking wet little copper band locked around her wrist. "Blessed-water-soaked bone, from a ghoul."

He started pacing, "You're not a Selkie, not an elf, nor a halfling…" He stopped and glared at her. "So what the hell are you?"

She spat blood on the floor. "A genie…" she hissed. "What's yer first wish?"

He smirked, "Tell me what you are."

"A jade liger."

His face twisted and narrowed, little hairs sprouted along his cheeks and his jaw creaked. He growled, "Why are you being so difficult about this? Just tell me what you are. It's not something worth this much pain," he demanded.

"If it's not worth it… why are you trying so hard… to find out…?" she asked.

He growled again, opening his mouth to speak, his jaw cracked harshly. He hissed in pain and spun around, breathing heavily. He glared at her over his shoulder and then threw the door open.

There were two guards standing outside, a man and a woman. "Take her to a cell. When the poison runs out in an hour or so, dose her again."

They nodded, heads bowed and trying not to stare as his eyes glowed amber.

Valour groaned as the chains were released from her arms. Her head swam, her eyes kept blurring out. She was pretty sure she'd thrown up once or twice already, and though all her wounds were healed, the pain was still there.

She was half carried, half dragged, and she could just barely make out her surroundings. They had just left a tent inside a camp, surrounded by people.

In the distance there was a howl, like a wolf, but there was something about it that made the back of her neck itch. Her 'supports' flinched and she swore the blurry people around her suddenly grew more frantic in their movements.

They dragged her into an actual building, a small place with five prison cells, only one of which was occupied. She was dragged to the one on the end and chained to a chair.

Her head lolled to the side and, as the cell door slammed shut, her vision went black. She dreamed a memory and it didn't take long for the nightmare to consume her.

She was back in the room. He was showing her drawings, an old temple with a symbol she recognised. The book beneath a silver circle. She remembered saying as much. She blamed her honesty on the venom destroying her thinking.

He then showed her another old temple complex. The silver circle was there, but there was a sword in front of a shield, underlined by a quill. At this point, the poison had begun to run its course.

Unfortunately, when the sarcastic answers came, so did the pain. He demanded to know what she was, and she woke up to an unfamiliar man's face and her arms were free.

She grabbed him by the throat and lifted him off the floor. "Who are you? Where am I? And where is Vivian?!"

She flushed a little at the slip. She hadn't meant to ask that last question, her head was just a little fuzzy still. It wasn't like the other woman was on her mind a lot, of course not. She just cared for her friend. Simple.

She heard him choke and loosened her grip with a yelp. "Oh my god! I'm so sorry, I didn't mean to hold you that tight, are you okay?!"

He looked at her weirdly as he coughed and she felt her face burn with embarrassment.

"Am I?" he chuckled. "Well, aren't you adorable? Sorry kid, no idea who 'Vivian' is. Now, if we're done with this whole song and dance, we need to leave."

"Leave?" She glanced around, blinking hard as she tried to get her mind in order. "Yeah... yes, yes we need to do that."

He glanced at her weirdly. "Okay. That's definitely not a good sign. Alright, I don't know where the keys to this place are, so what we're going to have to do—" He stuttered and fell silent as she marched over to the door, gripped the bars and ripped the whole thing off the hinges. "Is do that, and just walk on out. Okay then."

She stumbled towards the door, but her eyes twitched and the hallway started stretching, freedom getting further and further beyond her reach. Her rescuer gasped and bounced past her. She blinked as he reached out towards nothing, but then pulled a coat out of thin air.

A table swam into view and she blinked hard. Everything was normal so suddenly it made her brain hurt. The man was picking something off the table, a silver flask. He was handling it carefully, smiling at it, before putting it in a pocket on the inside of his coat.

She started walking towards the door again, the dull throbbing in her legs was fading. The cuts and bruises must be healing, she mused. Her torturer was keen in his tests. He'd even made a list, her healing factor at the very top.

She healed from small wounds rapidly but took longer the bigger and more serious they got. She glanced at the blood coating her ruined clothes and grimaced. She'd be feeling weak for at least a week, trying to replenish all the blood she'd lost.

But she gritted her teeth and strode forwards, the brown-haired man a step behind her. She went to open the door but he grabbed her wrist with an alarmed look. She bared her teeth at him by instinct, and he smiled, as if amused by her reaction.

"Guards?" he asked her.

She frowned at him; what kind of a question was that? Did he want to know if there were any? Or did he want to remind her that there were guards? One-word questions were always the worst and she felt the intense urge to flick him on the nose.

She sniffed the air and grimaced. All she could smell was the overpowering scent of dog, and it was everywhere. She understood marking territory, but this was taking the piss. It was like an animal had rubbed its dirty fur on *everything*. She ignored her nose for now and closed her eyes to focus on her ears.

No heartbeats, no breathing, no movement of any kind, she didn't even hear any nearby wildlife. She frowned. She could distinctly remember two people dragging her in, so where were they?

A light cough drew her back to the other man. He was smiling patiently, and she told him what she heard or—to be more precise—*didn't* hear.

"Okay... this is either an elaborate trap, or we may be walking into a horror story," he muttered.

"Horror, definitely..." she chuckled. "Werewolves are always bad news."

"A werewolf?" he asked her. Half his mouth curled up into a smirk, the other half down into a frown. It was a weird look, and it made him look weird. "That actually explains it. Werewolves on the full moon are incredibly territorial. Should another living being step into their land, they're consumed by the need to bite. This works both for us, and heavily against us."

"So we need to run?"

"No, slow but steady. Only run if you have to."

She frowned, but nodded firmly. She opened the door slowly, looking both ways, and started creeping away. She didn't care where the road back to Senway was right now, she just had to get out of the camp.

She heard the brown-haired man behind her, "My name's Valour by the way."

He stared at her weirdly, then smirked. "Nice to meet ya Valour. Name's Raven. I'd say it's a pleasure, but right now the situation's anything but."

She glanced around; the tents rustled in the wind. Something somewhere was creaking and there was a faint tapping, the plink of water dropping onto metal.

Her feet padded against cracked dirt and Raven's breathing was like thunder against the quiet. A wolf's howl blasted through the night. It was close, somewhere behind her, but she didn't run.

No telling what might happen if she did.

A shadow fell across her head and she shivered, looking up. Strange, there was a massive hole in the cloud layer, too perfectly formed to be natural. A sliver had slinked its way through.

She shook her head. Too jumpy. A clack caught her ear. She paused and focused, and felt dread when she heard a small rip, something sharp hacking through the ground. A huff. Something big breathed in, scenting the air.

Something big growled.

"Damn." She reached back and grabbed Raven. Before he could ask, she burst into movement, sprinting away.

The thing behind them moved fast, four heavy thumps striking the ground in a pattern. It gained on them quickly. She felt it nipping at her heels and had the horrible feeling that it was playing with them.

Fear kept her running. Kept her from tripping. She saw the edge, saw freedom, saw hope and then it all came crashing down as the wolf bit her calf, its teeth tearing into her flesh and bringing her down.

She hit the ground hard, screaming in pain as it sunk into skin and gnawed her bone. Raven rolled to his feet and jumped onto its back, wrapping his arms around its neck. It let go of her and reared back, and Valour stared through thick tears, her heart pounding with fear as it stood up straight.

At two metres tall, it towered over her. Its body was sickly, patches of pink skin stood out against dark-brown fur. The skin on its belly was hairless, stretched taught around its ribs to the point that she could see the rounded tips of the bone. Its muzzle was caked in her blood, its lips were peeled back and she could see through the viscous red, a rotted yellow and black. Its eyes were glaring down at her, dark orange and practically *burning* with hatred and a feral madness.

A clawed, human-like hand lashed back, grabbing Raven by the scruff of his shirt and easily tore him off and slammed him into the ground. It lunged down, jaws wide open and Valour whipped her arm across its face, frothing jaws smacking the ground just a scant few inches away from his neck.

She grabbed his shoulder and heaved, pulling him across the ground and away, and jumped at it. The wolf shot up with a speed that belied its large frame and punched her across the jaw.

Her head snapped to the side and she screamed as a burning pain tore into her shoulder. She grabbed its head with both hands and pushed frantically, but it just bit down harder. She could feel it, the werewolves curse seeping into her blood, twisting and clawing at the humanity inside her, but then a fire surged.

The wolf yelped and ripped its head away in a frenzied panic, skin and blood flying with it. Valour stumbled aside clutching her shoulder, her breaths coming in wet chokes. She lost strength and fell, the world fading away.

Raven pushed himself up with trembling arms. His eyes narrowed as his anger started to boil over. He'd come quite close to death, or worse, and the only thing that saved his life was the brave action of a girl he'd never met before.

He glanced at her wounds and her fallen body. She'd live for about ten minutes without medical help. He looked back at the wolf; the strangest thing was happening. It was clawing at its own muzzle, tearing at the flesh as though it was in pain.

He flexed his hand and the shadows around him shivered. He felt a prickle across his palm as the tattooed rune on the back of his palm tingled and crackled.

"I'm sorry," he said grimly. "I know there's a chance you might be a good person. I wouldn't know, I've never met you before. But to save her, I have to end this. Del'thuri."

He raised his hand and curled his fingers. Electricity leapt from his outstretched limb and struck the wolf. It howled in agony as the volts tore through its nerves, and with a grunt and a heave, Raven's lightning pushed it away.

He snapped his hand back and clenched his fist. Hiding it with his other hand, he looked around warily, a habit he'd never tried to break, then looked back at the wolf. He could see a smoking lump, but couldn't tell if it was breathing or not.

He shook his head and ran for the girl. Picking her up with a wince, he ran for the road.

13. A Turn

"Damn it all!" Raven growled. He had to set her down and bandage her wounds, otherwise she'd bleed out before he could get her to anyone. He was so busy putting pressure on her shoulder that he didn't notice someone approaching, until a sword was put up against his throat.

"Step. Away. Now."

Vivian seethed. Valour was on the floor. Valour was bleeding furiously. Valour was dying. And this man was sat next to her. There are a lot of conclusions one can draw from this, too many of them not good.

"If I let go of her, the wound bleeds and she dies." Raven winced as the blade twitched.

"If she dies, so do you."

"That's polite," he grumbled. "And exactly what I get for helping her out of that place…"

The sword angled as Vivian slowly sat next to Valour, and Raven noticed the unnatural glow on her skin. He recognised it immediately, but needed a second to put name to the feeling.

"You can heal her." He breathed in relief.

She glanced at him sharply and looked down at her hand with a strange stare. Fear, he realised grimly. "I wouldn't normally say this," he started hesitantly, "but now's not the time for personal hang-ups." She glared at him and he rolled his eyes. "The kid's in danger. She needs help. You're able to help her, so will you?"

She glared at him hard, but a stuttered breath from Valour made her wince. She hesitated for a second, then cast her sword aside and put one hand on top of her leg and slid her other hand beneath his hands on her shoulder.

"I can seal her wounds, but I cannot return to her what she has lost."

He frowned at her, trying to translate what she meant, then figured that she must be talking about the blood. "That's fine. That's all she needs. The curse she was bitten with won't affect her, can't affect her."

Her eyes darted up at him, then looked back down. "Curse? Never mind, tell me after."

She narrowed her eyes and he watched as the glow on her travelled down her body into her hands and into Valour. He watched the wounds heal, the light burning away the infection.

She sighed, her sleep slowly becoming a restful one and he huffed a relieved breath. "That's good. Good, good." He picked her up and nodded to Vivian. "I take it you're friends with this one?" Vivian glared at him and picked up her sword. She said nothing, but he didn't need her to. "Okay then, you got somewhere we can keep an eye on her?"

"Not anywhere I trust," she finally spoke. She glanced at Valour nervously and sized him up. He resisted the urge to chuckle in disbelief. A girl 20 years his junior was thinking she could pick a fight with him.

"But I do know somewhere she'll be safe. Are you willing to make a trek?"

He blinked, then looked at her narrowly. "What kind of trek?"

***

Two days later, Vivian knocked on the library door and stood back.

"Why would you knock?" Raven stared at her bewildered. "It's a library. Just open the door and go in."

"It is not *just* a library." She glared at him out of the corner of her eye. "Do you not see the sign? It is an extension of the Silver Premise. The Army of Light, a respected and noble order. We cannot just barge in without permission, especially not looking like this!"

Raven gritted his teeth. He had to give her that last point. They looked awful, covered in blood and clothes shredded to hell. The other girl even looked like she'd been stabbed multiple times in vital places. But one thing he *had* to point out.

"They put a library in a village where reading is a luxury, rather than a necessity. I bet you the owner got banished, oh I'm sorry, 'relocated' as an effort to spread the message of peace." He rolled his eyes, then frowned at the symbol on the door. "Though I am confused as to why a Premise building would be here. I thought they and the Ring buggered off years ago?"

"I do not know, and I do not care. Regardless of their reasons, they are a force to be feared and treated cautiously. Step carefully, who knows what they might take offence to."

He might have misjudged this girl. He thought she'd be one of those fanatics, like the lighter-minded nobles tended to be, but it seemed she had a healthy sense of realism about her.

He waited another minute, then annoyance got the better of him. "That's it." He raised his foot and kicked the door open. Ignoring her startled flinch, he strode inside and yelled out, "Oi! Medical emergency, I'm looking for Lydia!"

A voice shouted back across the room, "If it's an emergency, you shouldn't have knocked like a loser! Who knocks at a library door? It's a public establishment for god's sake!"

A different voice roared back from the opposite side of the room. "If you know it's a library, then you damn well know the rules! No shouting, so shut up the pair of you!"

Vivian grabbed his arm and dragged him around the first bookcase, where a table laden with books was. She swept it all off and nodded to him, so he put Valour down on it. He vaguely heard someone stomp around the corner, and Vivian intercepted them.

Valour was pale. He checked her wounds and they were still inflamed. The glowy kid's light had nixed the curse and allowed the wounds to heal naturally, but even with whatever this redhead kid had, a werewolf's teeth were something special, in a vicious kind of way.

See, in order to transfer the curse, their teeth were cursed as well. This left the poor sod with magic in his chompers that caused them to rot and decay in his chops, but the wolves healed them as quickly as they... corroded.

So, in addition to the insanity, the pain of their bones breaking and reforming their entire skeleton, they have killer fangs.

The other two were joined by a third, and he turned to them to start asking for medical supplies, then froze as he saw the librarian. "Ah. Hi."

Bastian stared at him bug-eyed and pale, then clamped his eyes shut and sighed in utter despair. "Great. You again. I take it this is your doing then?" He glared at him accusingly.

"Ah, no. Werewolf. She saved my life."

He laughed. "Ha! What a turn of events! So you're doing the right thing now?"

"Trying to."

"Well, that's all we can ever do. Move out of the way, you incompetent clot, an *actual* healer should check on her."

Raven backed off and glanced over to Vivian and the woman she was speaking to. The pair were talking lowly, looking worried at the unconscious redhead, and he nodded firmly. His job was done here, time to move on.

He took three steps towards the door before the woman called him back.

"I do hope you realise you're not done here?" she called after him.

"Excuse me?"

"My girl saved your life. You do know the implications, correct?" His eye twitched. "I suggest you balance it out as soon as possible."

"I already have. She would've died. I got her out of there."

"No, you carried her away from a dangerous area. This one here saved her life." She waved her hand at Vivian. "You should hang around; you might be able to save her life yourself. That and you may learn a thing or two."

Raven scoffed a second before Bastian and the latter glared at him for it. "I hate to say it, but I doubt he can learn anything here he doesn't already know."

Raven hid his smirk, but didn't say anything. He wanted to, oh how desperately he did, but the ensuing fight would make everything worse. Oh well, he'd have to settle for subtly needling the older man later.

"Oh, I know what he can do, trust me." She looked at his hands with an amused smile. "Mr. magic lightning here has made a bit of an impression on a dear friend of mine."

"A dear friend?"

Bastian choked. "You've been speaking with someone?" She nodded. "My word. And what poor unfortunate soul have you burdened with the curse of your personality?"

"If you must know, Adriana is a lovely girl. Mr. Spectre here saved her life a while ago. Some ruffians broke into her house and threatened her."

Bastian paused, then slowly turned to Raven with the deadest expression he'd ever seen. Even corpses looked more emotional than he did at that moment.

"Spectre?"

"Ahem, yeah, Raven."

"...Raven Spectre. *Really*?!"

"Oh give over, I was put on the spot. My first name was more realistic, but it got burned when I had an altercation with a distillery owner. Got my dumbarse blacklisted, so I needed a new ID."

"You changed your name; did you change anything else?"

"I was a detective. Did a bit of private investigating on the side."

"You changed your name and dropped a reputable career because no one would serve you alcohol?"

"... Well, when you say it out loud—"

"Not just out loud. If I think it, it remains just as stupid."

The conversation wasn't looking too favourable, so he decided to ignore him and turn to the woman. "How do you become a dear friend with a seer?"

She gave him a weird look. "How the hell do ya think? Mentorship."

"Mentor... so you're a seer as well?"

"Yup. Kid needed someone to talk to and cry about the nightmares and hellish sights. Plus that and the self-destructive view of herself when people eventually come asking questions and she might have to tell them the truth."

"The truth?"

"Our visions are of the future. Well, *a* future. If they or six other people need to die in order for the world to keep spinning, or to prevent something monstrously catastrophic from happening, we're usually the ones who have to politely tell them this. It's not good for your mental health, especially for a young one. Kid was one of the luckier ones."

"You have a strange view on the concept of luck."

"Oh yeah? She's a weak seer, vague visions, three times a month at most. I was lucky as well. My visions are powerful, I get them twice a week and I can force them, though that has a price. The unlucky ones? They either can't deal with the pressure or their minds snap."

"Oh. So she's very lucky then?"

"Yes. Now then, what can you tell me about the ones that attacked her?"

"What, she didn't explain anything?"

"She did. But then, she's not a detective."

"That's fair," he sighed and thought back. "They were new. Not to combat, but to working together. They had different specialties; someone took a stealth operative and a frontliner and expected them to work together. The fronter was undisciplined, let emotional thoughts influence him while on a mission."

"We don't need to worry about the Wise Bears any more," Vivian quickly butted in. "Valour and I assaulted their base and I killed the leader. Their forces should scatter."

"No," Raven disagreed, but he nodded in approval at her. "There'll be a scramble for power. If the leader is dead, someone will need to make a show of force, but if they have a lot of new blood? They'll have a lot of people trying to prove themselves. But you are right, we won't have to deal with them any time soon, if ever. You did good kid, more than I expected for someone your age."

She nodded and Lydia asked, "Did you find out who hired them?"

Vivian and Raven shared a confused glance. "Er, no? What do you mean?"

She rolled her eyes. "Some detective. Why would a mercenary group go after seers? Why would a mercenary group go after seers of differing strengths?"

"I know," Vivian perked up. "They were looking for information about the Final Moment."

"Ah," Raven sighed, smiling at Lydia weakly. "I apologise for my lack of foresight. A small-time mercenary group looking into something considered a world-ending event? Yeah, that reeks of something more."

"When we were listening in on their conversation in the bar, Valour heard the leader of the Bears call the werewolf 'lieutenant.'"

"Which means someone else is in charge. Which means someone was using the lieutenant as a middleman. Which means someone is very interested in the end of the world."

"What I don't understand is how they even knew about the seers in the first place," Vivian mused. "They had a sheet of paper with dates and locations, but not people. The best they had were weird, shaded drawings that were no help at all."

"A seer," Raven frowned. "That's the only explanation, but seers see people and events. They don't see specific places and dates." He glanced at the seer in the room. "Am I right?"

"You are," she frowned. "I have no idea. I can try and force a vision—"

"No," Bastian drawled out boredly. "You're still recovering from the last time."

"Oh please, you're still going on about that? I wanted to see if Valour would be alright. She was standing alone in a warehouse for god's sake!"

"I'm not talking about that. I'm talking about when you tried to force a vision during our poker game yesterday, when you got a nosebleed and collapsed, remember?"

"What? No, no I don't remember. When did that happen?!"

"During our poker game yesterday."

"And you didn't think to tell me?!"

"I considered it. But I couldn't be bothered to deal with your inane questions."

"My inane questions about my mental and physical health?"

"Eh, you were fine. A little nosebleed is good for you. There's too much blood in your head anyways. Plus you were trying to cheat, so I wasn't feeling very sympathetic."

"Unempathetic brat," she muttered, glaring at him.

"Cheating ignoramus." He turned away from Valour and nodded to Lydia. "She'll be fine. She'll need someone there when she wakes up or she'll likely exhaust herself back into another faint."

Lydia rushed past him. "When will she wake?"

"I'd give it another two days. She went through a lot of trauma; her physical injuries have healed up and her body will be fully repaired in a few days. Her head?" He bit his lip. "I'm not sure. But she will wake and she will get better. I know her and she can heal from anything."

Lydia nodded and stared him straight in the eye. "Thank you, Bastian." He nodded back. "Now bugger off. My granddaughter needs to be surrounded by beauty, peace and light when she wakes up, not ugly, aggravating and gloom that you constantly drag around."

"As always, you amaze me with your deluded blindness," he snarked. "Beauty? Light? Lady, the only light you carry is the glorious sense of misplaced self-righteousness and the flame of hypocrisy and tragic fallacy."

Vivian blinked from Raven's side as they both stared at the polar switches the both of them undertook. "What, what just happened?"

"I'm not too sure. I never thought I'd see the day when the crotchety git would meet his match. But the way she ripped into him; it was so beautiful I had to wipe a tear from my eye."

14. One Above

"You got beaten by a child, and a bumbling drunken fool."

Plato stared at the ground, his embarrassment clear to everyone watching. He was kneeling before the boss and the boss' partner. He didn't say anything, for if he did, he could trigger the man's rage. But if he stayed silent, there was a chance someone might speak up.

And they did.

"Judging by the burns the medic found on him, the victor used magic. Lightning manipulation. The girl was already reported to have enhanced strength and speed, so it must have been the man. It seems the fool, is not what he appears."

Savage glared at Seren as he delivered the small speech, then angrily gestured at a man holding a bunch of papers. "Who is he? And who is she?"

"Sir. We sent out feelers and got back his true identity. Malcolm Freeway. He's a detective with some small magic skill, but he disappeared a few years ago after an altercation with a distillery. The girl is a mystery. Lives with a grandmother in Solitude, a seer, no parents anyone knows of, and no medical records to date."

"Someone's tried very hard to leave no traces behind," Seren murmured. "Why? Oh well, it matters not. The girl and her group are of no further interest. We head forwards with plan A."

"No interest?!" Savage spluttered. "She massacred the mercenaries *I* hired, and then messed up *my* lieutenant! I am very much interested in seeing her dead!"

Seren sent him a disinterested glare out of the corner of his eye. "I have no interest in her. She has accomplished her objective, and she does not know of us. So long as we do nothing to rouse her interest, we shall not be enjoying her company ever again."

Savage resisted the urge to growl and smiled with a nod. "Agreed. I'll debrief this idiot, and get back to you if there's anything else."

Seren glared at him, "Do not engage the child, Savage. We are in a delicate situation, and cannot afford to bring notice to ourselves. We have had to move multiple times when *they* get close, and I can no longer be in the same place as him. Somehow, they can track him, and I did not account for it."

Savage inwardly groaned. He forgot that Seren was remarkably good at seeing through his deception and dishonesty.

"Fine. I won't attack the girl or her friends. Happy?"

He narrowed his eyes. The wording did not escape him, but he was too focused on his plan to call him out on it.

"If you bring the girl down on us, they will find him," he started slowly, as if talking to an infant or a puppy. "He will escape, he will tell *her* about you, about me, and then we will both be living on borrowed time."

Savage snorted. "I'm not afraid of any old vampire. We're too strong for that, we have people that can deal with it."

"She is not just 'any old vampire,'" he murmured softly. "She is *the* old vampire. One of the first. Her powers are beyond that of any currently existing, and she is far superior to either of us. She could kill us both simultaneously with a snap of her fingers."

"Oh," Savage said. But he was still unconvinced.

Seren knew this, saw it as though someone had written it across his forehead in bright pink. But Savage would soon learn. He knew it.

***

The lieutenant fell in a step behind Savage, head bowed just enough to follow his feet. He was shaking, not in anger, but fearful anticipation. Was his years of service enough to save his life? Doubtful. He'd seen the man cut open his best friend of 15 years because the other man had questioned one of his decisions.

Was his usefulness enough to outweigh his failure? He didn't know. All the uncertainty was killing him, twisting his gut and playing on his brain like a drum set. Though his life was in danger, the thought of running never crossed his mind. He could kill the other man easily, he was only human after all, and though his curse burdened him, Plato was still blessed with strength and speed greater than that of Savage.

But he couldn't. Was it fear? Yes, most definitely. But was that all it was? Not even close. There were rumours after all, oh there always are and will be. So long as people have tongues, ears, eyes or fingers, there will always be speculation.

But Savage and Seren had something that made them more. Was it magic? Seren is a seer, so it's not too outlandish an idea. And Savage? The man was a psychopath, but the things he did and was able to get away with? It bordered on the mystical.

They entered a room occupied by a single man; someone he'd never seen before in his life. The man had short blond hair and dull blue eyes, dressed in casual clothing. He didn't look like the kind of person that would consort with the kind of murderer and crazy that Savage was.

"Plato, meet your assistant." Plato frowned and glanced harder at the man. An assistant? That seemed quite unnecessary.

"Sir, with all due respect—"

"No," Savage interrupted him. "With all due respect, you were beaten quite handily by two people, even though you were in a far superior form. An insane beast you may have been, but your strength and speed far eclipsed their own."

"But the girl! She was far stronger than I could have expected—"

"And just what is she?" He paused, jaw opening and closing with no sound escaping. "You had time to figure it out, you have experience with all the different magical beings, cursed and otherwise, so why couldn't you figure it out?"

"S-sir, she is something I have never encountered—"

"Or could it be that you are losing your touch?" The wolf longed to intercede, to plead his worth and deny all claims that he was anything but competent, but everything he was saying had been interrupted. And he had no wish to be humiliated like that any more, especially in front of his future subordinate.

Savage stared the man down until he bowed his head in shame and shook his head, disappointed. "Lucondera is a monster hunter, and a tamer. He deals with the more... exotic and dangerous creatures that trouble people. He has a few pets to help him deal with the girl. You will have one more chance to kill this Raven, do you understand?"

He bowed, "I do. Thank you for the opportunity."

Savage sighed as he left. "A wolf, with the pride and instincts of a sheep." He waved Lucondera over and lowered his voice. "Check the temples, but be warned, we don't have the means to enter yet. Seren ordered an interrogation into what she knew of them. If she's smart and remembers, that's where she'll look."

The hunter nodded and left the room, leaving Savage to his musing. "Don't do anything to arouse her interest? Too late for that."

15. The Dream of a Promise

Sleep did not come easy for Valour. No, that was wrong entirely. Sleep was easy; a restful rest not so much.

To all those people who say you cannot feel pain in a dream, she had some choice words. The memory of agony clung to her. Like a leech, it sucked all the joy and peacefulness and left only fire behind.

She was back in that dark tent. The person was faceless, featureless, but the instruments were always the same.

A small silver scalpel, a bracelet made of bone and vials of poison that dripped acid into her veins and smashed hammers against the inside of her skull.

She felt helpless, trapped and fearful. That last feeling was especially horrifying. In the past two or so weeks, she had felt fear more than she ever had before.

It was a clawed hand of ice wrapped around her heart, squeezing like a vice slowly clamping together, pressuring, crushing, until her eyes rolled up and her breath could no longer pass her locked up throat.

There were shadows in the room, five of them. They were saying something. Static.

With a startled gasp, she was thrust back into the waking world. And with a shuddered gasp of exhaustion, her eyes rolled up and she fell back. If her head had hit anything other than a pillow, she would have been sent right back into the arms of the dream.

"Easy, you're alright."

The voice was familiar. That was the only thing that stopped her from freaking and lashing out.

"You're safe now. That wolf will not bother you again," the voice promised. "As long as I stand, he will suffer in the end." The voice grew darker, but the vengeful promises of retribution didn't frighten her. For some odd reason, she was comforted?

She opened her eyes slowly. The lights were dim and there was a window somewhere that was beaming in rays of dim starlight. She stared up and almost yelped. Vivian was smiling down at her, that part was alright. More than, really, but uhm... she had a bit, er, a *lot*...

"You have... blood on your... everything."

Vivian frowned and then looked down at the rags she was still wearing, even with the offers of a change in clothes. "Ah yes." She smiled at Valour, but the look was a bit... strained. "You have been out for three days since our arrival. Sleep is a luxury I will not allow whilst I watch over you. Therefore, whenever I find myself on the cusp of passing out, I simply... reset myself." She smiled at her disturbed patient.

"That's... absolutely horrifying, never do that again," she demanded. "That's... I can't even, oh my god." She couldn't find the words. All she could think was that they had to have a long discussion about this.

"Don't worry, what is death to someone who cannot die?"

"Something that should not be tempted, and something that you should not do regardless. Nor should you take it for granted, and neither should you do it again, because that is bloody terrifying."

Vivian smiled weakly. "You are an interesting character."

"What, because I tell you it's a bad idea to ki... I can't even say it."

"Indeed. When I was training, my father and teachers told me I should die in various ways, to see if I could build up both an immunity and tolerance to pain."

"... An immunity to death? Logical, but also what the f—"

"I know, it sounds bad," Vivian hastily interrupted, growing alarmed at her dismay, not having thought a careless comment could cause her this distress. "But truly, my death is not something anyone needs to be sad about!"

"I would be sad!" she yelped. "I'd be sad every time you die, even if it doesn't stick! No one should have to die multiple times. Oh my god, it sounds so weird every time I say it." She planted her head in her hands and started counting slowly, trying not to hyperventilate.

Vivian winced and put her hand on her shoulder, sitting on her bed. "My death, however many times it occurs, should only be a burden to myself. It's alright, *I* will be alright."

Valour sniffled, giving her a small smile. "Well, at least the recklessness makes sense now. But if I ever meet the man who encouraged his child to do these things, we will be having words!"

"As you wish," Vivian smirked, as Valour started glaring at the wall. Truly, it was like a puppy trying to be mad at anything. Ineffective and adorable.

"How does that work anyway?" Vivian hummed questioningly and Valour continued, "The whole dying and coming back to life thing."

"Ah," she grimaced. "That, requires a bit of story. What do you know of the Oélthrinír?" Valour shrugged, looking confused. "Understandable. To my knowledge, they all got bored of this realm a long time ago. Oélthrinír, are a species of magical beings. Think... ghosts, but made of magic, that can manifest with a bit of help."

"My mother," she grimaced, "is rather high up in the Luminescent Court. That is, the fairies who rule the day. She is also their most powerful enchantress. On the day I was born, she put coins inside my soul and 'blessed' me to rise every time I fell."

"Oh," Valour mumbled. "Why did she do that? Uh, not that I'm complaining or anything!"

Vivian smiled reassuringly, putting the frantic redhead at ease before she knocked herself out. "Of course not. The answer is, I don't know. My best guess is she needed me to do something, and for that she couldn't let me die."

"Okay, now that that's out of the way, I'm still stuck on the *how*?!"

She shrugged. "'Other' magic is a mystery to everyone but them. It's better not to think about it, but trust me, that's one of the questions I'll ask her when I meet her again." She frowned sadly, "*If* I meet her again."

Vivian glanced towards the window. "There are still hours left in the night. Sleep again Valour. If you are ready to wake properly in the morning, we shall speak more then. Okay?"

No, not okay. She wasn't ready to go back, didn't want to close her eyes and wake up back there. She wanted to stay here. At least this dream wasn't hurting her.

She frowned. Was this all a dream? It certainly felt like it. She was numb to physical feeling, but she still *felt* quite powerfully when it came to emotions.

Her eyes closed and she felt her fear rise then slip away, as she realised she had debated herself back to sleep.

Images flashed. Her dreams exploded before her eyes.

She was back in the tent. She felt her skin split as he ran that silver blade down her arm. She saw the pictures as he demanded what she knew.

Wait.

Pictures?

She didn't remember that. She focused, or whatever the equivalent was, and they came into stark relief. The drawings were obvious, they were buildings. He showed her pictures of a familiar symbol. The circle above the book.

Then he showed her a similar picture, but with a few additions. Beneath the book, there were smaller symbols. A sword overlapping a shield, underlined by a quill. Everything else was the same. It was a common symbol, so why would he want to know what she knew? Did he not?

No. There was no way. That wasn't the important bit. It was the buildings. The vision shivered and her sight unfocused, then the other picture was shoved into her face again. It was a temple. No. The temple was only part of it, a small part, it was more like a shrine.

There were others. On one building, there was a small detail, a sword on a shield. On another, there was a quill. All of them beneath that circle. It was starting to become clear, and someone was painting quite the unsettling picture.

When she woke up the next time, she knew she had to find Bastian. He was a member of the Premise; he should know something.

Unfortunately, she was rather distracted by the strange, somewhat amusing sight of Vivian looking completely awestruck at a cat that was sitting on the end of her bed. It was a brown-furred little thing, smaller than her knee, with green eyes staring at her.

The cat looked, dare she say, annoyed. Its eyes were half lidded as it occasionally flicked a glance at the other girl who was edging closer, only to flinch back with a little "Eep!" when she caught its eye.

"Good, morning?" she murmured, reaching up to scrub her eyes, ready to dismiss this strange scene as another deluded dream.

Vivian smiled softly at her, but still kept glancing at the cat. "Morning. It's good to see you well, Valour."

"... Do you want to pet the cat?"

She choked and flushed, staring at her wide-eyed. "What?! N-no! Of course not." She turned to the cat as a low rumble started in its chest. "I-I apologise for her, Mr. Spectre, she does not yet know!"

"Spectre?" She mumbled. Why did that name sound... wait. The guy from the camp? The one she saved from having his face bitten off?! "You're a cat?!"

The cat 'sighed.' And yes, it looked every bit as weird as it sounded. It jumped off the bed and, to Vivian's very visible disappointment, its form blurred and Raven stretched, cracking his back.

"Sometimes," he murmured, answering her question. "It's a trick I learned a while back. Helps me relax when things get a bit stressful."

Valour slumped back, staring at the ceiling. "People turning into cats. People turning into giant man dogs. People unable to die. Magic is so... weird."

She huffed and slowly rolled herself off the bed, which was actually a table she was just now noticing, and winced at the pain in her back and neck. "It would've killed you to gimme a pillow or something?" she whined.

Vivian shrugged. "Surprisingly enough, there aren't any sold in this village. Apparently someone's already bought them all."

"Someone bought *every*—oh, wait. Never mind, yearly mass sleepover at the great hall. I remember. People dump their kids so they can have a night to go and get wasted."

"That seems very irresponsible," Vivian criticised disapprovingly, and blushed in embarrassment as Valour paused to stare right at her, raising an eyebrow. "I withdraw my former statement," she murmured mournfully.

"As you should," she said. The half magic ghost had no right questioning other parents' choices, when their earlier conversation had shed light on some disturbing revelations.

"Where are you going?" Raven asked her, discretely putting himself between her and the door. "You just woke up from a little coma. You should be resting until Bastian gets back."

"I have no time to wait. I need to speak to him immediately."

"Okay, go back to bed. I'll go grab him and get him back here." He ignored her complaints, giving a look to Vivian. "Watch her? She'll likely hurt herself, make an injury worse."

"Agreed," she murmured, and Valour felt hands on her shoulders, guiding her back. It was a few minutes later when Bastian stormed in, berating a disinterested-looking Raven.

From the tail end of what he was saying, it was largely about her and how her awakening should have been brought to his attention immediately. Well, that and some snide comments about his coat.

He strode over and held his finger up, shining a light from the pad of his finger. "Any abnormal pains, specifically in your head or chest?"

"Nope. Can't you just use magic to find out anything wrong?"

He blinked and stared at her as though she were stupid, or had suffered quite a severe blow to the brain. "What? No, of course not. You need to stop reading fantasy books. They're screwing with your common sense."

"I don't think magic and common sense belong in the same sentence."

"You would be surprised on some accounts," he murmured, taking her pulse. "I once saw a trainee try to heal something that wasn't injured. There was no problem, but the spell was supposed to heal injuries. When it couldn't find anything, the intent and nature of the spell vanished, leaving the patient to be injected with pure magic."

Valour winced. "I remember you told me once; pure magic is like poison when it comes from other people. Did he live?"

"No. Quite the opposite. He blew up, killing himself, the medic and knocked his teacher through a wall. This incident was the inspiration for the revision movement. All medical education was overhauled and, suddenly, everyone was competent."

"So, how did you learn that skill?" Vivian asked Raven.

"I spent a couple of years running around Trivalga. One of their rainforests had a tribe of shifters, and I traded a few skills for the cat trick. I had a choice between a cat or a rhino. Didn't need the fighting help, so I went for the small escape artist. Served me well over the years."

"What skills did you trade?"

"Eh, just a couple of strategies, couple of spells, bit of lightening and a few sparks of fire. Made a couple of friends though, taught me how to properly cook a boar. Did you know their liver is edible?"

"I did not, and I could've gone the rest of my life not knowing."

Raven chuckled.

Valour stood up from the bed, cracking her back as she went. "What do you know about the Silver Premise buildings? Specifically, the ones with the book, sword and shield, and the quill?"

Bastian paused, looking at her strangely. "Not much, I was a medic. Technically, I shouldn't even be in charge of this place. But, people are often pulled from their calling, especially if the Premise needs something from you. What does the symbol look like? They love their codes, and different positions mean different things."

"The book was above the sword and shield, which was underlined by the quill."

He frowned. "Sounds like a training ground. But the only ones I know of are a combination of the former two. I've never heard of one that uses all three."

"What do they mean?"

"Well, the symbols are self-explanatory, really. The book, is the departments of history, wisdom and knowledge. The sword and shield, are the physical learnings. The quill, is an oddity. It represents the department of secrets, they who delve into the mysteries of everything. So why in the hell would the quill be with either of them?"

"I'm wondering why the hell someone would name a department 'quill.'"

"That's because you're a teenage brat with no respect for the beauty of subtlety. Although, I can't really blame you, considering with all your strength you've never had a discreet moment in your life."

She huffed loudly, displaying perfect mockery of affronted disdain, and then snickered as he turned his back, rolling his eyes at her dramatics.

"Now then, these two will take you to your grandmother's new house. It's just across the street from the old one, and they will be staying in the one next door. Neither of them are owned or occupied, and no one really cares. So, off you go, and for god's sake, remember my library is not a hospital next time."

Valour grinned at him and all three walked out of the door chatting about something inane. He really couldn't care less. Not trying to be rude this time, but he wasn't actually entirely honest with her earlier.

And it pained him to lie to her face. Honestly, the girl was one of his only friends after all, but some things were secret for a reason. He waited a few minutes, just long enough to make sure none of them were coming back, and then walked into the back room.

There was a small hall with only two doors. One led to his sleep chamber, the other he unlocked first with a white iron key around his neck and then he placed his hand on multiple spots. Small pictures lit up after every press, symbols of one of many ancient languages, this one more commonly used as protective measures.

"As I am the warden, Gala, I am the one with the key to definition, Asral, show the light that sees the path, Dirthir, illuminate the dark that becomes the path, Gala."

The pictures all glowed and the door *clicked* open. Inside was a small archive, though he acknowledged it was only small in his own opinion. But when one has seen the palace of knowledge and wisdom the Premise owned, everything becomes lesser in their eyes. Seven metres across, the only place not covered in some form of storage unit was the small table and single chair in the centre of the room.

He knew almost instinctively where he would find what he needed. Crossing over to the wardrobe in the far corner to his left, he paused to lay a hand on the symbol branded on a metal plaque. A bandage beneath a silver circle. To everyone else it seemed silly, not something you would expect to see as a symbol for the Premise, but to him it meant...

He wiped a speck of dust away, grimacing at his reflection in the polished, shiny silver and opened the door. He knelt down to look at the lowest shelf, the one he had never needed to look for, nor had he ever expected to need to.

He dragged out the box, hefted it over to the table and set it down with a *thump*. He wiped the dust off and opened the lid leaning back, as though expecting the papers to leap out and strike.

There, printed at the top corner of the first page, was the symbol exactly as Valour had described. He shivered as the room seemed to grow colder, though the wind had no place here. No windows, the door was sealed as soon as he closed it, the room was at a constant temperature, exactly how he preferred. Was it in his own mind? He doesn't have many doubts. It wouldn't be the first time his fear had chilled his skin.

He looked at the symbol bitterly. "A fool's hope I had," he muttered, putting it aside and pulling out a few more stacks. "And yet, it was one I dearly wished was true. Why here? So far away from everything, why here of all places?"

He resigned himself to a day and night of reading, some things old and some he had yet to see. It had been a long time since he had read up on the Chosen of the Light and their history with the Premise.

16. The Hunted

Valour grimaced as her eye twitched.

It's been happening ever since they left the library.

The twitch itself wasn't what bothered her, though it was quickly getting on her nerves. No, the thing that had her *itching* was the eyes she felt stabbing her back. She glanced at the other two every so often, but knew they hadn't felt it.

She shook her head and tried to focus on the tour she was giving. She had tried to tell them there wasn't anything of note, but Raven claimed they weren't in it for the sights. She'd been confused, because why would they want a tour if they weren't going to look at things?

Vivian told her they were looking at strategic points: high ground, ambush locations, bases, defendable positions, the lot. She'd just nodded and smiled; strategy like this wasn't really her strength. She was more of a charge in, hit 'em hard kind of girl.

Absently, she heard how her favourite shortcut alley was a decent ambush position, though she could do without the detailed explanations of how to cut someone's throat. Unnecessary, disturbing and not an image she wanted in her head.

It was early afternoon when they started planning. The new house looked almost identical to her old one, except the carpet was a bit bigger, there was a small dent in one of the walls, there was no crack in the window frame and a lot of other little things.

"We need to do some reconnaissance. We have nothing to go on and the longer we stay here, the more danger our base will be in," Raven said.

"Agreed. Our problem remains. Where do we find information? I am all for spying, but if we don't know where we're going, there's no point setting off." Raven nodded at her point, frowning in thought.

"We could wait until granny has a vision," Valour offered. "That's how I knew about Senway in the first place."

"A good idea, but we can't grow too dependent on it," Raven told her. "It'll turn us reactive and we don't want that unless there's no choice. For now, we take note of our options and our assets. We need to find whoever the lieutenant was working for, and stop him doing whatever he's doing that requires killing innocent people."

"We could go back to Senway, find the bar the lieutenant worked at and backtrack from there?"

Valour tuned them out with a frown. That feeling was back. She rubbed her arms, the room was starting to shrink, she glared out the window at the empty street out front. There was nothing there, but it was starting to irritate her.

She sniffed the air, but still nothing unusual. She strained her ears, but again nothing. She could only hear the heartbeats and breathing of the other two in the room.

"Valour?" she snapped back, looking at them wide-eyed. "Are you alright?" Vivian asked her worried, and Raven was looking at her, understandingly.

"What's got you spooked, kid?"

She shrugged, feeling self-conscious. "It's stupid, just nerves I think."

"It's not stupid," he shot her down. "You've been through a traumatic experience; your senses are heightened to compensate. Trust me, you'll get better with time and help."

She frowned at him, "You think?"

He nodded. "Yeah. I've seen it before. You're not the only one who's gone through some stuff. You're not alone, kid."

She nodded jerkily; she wasn't convinced. She smiled at Vivian nervously, missing the moment Raven narrowed his eyes at the window.

"So we should wait for three days. If Valour's grandmother hasn't had a vision before then, we leave for Senway and do some digging around. We look into the bar and then we put out some feelers. Agreed?"

"Yeah."

"Agreed."

There were two rooms in the house, one for her grandmother and Valour set up the second for Vivian to use. She then took a blanket and pillow and laid them out on the sofa. All she had to do for Raven was coil some tea towels on the floor and he curled up in his cat form.

She lay there for an hour, occasionally pinching herself to stop from falling asleep. The night ahead terrified her. Although the pain had faded, she still felt her chest tighten, her head swam and she fought the rush at the back of her throat.

Eventually, even the pinching wasn't enough. Her eyes closed and she drifted away.

And then the nightmares came.

And then the nightmares were pushed away.

She blinked.

Her arms were wrapped in silver chains and the sun blinded her, piercing through the soft, layered tent.

She blinked.

And she was free, standing in front of a smoking, twitching wreck. It was a body, the skin charred black by the most intense heat she had ever felt. The head moved. She stared into sorrowful, pain-filled onyx eyes.

She blinked.

The black-haired boy stood a head shorter than her, probably the same age, but the way he stood alluded to a pride and confidence forged by years. He wore silky clothes, with a symbol threaded into the right shoulder. The red tick in a semicircle looked vaguely familiar, but she couldn't remember from where.

"Kin," he proclaimed. She frowned at him and opened her mouth, but no sound came out. "Save. Please. Time. Out." He stared at her, pleading with her to understand, and she was upset that she couldn't.

She blinked.

The same boy was in front of a tall man. He wore a half robe, something she'd never seen anyone wear. Maybe he was a monk or a priest? He reached out with both hands and grabbed the boy by the face.

Their eyes glowed the same shade of blue and the boy's sharp fangs jutted out as he screamed noiselessly. He let go, the vampire slumped and he strode over to write on a piece of paper.

She blinked.

"Dream." He looked at her anxiously. "Stride. Help." She stared at him, willing him to tell her where he was, trying to beg him.

She blinked.

She shot up with a gasp, sweat stinging her eyes. Raven was standing over her, hands on her shoulders, full of worry.

An hour later, she was sitting at the table staring numbly at her folded arms.

"I've heard of it before, but only in legends." Raven bit his thumb. "The branch can only be learned by someone with an affinity for it. It's not bound to bloodlines like so many others. Unlike seers, Dream Striders are random. The gift is soul-bound."

"But how does that explain how they can find the seers?" Vivian rubbed Valour's back soothingly, the other woman in shock.

"It explains it perfectly," he murmured absently, mind racing.

"Then, please, for those of us not in the know."

"Every human with a connection shares a kind of, link. Family, comrades, strong friends and hated enemies. Striders can use these bonds, and temporarily create a connection with someone, using another person they have a connection with. The man you saw, he must have been a seer. The connection a seer has to another is tenuous at best. So he used his own ability to boost it, but even then he could only get a vision of the place and time they were going to be. Valour, the vampire called you 'kin?'"

She nodded slowly.

"He's a prisoner. He must've heard of your own imprisonment, got a decent description of you somehow, and used that to imagine you a comrade in suffering. He forged the connection and used it to reach out to you. The shakiness of the dream proves the connection is wavy, not that strong, but he can get words across to you. Sadly, it's one way, but it may improve with time."

"But this provides us an opportunity!" Vivian said. "We rescue this Strider, and they lose their seeker. We save both him, and the seers in one fell swoop."

"One problem," he said back grimacing, "We don't know where he is, and we don't know how to find him. We'll have to wait again."

Valour stood up suddenly. "I need to go for a walk," she muttered. The other two nodded, exchanging worried looks.

"Alright. I shall go to the library, maybe Bastian knows more of this," Vivian said.

Raven nodded in agreement. "I'll talk to Lydia. She knew Adriana. Maybe she knows this guy."

As she walked, she had to smile, even though she felt a flicker of annoyance. It was true that the road she walked was on the way to the library, where Lydia was resting and Bastian was doing what he does, but did they have to walk a few metres behind her? It was so obvious they were following her; she could scent them from a mile away.

She shook her head. The walk was supposed to be good for her, fresh air, exercise and all that, but her head was swimming. Her breath was speeding up, her heart was pounding and she felt the ground starting to crack as her feet came down harder and harder.

The roads were starting to twist, the colours of the world were blurring together, her skin was starting to burn and she felt an itchiness at the back of her eyes.

She smiled as the two reluctantly peeled off and she cut into an alleyway. Immediately, she fell to her knees, trembling as the heat vanished and in the shade of the two looming buildings closing in on her. She felt so cold.

Footsteps approached from the other end of the alley. She felt a moment of relief. Did one of the others follow after her? She sighed and relaxed as they got closer. She lifted her head with a smile, only for it to be wiped away by a combination of two things.

One, neither of the two are blond-haired men with spears taller than their bodies.

Two, both of them had scents she could track.

"Greetings." He bowed his head, looking distinctly amused. "I have to say, you are quite the confusing creature."

Valour blinked slowly. "Excuse me?"

"No distinctive features." He flicked his fingers as he counted from a mental list. "No extra physical abilities, no identifying personality traits. What are you?"

"Don't know," she muttered. Her head was starting to settle.

"You don't know? Hm. Well, it matters not. Disappointing it may be, but it is not necessary." He slammed his spear on the ground twice in quick succession.

Bamf

She froze.

It brushed past her thigh, close enough to dig its large, finger-sized teeth into her neck. The panther was larger than normal, the tips of its ears reached her chin and it had metal armour atop its spine, head and shins. A closer look revealed these extremities growing out of the beast. Except for one, the collar wrapped around its neck. This monster *grew* its own armour.

"This is my pet, Sheere. An Umbral Kynosar Sabra. You cannot fight. Run."

He slammed his spear on the ground a single time. A light-purple aura shimmered over the panther, before *Bamf* it vanished. *Bamf* She threw herself to the side, barely avoiding claws as they shredded the air.

"How did you do that?" She risked a glance at him. He was studying her intently. He slammed the spear again.

Bamf

A heavy paw whizzed past her ear as she ducked. "Incredible. Enhanced senses as well, it must be. Well, luck be mine today, you can't smell me."

Valour turned in a tight circle. She didn't hear the noise and she couldn't catch a glimpse of anything, be it the colour purple or the faint shine of metal.

"A hint, little prey." She glanced at him and he raised a thumb at her? "When one is on guard, be it a job or an emotional state, humans never look up." And he jabbed his thumb upwards twice.

Her eyes widened, her head tilted back and she froze as emerald eyes glared down at her. The thing was clinging to the wall, digging all its claws into the stone and somehow staying perfectly still, save the rumbling as it started to growl upon her seeing it.

Bamf

It vanished, far quicker than the other times, and a red-hot pain ripped through her stomach. She jumped back with a scream, stumbling and falling out of the alley. The wounds were lighter than she first feared, the cuts superficial.

She looked down the alleyway. He was strolling towards her, not a care in the world. The panther *Bamf*ed in behind him, prowling low to the ground, and she knew there was only one thing she could do. She rolled over to her feet, got up and ran.

Bamf

She sped up, the world started to blur past, but there were steady thumps behind her and the rough growling breaths as it kept pace, snapping at her heels. She crossed into the park and ran for the trees.

She weaved through and spun around, catching the panther mid run, and twisted her body, throwing the big cat through the air and crashing through a tree. It was up a second later with a roar, *Bamf* it lunged straight after and slammed face first into a tree.

Valour smirked and started jogging, then snagged a tripwire. Darts flew through the air. The majority missed but her left arm was impaled by three. There was a slight burning. She swiped her hand down and knocked them out, and felt the burn fade away.

The panther roared as it *Bamf*ed in, slamming its shoulder into her back and sending her flying. Hitting the ground, she rolled across another wire and a log flew above her head at chest height.

She rolled again but didn't get up, grimacing as she passed a snare on the ground. She got up and kept one eye on the dangerous animal, glancing warily at the woods around her with new vision.

She saw the weaponry on the floor but not where they came from. The trees were plain, small trunked and spaced out, though even that was tough to traverse for the panther, weaving through them with a snarl.

Valour shifted, the panther crouched, the collar glinted and a small sparkle of light flashing off the amethyst jewel in the golden band blinded her.

The big cat leapt and she ducked away. It landed and pivoted with a victorious growl and, with a snap, the snare wrapped tight around its hind leg and dragged it into the air. Even though this was her plan, Valour couldn't help the choking laugh that bubbled up.

It bared its teeth at her. She smiled sarcastically back at it, then *Bamf*. "Oh, I forgot he could do that for a minute there."

"You are no ordinary human," his voice shouted. "Speed, strength, the way you move. You are no tiger, no lord of the jungle. These woods are not your habitat."

"They're more my home than yours!" She spun around, growls from the shadows beyond her sight had her jumping at falling leaves.

"No, little one. A home? Never. Home is where you relax, where you feel safe. Were this your home, I would have killed you by now."

His spear whistled through the air and she ducked before lashing out. A paw came out of nowhere and smacked her aside.

"Mystics in human form... I have hunted them all, or so I thought." She coughed, pushing herself up. "Never have I met someone quite like me and twice in the same month as well."

"I don't hunt," she hissed, dodging claws by a hair's breadth.

"Of course not. But the instinct is still there. I watched you, you know? For a whole day." He smirked as she bounced off a tree, seconds before Sheere tore gouges into it. "For a whole day, I watched you interact and avoid other humans. Your hatred of them is instinctual but it cannot be a species trait. You are half human after all. And yet, not fully grown. You see me and can keep ahead of my pet."

Beads of blood whipped through the air. "Barely. I could say I'm doing humanity a favour, by putting you down. But, heh, who am I kidding?" Valour and Sheere disappeared from his sight, crashing through the bushes and between the trees with howls and yelps. "This, is what I *live* for."

Valour slammed into a tree, keeping it between her and the beast for a *second* to catch her breath. The hunter was fast, not as fast as her or a vampire, but every time she dodged and tried to counter, that bloody giant cat was there.

She'd swerve and dip and dive, and then she'd get scratched or scraped by claw or tooth. It was almost amusing how these light scratches were exactly like how a housecat would deal them.

The hunter lunged and his spear cut through the top of her shoulder, and she threw herself away with a yell. There was a line burning across her skin and she lunged at him with a furious growl, only to get caught by the panther's shoulder check.

She rolled away, panting heavily, and the air broke apart as the panther emerged from thin air. It smacked her hard and she hit the ground again. It was strong, she had to fight the urge to just lay there, her body was exhausted and moving was a fierce challenge.

She had an idea. It was vague, dangerous and not well thought out at all, but it was the best she could do.

She ran for the hunter and, just as she thought, the panther vanished. She dodged his spear but didn't go for him. She heard the *Bamf* and dived to the ground. There was a great whack behind her and the hunter flew through the air with a scream.

He hit the ground still screaming. He must have broken a few bones, she grinned. She stood tall and faced the Umbral whatever he called it. It stood frozen, staring at the hunter's fallen form with uncertainty. It was hard to tell on a feline face, but it seemed to realise just how badly it had messed up.

The collar sparked and the panther howled in pain. She twitched and stared in horror as it fell to the ground. Valour didn't even think. She ran for the jolting beast and grabbed the collar.

Her muscles seized and she yelped in pain. She let go and stumbled back, the jewel glowed mockingly, and she growled at it, then froze in realisation. She threw a punch and slammed it into the jewel. With a crack, it broke in half, electricity sparking wildly. She grabbed the two halves and yanked them out, the glow faded and the sparks stopped.

With a click, the golden band fell open.

Sheere stood up on shaky paws, growling fiercely. He looked down at the jewel and stomped down on it, crushing the stone into dust.

He hissed down at the collar, a lot of repressed malice appearing from behind a carefully controlled mask, and he looked up at Valour with a level of intelligence she hadn't seen in him before. He glanced at her fingers, the electric burns still sparking, and nodded to her.

She nodded back, despite how uncomfortable she was. Sheere turned to the hunter and started growling.

"I see," he whispered, smiling slowly in the face of Sheere's rage. "Heh. Ha, hahaha! Excellently done! Well played indeed! Turning the hunt back on itself, forcing the predator to run and become prey, I now see. I have become complacent. My edge has dulled. This will do nicely. Farewell mystic. May your fangs dull themselves on the hide of your enemy and may your instincts always watch your back. Trust them, for there will come a time when they are all you have."

He turned and smiled at Sheere again, with all of his teeth. "Now come, beastie. Let the hunt begin."

And, holding his broken ribs, he ran as quickly as he could. Sheere growled and *Bamf* vanished.

Valour sighed heavily and started walking towards the library. The claw wounds were starting to heal. The ones across her stomach were already pink and she rubbed the scar on her shoulder with a frown.

It was quite obvious the werewolf had sent him; he was the only one who knew. What she told the hunter earlier was right, though unintentional. She had no idea what she was. The only reason she knew she wasn't quite human was her granny. The woman had refused to hide her nature, but said the identity was dangerous. Something about how realising it herself made it easier for others to know.

She rolled her eyes. Didn't make much difference with the hunter. She wasn't really upset about it, though some days she did wonder… she stepped through a tripwire.

She paused and sighed as something she couldn't see whirred and rumbled. "Oh for the love of—" she said, "Eep!" as a swarm of darts flew through the air straight at her.

17. The Furless and the Clawless

Earlier that day.

"She looks alright so far," Vivian murmured worriedly.

"Looks can be deceiving." Raven nodded at the park entrance and they split off from their tail.

"So, what brings a noble down to these heights?" Raven asked her.

"My friend was killed. I have a duty to see this through."

"Ah, revenge. I suppose that explains the blinders." He smirked at her confusion. "Don't worry about it. But let me give you some advice. Revenge is a spiral. You'll never be satisfied. There'll always be something more you can do, someone else to blame. In the end, you'll just be a shadow of what you were."

"Speaking from experience?" she joked with a stone face.

"Yes." He smirked grimly at her surprise, but there was no humour. There was nothing in his eyes but resignation. "Trust me. Hate is a fire that consumes you, it burns so much, and it hurts so bad, that eventually you don't care who you hurt, just that they're burning too."

She gulped as he looked at her, his eyes blank and expressionless, mere cinders and ashes of rage long burnt out.

"How do I stop it?"

He looked at her sadly. "There are two things that can happen now. You can do the easy thing, or the hardest thing imaginable. You can burn the world until nothing remains and satisfy yourself with destroying everything."

"Or?"

"Or you can let go."

***

"Wow, if I didn't know any better, I'd say you look one foot in the grave."

"Sod off you disrespectful little pilchard," Bastian grumbled. He had bags under his eyes and his hair was heavily mussed like a mop. "I've been up all—" a yawn broke up his sentence, "night. Oaths keep me from speech, but I have something that can help our next step."

"Our?" he asked.

"Yes. Speech is prohibited, but I can take you."

Raven hesitated. "I don't know if that's a good idea," he advised cautiously. "You may not like what you find."

"And what do you think I'm looking for?"

"Hope. A reason why—"

The doors blew off the hinges and a man charged in with a bestial howl. Behind him, a squad of four ran straight at Vivian.

"For the Wise Bears!" one of them yelled.

Vivian lunged forwards with a snarl and Raven had a moment to shake his head in disappointment before the other man was upon him.

It seemed he lost himself to his instincts, clawing, snarling and biting. The man was every bit the animal his curse had forced upon him.

His nails were abnormally sharpened. Raven got a light scratch before he kicked him back. He glanced at the wound, then threw his arms up to block wide swings.

In his natural form, his limbs secreted a dark liquid that coated his nails and teeth. It's not strong enough to transmit the curse, but he winced as his own limbs slowed down and a fist broke past both his arms to slam him so hard in the stomach that he felt his feet lift off the ground.

Vivian hissed as a sword she wasn't looking at slipped past her arm, opening up a cut. These four were better than all the others she had fought, better equipped as well. They moved as a unit, they had no problem ganging up on a single opponent and no difficulties capitalising on openings and mistakes.

She parried a blow and swiped at the man, but her own attack was parried to her right and another blade swung in from her left. It bit into her shoulder and she swung her sword over her head, but the blond man released his weapon and jumped back rather than lose his hand.

She reached with her left hand and grabbed it by the hilt, tugging it free and dropping it as she lost strength in her muscles.

She glanced at Raven, whose hands were sparking as he tried to unleash his lightning, but failed as the lieutenant battered at his arms and kept him close. She glanced back at Bastian, who was staring at the duo's fight, looking disgusted.

Bastian marched forwards and slapped Raven on the back, and the minor curse vanished. He blinked and his arms tinged blue as a dim aura of yellow enveloped them. He raised his left arm and blocked a swing with his elbow, then jabbed him twice in the chest.

Plato stumbled back as his shirt started smoking and Raven raised his hands. Lightning blasted out and, for a brief second, all anyone could see was a flash of white, and then it ended. Plato was missing, but there was a suspicious trench dug through the floor near the door.

"That was pathetic," Bastian spat, glaring at Raven. The brown-haired man ignored him, glaring at the four as they regrouped, looking vastly less confident now the odds were tipping away from their favour. "What has happened to you, that you were almost beaten by *that*?!" He couldn't find a bad enough insult, resigning himself to a look of disgust and vague dismissive waves at the door.

"It's been a while," Raven muttered.

"Bollocks." Raven glared at him, but said nothing. "I know what shame you are feeling, but shying away from *that* isn't just going to get yourself killed." He pointedly looked at Vivian, her arm bleeding and exhaustion beginning to kick in.

Raven stared at her injury, face twitching as though he fought an internal battle. "Fine. Kid, switch."

He ignored spluttered protests and just threw himself towards the four mercenaries.

"What was *that* all about?" she hissed at Bastian as Raven caught a sword arm and ducked under it, throwing his captive in front of a stab.

"That, was an arse kicking that man desperately needed," he grumbled. "When I saw him some 23 years ago, he would have handed that werewolf his arse on a platter, one-handed during a cardiac arrest. How he became a drifter, alcoholic jester, I will never know." He paused to groan loudly. "I take it back. He's a noble idiot, that's how.

"I resent that," she grumbled. "Nobility does not lead to alcoholism."

"I beg to differ. Nobles are the best drunks; nobody knows though because they're rich enough to drink bottles at their houses."

The last of the mercenaries fell to the floor with a thump, arm broken and his jaw bruised. "You left them alive?" Bastian asked him. "You have changed. Vivian, grab a shovel. I'll get my knife."

The two stared at him in shock and he burst out laughing. "Ha! The looks on your faces! Nah, just toss 'em outside."

"Shouldn't we leave them for the police?"

"What police? Closest city is Senway, and that place is run by criminals. People know better than to commit a crime against someone else there, because you don't get arrested, you get killed. This lot failed, and mercenaries who fail easy missions like ambushing an old man, a teenager and a homeless-looking vagabond get repurposed pretty quickly."

The door thudded open as someone violently kicked it and they staggered back in shock, staring as Valour walked in, angry, exhausted and overall looking done with life.

"If it's not any bother," she deadpanned, "can someone please remove the darts from my back." She turned around, showing how she'd developed into a hedgehog with how many pointy things stuck out.

18. The Lost and the Found

With every dart pulled free, the curses uttered by Valour grew more creative and fouler. With all the poison running through her veins, she was truly grateful for whatever she was, but she also longed for something less resistant, so that her torment would end.

Bastian was pulling the darts out and dropping them into a bowl that Vivian was holding. He had pulled the first dart out, took one look at the purple beads coalescing on the tip of the metal needle and immediately stabbed it back into her so he could go get some safety equipment.

"Quit your whining," he had grumbled. "The most you'll have is a migraine and some itchiness. Me? This'd actually kill me."

Raven was asking Lydia questions. Her granny had gone on a walk before they arrived. In her own words, she was annoyed with Bastian and needed some air, before she boxed his ears.

And the woman looked more than eager to do it still, even being an hour away from him. The questions about the seer had drawn a blank. She didn't know who he was and a forced vision showed nothing of value.

Bastian chuckled as he pulled out another dart, not a hint of a tremor in his hands. "I, on the other hand, have amassed exactly what we need," he boasted, looking at Lydia haughtily, smirking as her eye twitched.

"Except you can't tell us," Raven pointed out.

"Quite," he admitted. "I cannot tell you about these buildings, their purpose or what their allegiance is. What I can tell you, is that I found a picture of some familiar symbols in one of *my* books."

"But we knew that they were the Silver Premise already, so that's not helpful," Valour grouched.

"It isn't. But my book wasn't just about these symbols. They were about the Light's Chosen. The Benevolent."

"Oh." Raven's face fell. "Well god's damnit, of all the foolish, forsaken…" He turned and kicked a shelf. "DAMNIT!"

"Well, he's not happy," Lydia snarked. "What's his deal?"

"A bad experience, leading to a few years of bad choices. Do not worry, he will snap out of it soon." He disregarded the man as he stropped.

"Sorry," Raven muttered, running his hands through his hair and tugging at it. "But when someone messes with a place belonging to the Light or Dark, they tend to take notice."

"He is correct." Bastian apologised to Valour and tugged a dart out of a sensitive muscle, not reacting as she growled. "The Light in particular tends to be sensitive about its territory. If our foe is encroaching, then it shall know. If it knows, it's Chosen will know."

"The Chosen will tell the Premise, and the Premise will send a force," Raven hissed. "And when they do, the Ring will send a force to attack them. Luckily for us, it won't be another Chosen, just a task force or an assassin squad."

"Luckily?" Bastian asked doubtfully. "You know as well as I what shall happen after."

Raven started pacing. "Of course I do. They'll send a knight, someone to survey the place for strategic value. The King's wizards will sense the presence entering the island borders and send a force to repel them, peacefully or otherwise. Depending on the larger plans in place, the knight will retreat or carry on. No one has a foothold in Brinia yet, so our island has no value to them. We just have to hope they have bigger interests elsewhere."

"Wait." Vivian frowned. "If they don't have a presence here, why were you banished here?" she asked Bastian.

"Because neither of them have presences here," he repeated dryly.

"My gods, what did you do for this drastic punishment?"

"I did the one thing a member of the Light must never do. I gained the one thing it is absolutely forbidden for us to have. Doubt." He clammed up after that, refusing to speak any more on the subject.

"Why are we worried about knights? What about the Dark's Chosen?"

Raven snorted and Bastian let out a small smile. Both of them looked at her like she was a child that did or said something endearing.

"The Chosen of either have no real obligation, though the Light is quite good at choosing those who stay loyal to the Premise. The Chosen have no obligations to either of the armies, but the Light has always been more united than the Dark."

"What he means, is that the Chosen by the Dark tend to either strike out on their own, or ally themselves with the Ring in exchange for concessions. Although the goal is always to deal damage to the other, and work towards the great victory for their side, to be Chosen is sometimes a reward for a deed, or an aspect that takes a liking to you."

"We'll be lucky if there are only three Chosen per generation, but to be allied with the armies is not a requirement. Take the Great Uniter for instance, a man in Trivalga who, 300 years ago, united the warring tribes of the Ancient Forest. He was a satyr who gained the favour of the Light, but had never even heard of the war."

"And Lord Bayler," Raven muttered, "the man who caught the eye of destruction by starting the wars. He destroyed the Unity Stone and assassinated several figures and blamed various tribes. The following seven generations of slaughter granted him the blessings of the Dark."

Vivian nodded slowly. "So these temples have something to do with the Premise and, therefore, the Light's Chosen? And because they do, we have a very real chance of being enthralled in their war?"

"Unfortunately, if our enemy is seeking knowledge on the Final Moment, we may soon be seeing the end of the war, and not in a good way."

"Hang on, if it's final, as in the end of everything, won't that be a Dark victory?"

Raven and Bastian exchanged an uncertain look, which was quite frightening in Valour's opinion.

"The Light wins," Bastian said, "if the Dark loses. The Ring seeks victory by subjugation, for what point is there of ruling, if there is nobody to rule. The Light wins, by the complete eradication of the Dark."

"So, the Dark is good, and the Light is bad?"

"No," Raven immediately shook his head. "The Ring has proven time and again it has no problems ending the lives of millions if it means that their plans are completed."

Vivian frowned. "So the Light is good, and the Dark is bad."

"No," Bastian smirked without humour or amusement. "The Light has kidnapped and raised soldiers to be brainwashed into fighting their conflict, and has no problems killing innocent souls should they be 'tainted' by the Dark."

Valour grimaced. "So, neither is good?"

Bastian sighed. "The Premise has some of the most powerful healers and ancient medical spells. They have eradicated most plagues and healed the sick and wounded, providing support to many who have lost homes or livelihoods to natural disasters, or the actions of people."

Raven bowed his head. "The Ring has provided protection and support to the innocent, who are hunted down simply because of a potential that leads to something the Premise consider 'bad.' They are the proud owners of many institutions that support the refinement of talent and love for the arts, for the sciences and the development of all races."

Valour frowned, "So... neither is completely good, neither is completely bad...?"

"Everything's a shade of grey," Raven nodded approvingly. "Best thing is just to stay out of everything and deny any invitations that make it seem like you're picking a side."

Bastian nodded grimly. He pulled the last dart out and threw it into the bowl with contempt. "Despise that poison..." he muttered. "Raven, fetch me the map over in the non-fiction zone."

He turned back to Valour as the other man strolled off and wiped away the bits of blood that had surged to the surface. "There we are, poison's burning away and the marks are healing nicely. If there are any complications or pains, tell me immediately. Understand?"

"Yeah," she grinned, standing up to put her shirt back on. "Thanks Bastian."

Raven returned and rolled out the map over the table she was just laying on. The island they were on, Brinia, was divided into several pieces.

"We are over here, by Senway." He pointed to a segment in the very centre. "What we may or may not be looking for could be here." He pointed to a spot to the east, still in the boundaries of the section and near a large spot of blue, with small lines running throughout the island and into the sea. "There are other spots of course, but we shall start with this one."

"Seems easy enough." Vivian frowned. "What's the catch?"

Bastian nodded in approval. "There may or may not be a lock, but an iron key is not sufficient for magic. We do not need to bother with that yet, we simply need to go there. If Valour gains a dream, we shall adjust accordingly."

***

The party of four left Solitude by the eastern road, leaving Lydia behind in a 'safe place.' Valour's grandmother insisted that she was safe and no one argued, though all held doubts about the security, given she didn't tell anyone where she was going.

The moment they passed the temple's vicinity, all of them could feel it. A heat that caressed the skin, a welcome and a warning all in one.

There was a small village at the base of the path, long abandoned. The houses were cold and the gardens were overgrown, weeds and nettles in abundance over everything.

"What is this?" Vivian hissed, rubbing her arms as goosebumps popped up over her skin. "It feels..."

"Like a ghost town," Valour offered nervously, peering around at the shadows, expecting something to leap out with every twitch.

"It's a consequence," Raven muttered bitterly. "Wherever either of them go, no matter who they are or who they work for, this is always the result. They like to justify it, 'before creation comes renewal,' pretty words, a nice sentiment, but no matter how you dress it up, the innocent always suffer."

"And yet, good is always achieved. People die, yes, but we are not gods. We cannot save everyone. We must trust that their lives were not lost in vain," Bastian murmured, though he looked just as bitter as Raven.

"Again, the justification of those who do not care," Raven murmured.

It was strange, Valour reflected. Though their words suggested otherwise, they weren't actually arguing. More like quoting an old argument, one neither of them truly saw the point of.

There was a path beginning in the centre of the village that led up to the buildings themselves. The stone was hot but not burning, yet the grass and other plant life shied away from the heated shroud it produced.

They entered the courtyard without incident. The temple was in as much disrepair as the village below. Likely the only thing that kept the outside from gathering layers of dust was the sudden bursts of fierce wind.

"I have to say, I kind of expected something... I don't know, *more*," Valour said, looking around with disappointment.

"Uh, kid?"

She looked back with a curious hum and flinched at their disturbed expressions. Vivian was pale, looking around nervously and scratching at the back of her neck. Raven was shuffling his feet, hands in his pockets and staring at the ground like a chastised youth. Bastian was staring at the smallest building, the shrine of the temple, with his head tilted as though he was listening to something.

"You cannot feel that?" Vivian asked sceptically.

"Feel what?" She cocked her head to listen, but heard nothing. She closed her eyes to feel and sniff the air, but there was nothing except the warmth of the sun and no scent on the air, save the three before her.

"This isn't right," Bastian declared, scowling and marching for the building marked with the book. He placed his hands on the door and symbols lit up. "Wait, what? These aren't the…"

Raven stepped forwards, frowning as he studied them. "Uh, Bastian? Hate to be that guy, but those are Nordren runic locks. They're neutral magic, and correct me if I'm wrong, but the Premise tends to lean towards the Althura Sigils and the Arthuran Sun Script."

Valour inched over to Vivian to whisper, "Do you have any idea what they're talking about?"

"Somewhat," she admitted reluctantly, displeased with the amount of knowledge she was lacking. "Nordren runes form a language that deals with defence and offense. The Sun Script is based on blessings and powerful spells to influence the self and others. For example, I know of a Sun Script spell that banishes luck from a foe. The Althura Sigils are misdirection's, illusions, confusing the senses and producing powerful shields."

"Ah, okay." She looked back at the other two as they bickered. Raven reached out to touch a picture and Bastian slapped his hand, barking obscenities at him. "This is going to take a while."

19. The War

Valour stared at the last rays cresting over a distant mountain with increasing disbelief and irritation. Of course, this anger wasn't helped by the attractively smug face her opponent was currently wearing.

She looked down at the cards in her hands and admittedly had no idea whether the group of coloured images in her grasp were any good or not. Vivian had given her a crash course in what she says is a popular card game called 'Back Home.'

A number of rules had been 'conveniently' left out until opportune moments when suddenly a weird mixture of cards that looked like they had nothing to do with each other were a 'Clam Royal' or whatever the other girl said.

Valour was gearing up to accuse her of speaking nonsense and taking advantage, but the sheer delight Vivian tried to mask and the little grins that lit up her face stayed her hand and made her smile herself.

Of course, the little smirks and boasting eyes quickly turned her smile strained.

There was a bang of smoke over by the door and a loud curse as runes faded away, the symbols they'd drawn on the floor amounting to nothing, especially not what they'd hoped.

"I never imagined I'd find such a strange reason to hate the Premise," Raven grumbled as he limped over to slump on the floor, rubbing a scorch mark he'd gotten from the 'warning' the door had given them.

"Indeed," Bastian sighed. "Alas, the greatest foe is normally the one you would least expect. Bloody doors." He slumped down next to him, both of them dejected.

"Maybe you're coming at this the wrong way," Vivian said, picking up the cards Valour had thrown down and shuffling them. "Maybe there's a key. I mean, nobody really wants to draw a runic scheme on the floor every time they want to go inside. There'd be complaints and protests after the first week."

"If that," Bastian grunted. "But it's useless. If there is a key, then we cannot enter, and this trip has been for nothing."

"Not nothing," Raven drawled out. "We've learned several things actually."

Valour took this moment to get up and wander about. All this talk of keys and learning had given her an idea. She certainly wasn't going off of a vague notion in order to avoid her pride being trampled once again by the queen of cards, oh no. She would never be so exasperated by simple bits of cardboard and ink.

She wandered around the courtyard, skirting the edges of the overgrown garden and the empty moat surrounding a broken pedestal.

"For one, the Premise had a temple here. Their purpose may be beyond us, but they were here. Second, this place is old. So old, it must have been built, what, couple hundred years ago? At some point, it was abandoned and then it lost the Light's protection."

Something glowed in the grass and Valour's pupils widened. She dived for it and snatched it out of the grass with a wild grin. It was a small piece of glass but the part that caught her eye was the ring of gold around the edges.

"No! Valour! Drop it!" Bastian shot up, glaring at her. "You know damn well what shiny things do to your brain, now let it go!"

"I refuse."

"I swear to the gods, I shall not allow another bracelet event to happen!"

"As you say."

"Stop ignoring me damn it!" He waved a hand at the other two impatiently. "I'll explain in a moment, just take it from her before she gets worse."

Raven stared at him blankly. "I refuse, and you know damn well why I do." Bastian frowned at him and stepped in close to start a hissed conversation.

Vivian crept close and froze when Valour *growled* at her. "I know what this is like. I know what it is to see something, and have your blood drown you out. I want you to know, that I shall not take it from you."

Valour glared at her suspiciously with unfamiliar eyes and her heart almost broke.

"I know what these things mean to you. They are precious, they are something to admire. Shiny things, beautiful things, and when you possess them, others have no other option but to admire you. It is your pride, and your happiness. When they admire you, they do not dislike you."

Valour huffed and stared at her, the shiny object in her hands drooping in a loosened grip.

"Come to me, I will not move. Anything that happens here, it will be because of you, and because you make it so. Not your instincts." She held her arms out like she was asking for a hug and stayed perfectly still.

Valour stared at her and she knew the girl did not acknowledge her words or the meaning, but by the waters of the Day, she hoped the emotions she poured into her voice had been heard.

And then the girl took a single step, and she hoped. Valour stalked over to her and she felt nervous, but never did a hostile thought cross her mind. And then she held it out. Vivian blinked, looking at the lens, then at the expectant frown the lost girl had.

She reached out hesitantly, prepared to snatch her hand back at the slightest hint of aggression. But Valour just kept staring. When she took it from her, the girl smiled proudly.

"Thank you," she smiled, and Valour's happy little smile turned into a joyous beam. "It seems we both have burdens to bear, alongside the gifts of our blood."

The lens was a simplistic thing, though she noticed a few carvings on it, one of them quite prominent. She frowned, "Argol. Power, the beacon and the sun. Where did you find this?" she asked Valour, who just smiled at her. "Oh, right, I apologise."

She looked back at the door to the temple and frowned. She looked over the locks and then at the other doors on the other buildings. The runes used were different, all in different places and in different schemes, all save for one.

The rune carved into the stone frame above the doors, Argol, the elegant backwards 'S.' "Why would that one be on all of them? It doesn't even have anything to do with locking anything..."

She frowned, then moved forwards into the light, holding the lens up in such a way that the light shone on Argol.

As she expected, the rune began to glow. But what she didn't foresee was the runic lock fading as a new series of runes *behind* the lock began to glow, powered by Argol.

"Oh." Raven stared at it blankly, stepping past her to look more closely. "That's... a curse dispeller. The lock wasn't a lock, it was a curse? What the hell?"

"But that makes no sense," Bastian scowled. "The Council of the Premise outlawed the use of cursed runes; the proclamation was that they left a stain on your soul that the Dark could use to subjugate you."

"Yeah, and that would make sense, if the Ring hadn't outlawed the use of soul subjugation centuries ago," Raven uttered dryly. "Surprised everyone. Apparently, there were lines even the Dark won't cross."

Bastian waited for the light to fade from the runes and pushed the door open. For a temple that had not seen use in a long time, there was a strange lack of dust and dirt on everything. There was a large tapestry covering the far end of the wall, an archaic and frankly amateurish drawing of the sun. In the centre of the room were three statues of featureless beings.

"The first champions of the Light," Bastian informed them absently. "Touch the middle one, all of you. And don't look at me like that. It is necessary, I assure you."

Raven held out his hand, preventing Vivian from going first. He touched the statue and waited for a moment, until Bastian nodded. He waited a moment longer and then nodded at her.

Absently, she noted that the older man was making sure it was safe and she smiled a little bit. It made her happy to know he cared, even if she knew care for her safety was not needed.

She touched the statue. A second later, Bastian nodded, and she pulled away disappointed. Seeing Raven go through the exact same thing, she logically knew nothing special was going to happen, but she was still a little bit let down.

After Valour did the exact same thing, Bastian let out a little sigh of relief.

"Excellent. Now I can tell you what I know without the oath magic crushing my heart."

"Wait, what?" Valour chose an excellent time to come around, Vivian thought with a small smile of amusement.

"This place, this group of buildings, they are a joint training facility. The wisdom, knowledge and power gathered by the Silver Premise across time and gifted to those chosen by the Light. The greatest warriors, the most intelligent scribes, all would be summoned when a Chosen presents themselves. They would gather in one of these buildings and they would train to fight the forces of the Dark."

"Huh," Raven whistled. "I always wondered, you know. Little bit disappointed if I'm honest. I expected palaces, great pens with captured monsters, not high school. Bit Dark for something supposed to be Light, don't you think?"

"High school is not Dark, Raven."

"Tell that to teenagers everywhere."

"Shut up. I don't know why our enemy researches these places, but I do know where to start looking. For now, Vivian and Valour, I suggest going through the combat building and seeing if you can find any equipment of use. I shall go through the archives and see what remains."

He strode out, leaving the others staring in confused silence. "Damn it," Raven murmured. "Alright, do what he says. I'll find out what's up." He took a moment to look them both seriously in the eyes. "This place is dangerous. The Chosen have abilities beyond the common mage. Whatever they've left behind could be dangerous to the touch. If you have doubts, don't touch."

***

Bastian entered a room with a reverence he had sworn never to show again. But even with his years of bitterness and betrayal, a smile of wonder and joy wormed its way past his unfeeling mask.

"The Grand Mage's office," he breathed in awe. He ignored everything, the green pastured artwork on the wall, the fancy and elaborate little keepsakes on the wooden shelves, going straight for the iron box in the corner of the room.

"Let the path be laid out clear of the mist and of the darkness that seeks to beguile, Gala."

A rune formed on the box shaped by his will and magic and the door sprung open, the locks breaking under the force of the symbol.

He reached in and pulled out a thick book. The cover was worn, a leather hide with a simple strap holding it closed. He tugged it open. He skimmed through the pages, but after ten minutes, he threw it on the table with disgust.

"Not found what you were looking for?" Raven leaned against the door frame with his arms folded, a look of sympathy on his face.

"I suppose this is where you say I told you so?"

"Maybe in a minute or two. But while your situation isn't unique, it's just not going to be written down where anyone could find it."

"I just… there has to be a reason, there has to be…"

"Something more," Raven murmured, eyeing him as he slumped down behind the desk. "A reason why it had to happen. That doubt leads to corruption, or something that a dark mage could use to turn you, or worse."

"My banishment was not because of petty fear. It *can't* be."

"The people who took you in couldn't have thrown you away, cast you aside because they feared what you might do or what you might become, based on a moment when you asked questions they didn't like."

He groaned in abject misery, rubbing his face harshly. "What am I doing? They need my help and I waylay them with *this*, with *my* misery…"

"To be fair, this place holds a number of things which could be helpful. It's not a waste of time at all, but I do think you owe those kids an explanation and an apology."

"I do. Come. If I hesitate, I fear I shall never stop finding a reason to delay my moment of shame."

"Fair." They left the room, Bastian grabbing the book to take with him and Raven smirked, glancing at him out of the corner of his eye. "Oh, by the way. I told you so."

"Go to hell."

***

Valour and Vivian abandoned the search when they heard Raven shouting for them. Not a moment too soon, as they were just about to call off the search on their own. The only things they found were covered in rust or broken beyond repair. It seemed whatever magic kept the buildings clean did nothing for the objects within.

They told Bastian about the conditions and he rolled his eyes. "The warriors have always been particular with their equipment. They say that using magic to maintain their weapons makes them lazy and encourages shortcuts. I had hoped this place might be different, but clearly I was wrong."

"So what do we do now?" Valour asked.

"Now, I apologise," Bastian grimaced. "I have not been entirely honest about my intentions. When I suggested we come here, I had hoped to find some information regarding past banishments, like my own."

Vivian nodded in an understanding that Valour found confusing. "You seek knowledge on why they could have abandoned you. To know what you had done that would make them see you in such a way, that leaving you was the only course of action." And she understood. But she still had questions.

"What happened that caused you to doubt? What did you say or do that caused your banishment?"

She had asked these very same questions many times over the past years, but he had never told her, staying silent with such a look of pain that she lost the will to continue.

"... As there always was, as there always shall be, there was a lord of magic. A Dark one. He was different from the others. He did not work with the Ring, nor did he seek allegiance with them. He did not receive an aspects approval, nor was he chosen. He gathered an army and he started his conquest by capturing islands around Ereglos, the Land of the Silver Premise. He came the closest anyone ever has, or ever will, to defeating the Premise. He captured half of that continent. The victory of the Dark was at hand. The Light was being beaten. Until a small task force was gathered, for an assassination mission. The first ever assigned within the Premise."

He sucked in a deep breath, his face pale as he recalled unpleasant memories. "They pulled in two warriors, three mages and a medic, and put a sword in all of their hands."

Raven shook his head in disgust, "The Council, in all their infinite wisdom, pulled a healer away from his calling? Forced a practitioner of the medical arts to break his oath and cause harm to others? Shameful."

Bastian ignored him. "We infiltrated his fortress, made our way to his operations room and then…"

***

The room went silent. There were men and women everywhere, none of them fighters. There were no knights, no armour, no weapons, not even the faint hum of magic being readied for a spell. That should have been their first clue that something was wrong.

The second? When no one tried to run or attack them at the very least. They looked up from their papers and conversations about battle tactics, admired them like glossy furred beasts in a zoo and then went back to whatever they were doing.

Six armed strangers just walked into their most heavily guarded sanctum and they didn't care. Didn't even blink at the weapons in their hands. Oh, there was fear alright, but only flecks and it was sparse in the crowd.

And then they saw *him*. His back was to them, covered in a long black cloak that, as it caught what little light there was, revealed itself to appear like it was made of feathers. He was speaking with a dignified-looking man in a smart uniform of grey and dark green. The uniformed man looked at them, but, like the others, it was not fear they saw but disdain.

He was told to leave. The man saluted and then ordered everyone out of the room. They left through side doors, avoiding the large exit behind the group of assassins.

The Dark Lord turned to face them. As soldiers of the Light, they were taught to control their emotions, to suppress them when needs be, even the medics. But even the eldest and most distinguished amongst them faltered when they came under his burning red gaze.

It was then that Bastian had the numbing realisation. He knew then and there why no one was afraid. Why would they be, when this monster guised as a mortal man was at their side?

The two warriors were the first to die.

One charged and swung his blade, but the Dark Lord avoided him, moving around him with an unnatural grace, and then clapped his hands on both sides of his head. He had seen someone discombobulated before, healed enough burst eardrums to know the horrifying effects of such a simple move, but never before had he seen someone's eyes burst and their brains leak out of their ears.

The other warrior yelled in horror and grief, and then charged in a vengeful rage. The lord broke his arm in three places and used his own sword to disembowel him. He slumped to the floor, gasping out a prayer to the Light and crying as he tried to put his intestines back in with a shaking hand.

The mages were both overwhelmed by their fear, spells were cast with trembling voices but were broken by the doubt brought on by the rushing terror. When the last warrior died, a ball of fire was thrown, but it was backhanded by a casual wave and splattered against a wall. A hand gestured at him and the mage who'd thrown it was picked up off the ground and slammed into the scorch mark.

He died screaming as his body was melted into the stone.

The last mage held out a hand and invoked the name of a rune and, with a small chant, he summoned a single bolt of lightning. The lord caught it, allowed it to travel through his body, then channelled it into his hands and amplified it.

The resulting electricity was so powerful it set the mage's skin on fire and burned him until he was just ashes.

Bastian was not afraid to admit he dropped his sword and started crying. He also vomited, seeing his comrades slaughtered in such a way. He looked on as the lord approached him but he couldn't hate him. The emotion was lost in the maelstrom of fear, regret, sadness and a whole host of other feelings that meant the same thing.

But death did not come for him that day.

The lord grabbed his chin between two fingers and stared at him curiously. "You are not like them... I see no blood on your hands, nor can I see any ghosts that haunt you. Why you?"

Before Bastian could say anything, likely a plea or something equally as damaging to his pride, he saw a bright light through the window at the front of the room. It was the one that overlooked the front keep of the fortress and the one through which you could see the sky.

He had a fleeting belief that the gods were sending him a sign, some aid to say his life was not yet done or that his faith and goodness was being rewarded. He smiled with joy and hope, and then passed out as everything around him exploded.

***

"I later learned that my task force was never meant to succeed. Apparently, it was a miracle we even made it into the fortress itself. Though I have to agree with that last part," Bastian grimaced. "You would not believe how many planets had to align, how many celestial events had to take place for even one iota of that idiot's plan to succeed."

"What happened to the Dark Lord you faced?" Valour asked, awestruck as he wove the tale.

"The Council believed him too distracted to notice when they activated their greatest weapon. The Stronghold of the Premise. The oldest, most powerful artefact the Light has ever created. Utilising over three centuries' worth of charge, it launched a spell so powerful it devastated the defences and destroyed the fortress. I was spared by the whim of destiny, but the Dark Lord was not so lucky," he uttered grimly.

"So, the Council willingly sent you into a death trap, used you as bait so that they could launch a… a big… a bomb, they launched a bomb, and knew they were going to kill you and your team?"

"Indeed. But in the grand scheme of things, our lives equally balanced the scales when they were also ridding the world of a Dark Lord. It was very awkward when I showed up at my funeral, as that one twit I hated was giving my eulogy."

"And your doubt, it was if the Council were willing to kill their own people…"

"Then how is the Premise any different from the Ring? They use their people like pawns and cast them aside when they no longer have any use or use them to draw others into a greater trap so they can wipe the board." He smirked without amusement. "The truly terrible thing is that you don't know which side I just described."

***

When Valour fell asleep that night, in a sleeping bag placed on the floor of the shrine, she dreamt of lightning and fire, of blood and broken bodies.

"Cheerful." The Dream Strider muttered, kneeling on the floor. He looked exhausted, covered in scratches. Valour crouched by him and grabbed his shoulder, trying to silently convey all the support she could muster. It must have worked in some vein, for he smiled at her thankfully.

"Faralla. Timbura." She stared at him blankly. Had he just decided to start speaking in a different language? Not only was that extremely unhelpful, but also a bit concerning. Had he hit his head? Was he losing his sanity? Was he ever sane in the first place?

He looked at her blankly, "Not. Helping." Oh, so he could read her thoughts. Interesting. Disturbing. He shook his head slowly, "Dream." Okay, so he could read her dream thoughts. Interesting. Disturbing. He rolled his eyes and then blinked at her.

She blinked.

The ceiling was cracked. No dust though. That was some spell. She really had to learn it for when she went back home.

She woke everyone up and that made everyone mad at her, but she ignored it and told them. Interestingly, they all shared the same reaction. They all groaned in misery, but Vivian was the one with the strongest gripe. She slumped back and lay out like a starfish, going "Graahhahhaha…"

"Faralla is a former noble family," Bastian informed her grumpily. "They lost their title when the Premise accused them of consorting with the Ring a few hundred years back. A wrong accusation based on 'evidence' supplied to them by a rival family, but when the Faralla head tried to seek revenge, he did so by siding with the Ring. However, after the fierce battle, the Premise was victorious and the Ring abandoned his house to die on the battlefield. The head was executed, and his family was soon to follow, but the King and his army arrived and banished both Light and Dark from Brinia."

"The Faralla have hated both ever since," Raven winced. "And Timbura, the village they're situated in, has stood as a monument to neutrality ever since, spitting in the faces of both armies. That place hates everything to do with either, and deals with 'trespassers' quite harshly."

"So then why would they assist our enemy? If he seeks the end of everything, surely they should stand against him?!"

"If they know he is there at all," Bastian mumbled. "He could be hiding anywhere within the boundaries or even just outside of them."

"He could even be a noble, housed in one of their guest houses," Vivian offered. "But I can get us in and I can also get us housing, food and information."

Raven and Bastian gaped, astonished at her words, much to Valour's confusion and concern. "You can? How?!"

"My stepmother's maiden name is Alura Faralla," she explained. "My father's compound is on the edges of Timbura."

Bastian blinked slowly. "Uh, no offense my dear, but why are you not burning this place to the ground? From what I know, the hatred of the Premise is generational."

Vivian glared at him, but her gaze softened seconds later. "My stepmother hates the Premise, but she claims to have no choice. The rage is inherited. She says she had no choice, and it has impressed upon her the beauty of free will. She has given me the knowledge of what occurred and allows me to form my own opinion. I have no love for either, but their weaponry and wisdom is useful, if it is salvageable."

"I see," he murmured mournfully. "All it takes for one to appreciate a gift is to have it taken away and placed out of reach."

"Not always," Raven sighed. "But depressingly often."

20. Abomination

Even as he received a troubling report, something that could prove disastrous in the end and ruin all he had planned, Seren did not take his eyes off the thing lying on the table. The man giving the report was dressed all in black, a stereotypical spy, but there was something strange about him.

His skin was pale, not unlike a vampire, but even vampires had some measure of life within them. This thing did not move like a human or a predator of the night. It did not move with the sometimes unseemly and awkward moves of a human nor the grace and natural swagger the top of the food chain provides.

No, this creature was neither, a thing made of magic and given life by a ritual created by a Dark practitioner many centuries ago. Seren had paid for this knowledge some time ago, but had not found it necessary until now. Until Savage had stupidly gone and antagonised a potentially powerful enemy not once, not twice, but three times.

Granted, Seren took some responsibility for the second time, but now steps had to be taken. Now weapons had to be built. He sighed loudly, halting the report as he stared at the ceiling sadly, mourning the time when he didn't need to waste all that gold and hire even more mages just for the simple task of killing the world.

Savage entered the room and froze as Seren's spy turned his head a hundred and eighty degrees to stare at him.

"Leave us. Your job is done. Wait in the hold for new orders." The spy's head turned back and it bowed to him, striding towards the door with stiff movements, like its joints were filled with sand.

"Golems? *That's* what we're stooping to?!" Savage snarled at him.

"How amusing. The serial killer, psychopathic sociopath wishes to speak about levels."

"You know damn well what I mean! Those... things have no souls! No blood, no life, they're autonomous things with no loyalty, no respect, no restraint!"

Seren stared at him with surprised mirth. "Again. *You* wish to talk to I about these things?"

Savage hissed and spat on the floor. He was about to leave when he saw the table and the thing on top of it. "What the hell is *that*?!"

Seren turned back to it, just in time for people dressed in white surgery outfits to enter the room, carrying a large body part. "You tell me."

His anger and vitriol was long forgotten as he stared at the amalgamation of body parts with awe. "A human larynx, human head. The teeth, tongue and eyes removed, all hair burned off... that torso is a troll's, that heart... an Umbral Kynosar Sabra. I recognise it as one of the trophies that idiot hunter displayed in his tent."

"Ah yes, Mr. Lucondera," Seren smiled serenely. "Since his disposal, or imminent death by teleporting panther, I have... repossessed his belongings. The lungs belonged to a salamander, the legs a leaping cave toad and the arms from the hide of a basilisk. Since giant snakes don't have arms, we needed to carve hands out of the body and transplant the claws of a venomous Hyrantheer. Sadly, they only have the two spikes, so we needed five specimens."

Savage stared at it with a creepy grin that was getting wider by the second and with every word spoken. "The ultimate killing machine." He frowned. "So how are you bringing the thing alive? Doesn't matter what you put into that thing or how much blood you pump into it, it's still dead."

"The same way I brought my golem to life."

"That'd take a *lot* of magic."

"Did you know, this land has something in common with both the Ring and the Premise?"

"I did not, for I never cared to know."

"This is the place where all those who seek retirement, or are disillusioned come to be. Sadly, when one lives their life full of magic and action, the boring and simplistic ways of a peaceful land becomes quite aggravating. And so, they sell their talents to the highest bidders. Some become advisors of nobles, but they can't help but carry their grudge. Did you know, that even though the King still upholds his ancestors' banishment, he has ex-members of the Silver Premise inside his court?"

"Again, I did not. Never cared."

"And when I told them this, several old members of the Ring were quite upset, quite upset indeed." He smirked satisfactorily. "I told them my plan, a little bit of the grand plan and they hopped on board immediately, provided they can assist me when the time comes."

"Ah." Savage made a sound of realisation as he caught on. "You hired a bunch of them to bring this thing to life and created that golem to test the procedure and make sure it worked on something smaller. You probably made other things to make sure there'd be no problem raising this thing."

"Indeed." Seren smiled happily, skilfully lying to the other man, effortlessly concealing that he had a purpose for them beyond mere tests. The spy golem, for instance, had told him many things that Savage had been hiding from him.

He knew that the hunter had lost control of his pet, because the golem had been in that very room when Plato had given the other man his report. Speaking of, actually...

"Now, I have something for Mr. Plato." He reached into his half-robe pocket. The thing was awfully deep and wide—you could fit two flasks in there side by side—and pulled out a little vial full of silver liquid. "Something I bought from the Ring members I hired."

Savage took it and popped the cork, taking a whiff of the vapours that escaped the confinement. "Wolfsbane?" he muttered in surprise, and then took another sniff. Seren smiled a little when Savage grew annoyed at being unable to identify anything else.

"Wolfsbane, and a few other bits and pieces that allow him access to his beast's full capabilities, for a brief time. Call it a gift for exemplary service over the years." Seren smiled again.

The potion was heavily toxic, and even though it did as advertised, it would also kill the man slowly and painfully. A fitting punishment for both, seeing as he couldn't yet wash his hands of Savage, as the man's criminal connections were too valuable. For now.

"A nice offer," Savage nodded. "Securing the man's loyalty and making our tools stronger at the same time."

"Indeed. I have more use for him, so it only makes sense." A light warning. Savage was going to kill the man when he arrived, but that he wouldn't do just yet. He would have to satisfy his homicidal desires elsewhere.

"So, what are we going to do about the Strider? I mean, when he goes, the vampire lady is going to come after us. That's what you said, right?"

"Indeed, I did. It is unfortunate that our ally, Mr. Gordova, kidnapped him without our knowledge or consent. It is equally unfortunate that a two-week festival has been arranged and he will be the guest of honour. A festival where the dress of choice will be robes, much like my own."

Savage blinked at him, completely lost. "Uh, I don't know of any festival that lasts that long..."

"Of course, the festival will be thrown in the honour of the Faralla, as thanks for their patronage. All the family will be there and Mr. Gordova will greet them. He shall have Mr. Plato as personal security and Mr. Gordova will have full command over his lieutenant."

"I still don't see what this has to do with anything?"

Seren screwed his eyes shut and sighed. The level and quality of intelligence around him was astonishing. One moment he could be the equal of any genius with his insight and the next? Well…

"It is called a feint. I am going to attempt to throw them off my trail with a duplicate. He will dress like me and he will act as though he were the one in charge of this operation. When they kill him, they will lower their guards, imagining their victory over me."

"Ah, okay, now I see. So, what kind of festival will it be?"

"I do not care. Mr. Gordova will handle this."

Savage nodded and Seren breathed heavily through his nose as the other man's gaze kept going back to the creature.

"You have a question. Ask, stop the fretting."

"You said the legs came from a toad, I just… how does that help with anything? What does it contribute?"

"The leaping cave toad has some of the strongest leg muscles in any predator." He ignored Savage's quiet snicker at the words 'toad' and 'predator' being in the same sentence. "It can jump upwards of twenty metres and has enough muscle strength to kick through steel."

"… I'm sorry, what?! A toad can… what?!"

Seren smirked to himself as Savage stared at everything, bewildered and his sense of reality completely shattered. Maybe it was a good thing to keep the idiot alive. He was finding very little humour in things these days, and breaking people was oh so fun.

21. A Festival of Confusion

After four days travel.

The fireworks screeched through the air, coloured trails of smoke left in their wake, and exploded into lavish colours. Reds, greens, pinks all illuminated the night sky as screams of joy and gasps of admiration accompanied the explosive sparks and pictures that sought to paint the troposphere.

The group moved quickly out of concern for their fourth, Valour, who gripped her ears with both hands and snarled at the sparks, but whimpered with every thunderous *SNAP*. Vivian rubbed her shoulder with a gentle whisper as Raven led them down the road, his expression clearing the path of any merry-goer that sought to block them for any reason.

Bastian glanced at the few people they saw with a hum, narrowing his eyes. He shook his head; they had other priorities. From afar, they had seen the light show and been impressed and awestruck, but as they got closer and the sounds grew louder, the problems started to rear their ugly heads.

The road they walked split off not far from the entrance to Timbura, onto a stone-layered path that seemed to shine with the amount of care given to it, unlike the one that led further into the village.

"Not far now," Vivian whispered to Valour. "See? Just there, we can go in and set you up in one of the rooms. We can blot out the sounds and watch the lights without the horrible noise."

The home of the El Lock family was large, grander than any mansion, yet less than a castle or small fortress. The open gate gleamed with bars made from silver and the stone archway was decorated with images of kelpie, horse spirits that inhabit bodies of water, erupting from rippling lines painted on the stone.

The wall that surrounded the building was low, only two metres tall, which was an abnormal level of security for a noble house. They entered the gardens unhalted by the guards, who took one look at Vivian and bowed, backing off to their posts.

Vivian took the lead with Valour, taking them past detailed hedge sculptures of horses and arches. Before the door leading into the large building was a big fountain, a large statue of a woman in a long flowing dress and many bracelets up to her elbows. Resting on the edge was another female, looking up at the stone woman with a sad smile, wiping away a single tear.

"Matt'her," Vivian called out, a strained smile on her face.

The woman snapped around at the call and covered her mouth with a hand as tears began to flow. The woman with flowers in her long braided ginger hair ran for her and threw her arms around Vivian's neck, sobbing loudly.

"Vivian, ma datt'hir! Lev tell pronere!"

Vivian relaxed, sighing in relief at the words. "Matt'her... Vel quory..."

She moved back, wiping her face with one hand, the other still clutching her shoulder. "Never apologise, my dear heart. I know of the anguish a loss can give you and I understand the actions one must undertake. But please, do not leave us like that again. Hy drimer canth laik uit."

Vivian embraced her stepmother tightly, apologies on the tip of her tongue, but she did not speak them. She would make it up to the woman she cared so much for, but words only got her so far. Shiny jewellery or big stuffed animals were in order. The woman was a fan of the big cats, just like her, so she already had a plan.

Alura El Lock née Faralla smiled happily at her daughter, looking her over for injuries. And though she couldn't see any, she knew Vivian's 'special condition' made looking rather pointless, so she asked.

"Now, what have you been up to? You were leaving for Senway, yes? Did you find what you were looking for? And did you encounter any trouble?"

"Let the girl breathe, Alura," a voice drawled out. Vivian paled and stood tall as the large black-haired man strode out of the manor.

Dressed sharply, the jovial-looking gentleman portrayed the essence of grace and nobility, his smart clothes and neat hair on both his scalp and chin cut close, yet still bold. He did not appear particularly sharp, until you saw his grey eyes and the storm behind as calculations and plans were plotted in plain sight.

"You know she is fine, for she stands before you. And no trouble can outlast her." He smiled in amusement, yet his eyes betrayed his words as he glanced rapidly at all her vital areas, slumping slightly with relief as he saw her good health.

"Just because she can reawaken does not mean I wish her to sleep at all!" Alura growled at him, disguising Vivian's ability effortlessly in the presence of 'strangers,' even though it was rather confusing to those who did not know.

"I believe we should retire to one of the greeting rooms," he said, looking at his daughter's companions with curiosity. "This tale should be a good one."

***

Vivian sat flushed on one of the chairs as her stepmother cooed over Valour. The young woman did not mind, as she was wrapped up in one of the fluffiest blankets she'd ever had the fortune to wear, the little 'hood' up and over her sensitive ears and dangling over her face as she stared up at the woman with wide sparkling eyes.

She long forgave the invasion of privacy as the ginger woman oohed and ahhed in her language, petting her head and scratching a relaxing spot she didn't know existed behind her ear.

"My, this one is so adorable! Where *did* you find her?" she beamed.

"Well, she found me, actually. I was fighting a group in a warehouse, and when I won I tripped, and she caught me."

Alura gasped in exaggerated delight. "She saved your life?! Unnecessary, but so appreciated! Thank you little one, you have my appreciation and my favour!"

"Matt'her," she sighed.

"You were fighting?" her father, Jonathon El Lock, asked curiously. "And how did your first fight outside your tutors go?"

She paled, remembering her little incident. "Uh, well. Quite well. Not too badly, not too easy, but I managed it." She finished her 'report' with a smile so obviously faked.

"You slipped, didn't you."

"I did..."

Jonathon sighed. "Is there anyone we need to silence? I must stress once more, the importance of silence. Should your ability be known, we can go to ground, but I would rather seek alternatives."

"There is no one I do not trust who is aware of my, situation. The enemies have been dealt with, and I have been cautious not to let my guard down."

He sighed in relief. "Good." He looked her in the eyes with regret and sadness. "I'm sorry that I asked this of you. If I had any other choice, I would not have placed this burden on you so young."

"It's fine, father," she smiled reassuringly. "I understand."

He smiled back. "It isn't, and you shouldn't have to. But that is how the world is. Now, tell me of your situation."

He listened as she retold everything, narrowing his eyes at various parts and glancing at the people in question as they came up in her story.

"—and that is all I can say without revealing personal information, told to me in confidence."

"I see." He sat back with his arms folded, staring at her intently. His eyes were moving minutely as his mind blurred, the facts coming and going, lines being drawn between the events.

"We must keep this silent," Alura spoke up. "At least for now. With no proof, we have no case. And with the King's death, his eldest taking up the crown, he will allow nothing to interrupt the mourning period."

"Blast it," Jonathon sighed. "I had hoped Alliniad would have died or given up his claim. He is too weak-willed and meagre to be the King. It seems the solitude shall continue. What you speak of is important, but not one that will be taken with the amount of attention that is needed."

"At least not yet," Alura said. "Unfortunately, unless a higher up is captured or written documents are procured, there is nothing we can legally do."

Jonathon smirked. "Agreed. But this is our village, our home. If this enemy of freedom believes he can get away with this, he has another think coming. I will reach out to our contacts in the village, and find this Dream Strider."

"In the meantime," Alura grinned sharkishly, and Vivian felt a familiar shudder of fear run up her back, "you simply must enjoy the festivities. The village people decided to throw us a festival, and it is fortunate you arrived here at the opportune moment."

Jonathon winced. "They wanted to make it last two-weeks, but we vetoed that. They don't have the supplies, and it's rather foolish. We talked them down to a single week, and that's as far as they were willing to fall. There are two days left for you to enjoy, so take the time off. Have some fun. We will deal with everything else when we have the time."

Alura clapped her hands gleefully, but Vivian sensed something more, something evil. Great peril was on the horizon and yet the coils wrapping around her neck felt so close.

"Time for your dresses! I have the perfect outfits for you to try on, and for your friend here as well!"

"Gentlemen!" Jonathon suddenly shouted with a wide grin. "I have some top-shelf whisky in my office and some more questions of a personal nature. If you'll please follow me?" And without looking to see if they followed him, the Lord El Lock ran from the room like he was fleeing a natural disaster.

"Hmph. Pansy," Alura sniffed, lifting her chin as she glared at the closing door. "Now then, as that is out of the way, shall we?"

Vivian grimaced, completely pale as she slowly resigned herself to her fate. Valour, on the other hand, was smiling happily as she folded the blanket and placed it on her chair.

"Sure! Let's go, I can't wait!" Alura smiled at her proudly with a certain glint in her eye and Vivian felt so bad for her unfortunate friend.

It has happened to many others in history. Of course, no one would willingly admit to the perils they faced and thus left their fellows without warning of the nest of vipers lying in the north. It was an admittance that would damage their pride and thus went acknowledged, and it was a trail Vivian would follow to the bitter end.

Did that mean her friend would fall victim to the alluring siren's song of sweet silky velvet and iridescent jewels of splendour that would adorn her skin? Indeed, and like those ships that crashed ashore, and those sailors who would embrace their killers with soft smiles and eyes full of love, she would soon know her end. Or at least wish for it.

Oh well, at least she did not have to suffer this indignity alone.

***

"I hate you."

Vivian just smiled. It was a brilliant day. The sun was shining brightly, the air was warm upon her skin and the birds were singing beautifully.

"There shall be vengeance. And the depths of which shall make even the greatest abyss shudder in revulsion and fear."

Ah yes, all was well with the world. Oh, and a minor detail so small that it didn't have anything to do with anything, she only had to try on two dresses before Alura was satisfied. Of course, someone *else* wasn't so fortunate.

Valour glared at her with life-ending malice, the silver glitter around her eyes shimmering. She was in a long-sleeved dress of azure, bracelets of opal and sapphire adorning her wrists.

It was dress number seventy-two and deemed 'the one.' The dress had been worn and chosen in the fourth hour after they started and Valour had immediately collapsed.

Vivian could not afford to show pity, for she had been offered none in the first place. She had sacrificed her friend in a well-thought-out strategy, seeking to exhaust her stepmother with a new dress-up doll.

To her joy, it had succeeded. To her sorrow, it meant that her friend now sought her likely painful demise.

***

Valour strode down the path with the fakest smile she could muster. She felt eyes on her and cringed internally, suddenly reminded of all the times she'd felt that sensation and then been attacked.

She started breathing a little harder. She felt the wind, a soft breeze, suddenly a hammer that battered her skin.

A hand was placed on her shoulder and she almost ripped it off when Vivian's scent shut her down.

"Thank you for waiting, Valour," she smiled as she spoke unnecessarily loudly, guiding her along.

The other woman had led her off the centre of the street and into the shade, where she wouldn't be so noticeable.

"Thank you," she whispered with a sigh. "That, I don't even…"

"It's alright, don't worry about it," she smiled, but Valour could see the worry. She shook her head and replaced the smile on her face, grabbed Vivian by the hand and led her back into the streets.

***

Vivian smiled, hiding the tumultuous feelings building up. Something was… strange. The crest of her family, both of them, was everywhere and, yet, no one was reacting to *her*.

Sure, it was a little vain of her to think this, but for a festival to be thrown for her family and yet no one has noticed that her family was not present? Or that the heir walked among them?

She shook her head. She was thinking too much and thinking with her pride rather than her head. And yet, even when she did that, something was a little off.

Some of the booths they went to, the prizes they offered were common little things you would find in a local shop, just painted or prettied up a bit. Usually, when a festival was thrown, everything was a bit more… professional.

She tested it a bit, while Valour was grinning as she tossed a mini hoop around a bottle. She stared rather intently at the strangely coloured stone on the wall and noted the owner's reaction.

His smile grew a little more strained, his eyes darted nervously and his hands started fidgeting. She was about to question him when that very same stone was plucked off the shelf and thrust under her nose.

She blinked at it and then looked at Valour, confused.

"I saw you looking, so…" she smiled nervously, still holding out the stone.

"Thank you," Vivian smiled, accepting it graciously. She knew she had done the right thing when Valour beamed at her, but when the girl turned away, she looked at the stone more intently.

The paint was chipped away at the bottom, revealing an ordinary rock underneath. She pocketed it anyway, smiling at Valour's not so subtle glance back.

As they wandered around, she couldn't help it. She noted some things that were for the seasonal festivals, old booths dragged out and repurposed, small food items that were obviously leftovers needed to be brought out, there was even a banner from the summer festival two months ago.

The people of Timbura take festivals quite seriously. As the only consistent form of major entertainment they get, they take the time to go all out every time. This seemed… rushed.

Valour suddenly sniffed the air and gasped in delight. "Roast chicken!" Vivian glanced at her and sniffed the air as well, but all she could smell was the overpowering scent of sugary powders. "Come on!"

She shrugged before following with a small smile, just acknowledging the redhead's nose as far more powerful than her own.

She followed Valour all the way into the centre of town and almost ran into the girl as she froze in place. "Valour?" She looked at her face in worry as the other woman showed a mixture of conflicting emotions. Bafflement, surprise, suspicion, anger, fear, all mixed up in a cocktail that twisted her expression in amusing yet concerning ways.

She glanced where she was, her mouth fell open and she felt her eyes bulge.

There, in a spot dead centre of the square, in a space actively avoided by everyone else, were three men. One of them, a blond young man around their own age, another with short black hair and a weird half robe and the last was a familiar werewolf she had only seen once herself.

She groped for her sword, cursing as she remembered she wasn't allowed to bring weapons into town, before she grabbed Valour's wrist.

"The other guy smells like roast chicken," Valour absently murmured, her eyes swimming as she stared at the lieutenant.

"It's alright, Valour," she soothed, though she felt anything but calm herself. Rage. That's it. She put a name to the unholy fire that threatened to burn all thoughts but death away, and she was half tempted to let it. She tightened her fist and felt her knuckles pop.

She could do it. She could charge over there and beat him to death. She didn't need a weapon, she *was* a weapon. Her muscles tensed, her sight tunnelled and Valour whimpered as her grip turned bruising.

Like a switch, everything turned off. She stared at the other woman in horror. She glanced once more at the three men, then wrapped her arm around Valour's and gently started leading her away, murmuring apologies as they went.

***

They passed through, ignoring everyone as Vivian sat Valour down on a couch, got her the fluffy blanket she adored at first touch and then started pulling out her spare armour and changing her clothes.

Down went the crimson dress, on came the leather trousers and rough woollen shirt. She strapped on a cuirass, her gauntlets and grieves and belted her scabbard.

"Well, this is quite the turnabout." Bastian slapped the back of Raven's head as he passed and knelt down by Valour as he started to check her arm. "Ow. Oh, come on, it was a legitimate worry," he complained. He turned to Vivian, who faltered. "What's wrong?"

"The werewolf is here."

Raven's eyes flashed and she flinched at the darkness, before he blinked and looked at her seriously. "You're not facing him alone, or at all if I have anything to say about it."

Alura sashayed into the room with a deceptively peaceful smile. "I am in agreement with your friend, datt'hir. Unfortunately, if you seek to detain this man, then I or another elder of our house must be there as well."

"Wait, what?" Raven glanced at her in shock. "No, none of us are facing him. My plan was to collapse a building on him. None of us are going to *fight* him."

"Why not?" Bastian asked absently. "You fought him in the library, so why not face him head-on?"

"Because that was the middle of the day! Everyone knows the curse gets stronger under the moon. It's only when the bloody thing is full is a transformation possible!"

"I didn't know that," Valour chirped with a forced smile.

"I know, kid," he softened, "I'm sure that's why he said that, to lead me on."

Bastian hummed, "That's true. He tends to leave important details out unless he's reminded. He's an idiot that way."

"Go to hell."

"Already do, every time I'm in your presence."

"Do not concern yourself with my safety," Alura interrupted. "I am a daughter of the house of Faralla and a friend of the Day Court. I have the means to defend myself."

Raven shrugged, "Alright then. But like I said, we're still going to—"

"Their leader was there," Valour interrupted. Raven glanced at her in shock and she expanded. "The man from the dream, the seer. Same hair, same clothes, it's him."

Raven frowned, sharing a glance with Bastian. "Scrap that plan then. We need to take him alive, find out what he knows. We get him to name every one of his accomplices, every one of his plans. We end this threat before it gets out of hand."

"Raven, it's never this easy," Bastian lightly warned him.

"I know. But we have to take the chance, even if it's a bad one. We go in there assuming it's a trap. If we get in over our heads, we're out.

Agreed?" After a round of nods, he nodded himself. "Alright, here's the plan."

22. The Bright Side

Plato groaned as he slumped in a chair. Something was wrong with him. He was itching in various places, sick to his stomach and feeling a blinding headache.

"How long have you been feeling like this?" Gordova asked him curiously, not an ounce of pity in sight.

"Since the potion wore off an hour ago," he grumbled. He could feel himself getting better, slowly, but there was a strange pit in his gut. Something was wrong, but he didn't know what.

"Wait, potion?"

"How do you think I got here so quick?" he growled. "I tested a new potion the boss got me. I had everything, the speed, the *power* but none of the drawbacks. It was *incredible*. I ran, faster than any horse, and made an eight-day journey by foot in only four."

"Eight days? Where the hell were you that was *eight days* away?!"

"None of your business," he growled.

Gordova's eye twitched. "I see. Well, if that's none of my business, then I can safely say neither is your health."

Plato rolled his eyes, grimacing as needles pierced his brain. "Leave it be. What was that kid speaking to you earlier?"

"I don't know, something about a dark fog hanging around me, working with the bleak circle and looking really smug about something. I called him an idiot, told him to back off and he just looked at me like he was going to throw a strop, stomp his foot and everything. What's up with you?"

Plato was staring at him weirdly, as though Gordova had spontaneously shouted praise for the peace ideal. "The bleak circle. That's what he said?"

"Yep."

"And you didn't think to notify me?"

"The thought never crossed my mind."

He rubbed his nose with a deep groan of misery. "The bleak circle, is what the—"

The door to their little house was kicked open. Plato was up on his feet with a pained snarl and Gordova dived behind him with a yelp.

To their surprise, a familiar brown-haired man strode in, before turning to the doorway and offering a hand to assist a lady into the room, helping her over broken bits of wood and splinters.

She bowed her head to him with a thankful smile, before surveying the room with a disdainful sniff.

"I expected better. Hy Guith. Tell me, are you always this gauche with your living arrangements?"

Plato shared a confused look with Gordova. "You are trespassing in my house. I suggest you leave immediately."

***

Well that's interesting.

Raven cocked his head as the lieutenant spoke. The werewolf was standing in front of the other man, his so-called leader, but it wasn't to protect the man. No, he was one dirty look away from throwing himself at the two of them.

And he saw the fear on the other man's face and, as a self-proclaimed master of deception and disguise, he could confidently say that either the man was far better than he was or something was a little off here.

"We know you have an unsanctioned prisoner somewhere in this city."

The man at the back twitched. Raven smirked as the fear and confusion showed before he hid it behind an impressive mask. Well, that rules out being better.

"Relinquish him to us, and our judgement may be merciful."

Raven noted that the woman didn't make a promise or an oath of any kind. On their way here, her daughter had told Alura just why she was so angry with the cursed man, and Alura had been almost apocalyptic with rage. It was a testament to her self-control that she calmed herself down so quickly and was facing him with just a smile on her face and fire in her eyes.

"And if we refuse?" The man at the back glanced at him annoyed but didn't say anything. Another strike in favour of Raven's theory.

"Then I will bring you to heel," she smiled serenely.

The werewolf growled angrily and his eyes twitched. Raven blinked. The other man's pupils dilated, his forehead beaded with sweat and his outstretched arms shivered. Is he poisoned?

The werewolf lunged at them and Raven swore as he was caught off guard. Alura whipped her hand before her and the cursed man slammed into a dome of shimmering silver. He howled as his skin started to blister and smoke, throwing himself back.

"What have you done?!" he howled.

"Argentum Foréln," she drawled. "A shield laced with the properties of silver, though it does not make the metal itself, to my disappointment."

Raven frowned as the wolf fell to his knees. That should not have happened. Yes, silver is quite painful when it touches one of the bitten, but that shield should not have brought him down so easily.

Alura shared his thoughts, looking at him confused and a bit unsure of what to do next. He frowned but addressed the elephant in the room.

"You're not the seer we're looking for, are you." He did not question but stated as he glared at the other man.

Gordova looked between Plato and the both of them, and promptly decided that surrender was his only option. "I-I'm not. My boss set me up as a red herring, I don't know anything about anything, I'm just in charge of the guy in the basement."

"Why did your boss abandon this place? The Dream Strider is his best asset right now, his only way of finding other seers."

"The seers aren't important any more; they never really were. Boss just wondered if any of them could tell him an easy way to get what he wanted, but they couldn't, so he dropped it."

"And just what does he want?"

Something crunched behind them and they spun around. A blond young man glared at them all with piercing green eyes, wrapped in a shawl of pure white over clothes of a deep purple. On the centre of the white silk was a silver circle that surrounded a pair of scales.

"Disgraceful. I see the abhorred legions turn on themselves once more. This conspiracy of yours keeps getting—oh no." He froze as Alura turned to face him with a scolding look and a reproach on her tongue, but she froze, staring at his face.

"My, how the tables turn," Plato murmured, staring at the two with the look of a man who'd just seen an act of the gods.

And Raven couldn't understand because he saw the exact opposite. He saw generations of hatred consume a gentle woman. He saw a noble who carried herself with a grace earned by years of dedicated training turning into a terrifying beast.

"YOU!" The scream was shattering, the anger and the sorrow seeking to break both his ears and his heart at the same time. Alura's hands flew for the young man's neck and waves of unfocused force were flung haphazardly.

The young man stumbled back, deflecting the blows, and Raven gasped as he was hit in the stomach and propelled through a brick wall.

***

"Woah!"

Valour yelped as the right wall of the house broke and a blur rammed into the neighbouring house, before falling to the floor in a heap.

"Bastian! Check on that, we're going in!" Vivian yelled and charged forwards. Valour hesitated for a second and then sprinted past her and straight in.

She had a second to take in the room and assess the threats.

Alura was facing off against an unknown, having a hard time as her wild blasts were deflected off to the sides by focused, powerful shields. The lieutenant was on the floor, hand in his pocket and pulling out a glass vial, the boss behind him.

The next move was obvious. One threat down, two still standing. One was a non-threat, given how he was paralysed by fear, the other was facing a tiring Alura, who was throwing away her energy in a fit of rage.

She sprinted for the unknown and threw a punch, but the blond man somehow seemed to know she was coming and spun around, catching her fist in an open palm. He winced as his hand buckled under the force, but smirked.

"You cannot hide from the Light," he claimed in a really strange voice. It was as if he was trying to be wise, copying something he's heard, but wasn't really successful. That combined with the condescending head tilt and it all just ruined the effect he was going for, making him seem arrogant.

"What the hell is that supposed to mean?"

"It means—" A wave smacked into his back and he did a flip as he was blasted across the room. Valour's smirk fell as he stood up quickly and waved his arms at her.

A sphere of light expanded around him, shooting out across the house. She braced herself, but it did little more than brush her hair. The same for Alura, but Plato yelled out as he was knocked back, smacking into Gordova and they both fell.

"Wait, that was supposed to…" He stared at her blankly, then his face fell. "Oh no, I've made a terrible mistake."

"You sure have."

Vivian hit him across the back of his head hard with the hilt of her sword. Valour nodded to her, but Vivian just glared back.

"You can run, way too fast. Next time, wait for me." Valour grinned sheepishly and then they turned to their targets, just as Plato gulped down a mouthful of the liquid in the vial.

"One last drink before it all ends?" Vivian smirked maliciously. "Surrender, and you will be left unharmed." She lied. She had no intention of not hitting him at least a few times.

Valour glanced at Alura. The woman was still glaring at the fallen man behind them, baring her teeth like some wild animal.

And then a heart in the room started beating faster, too fast, like it was about to explode. She blinked as she looked at Plato. Normally, she would have to focus to hear someone's heart, as her ears weren't as strong as her nose after all.

Speaking of nose, a strange sour smell was in the air. It was familiar, but not in a pleasant way. And then Plato howled and the windows shattered beneath the force and pitch of his cry.

Valour flinched, stunned by the loud pain and joy she heard, the mixture a concoction that blasted her eardrums.

He lunged for Alura, the woman so distracted she ignored Vivian's warning cry, screaming in pain as his teeth broke the skin of her shoulder. He jerked his head, throwing her to the floor.

Gordova ran up with a grin, "Excellent work! Now, finish these fools—"

It was the height of irony as the man spoke of fools, for as he ran up behind a beast running on pure instinct, his throat was bitten and torn by the werewolf's teeth. Plato threw the dying man at them and then sprinted past in a blur.

Valour hesitated, but Vivian yelled at her to go. The redhead nodded and charged after the lieutenant, but all she saw was the trail he had left. She ran through the throngs of people and down the street. She glanced at the floor, noting the indents of powerful steps.

She ran until she reached the edge of the village and looked out across the roads with confusion. He was gone and there was not a trail to be found. She had lost him. A human had outrun her and she had no trail to follow.

***

"Ouch," Alura mumbled, staring up at the ceiling with fogged eyes. "That was highly embarrassing. Datt'hir, do me a favour, would you kindly?"

"Of course matt'her," Vivian mumbled, staring at the wound and tightening her grip around the woman.

"Never mention this to your father. I dare not imagine the hilarities he would weave at my expense. Even the threat of a new bed upon the couch would not deter him, I fear."

She chuckled throatily, tearing up. "What happened? You just... snapped. I've never seen you like that before."

"That," she grimaced heavily, "was why I value free will. Vel quory lev gat ol weet hath. It is not something I thought I would feel in this place. Tell me, is he still there? I dare not look, for the rage will take me once more."

She glanced over; the blond man was still unconscious, with his face firmly in the ground. She winced; she wouldn't be surprised if his nose was broken.

"Yeah, he's still there. Not moving any time soon though," Alura huffed, irritation clouding her face.

"Vivian!" Bastian ran in, followed by a scowling Raven. "Are you alright?"

"Bastian! Wounded, we need a medic!"

He hustled over and examined the bite on her shoulder. "Excessive amounts of cursed saliva." He pulled a face as he wiped his hands on his robes. "Not the turning kind, but heavily weakening and damaging to the immunity system. Here." He pulled out a vial of blue liquid. "Good for all curses and poisons."

She gasped in surprise. "You have a cure-all potion?!"

"No, don't be ridiculous. No such thing exists. I have a *slow-all* potion that will prevent the curse from spreading, mitigate the effects, until we find or make a proper cure and give it to her within the hour."

"What happens after the hour?"

"The potion runs out, and she starts screaming. I hope I don't have to tell you why, but screaming of any kind is terribly grating." He turned to Gordova. "Oh. Well, in my expert opinion, he is dead. Oh well. Life begins and life ends. Quick prayer and we're moving on."

He turned to the blond man and froze.

Raven hissed in pain as he straightened his back, trying to click it. "I have been thrown through far worse things than a wall, so how is it, that this one hurts just like the rest?" He frowned at Bastian as the old man stared in growing horror at the lad on the ground.

"What's the matter? You look like you've just seen—" He froze, staring at the blond man as well. "A ghost. Oh crap."

Valour skidded to a halt as she crossed the doorway, holding her hands up pre-empting the surprise attack she believed was coming, but was confused when the two ignored her. "Okay, little weird."

"Valour, I need your assistance!" Vivian called her over.

"Vivian, dear, I am lighter than most feathers, I do agree with what everyone says." She ignored her daughter's disbelief. "But your friend may need some—woah!" Valour scooped her up and held her easily in her arms. "... Well, I am impressed," she murmured.

Valour just grinned at her and then turned to the other two. "Are you guys okay? We still need to find the Strider—"

"Basement, dear."

"Thank you Mrs. Alura. I need you guys to get him out of the basement. Uh, guys?" They completely ignored her and she started to get annoyed. "Raven! Bastian!" Raven turned to her with wide eyes and a look of fear he was not able to hide. "A-are you okay?"

"No," he bluntly groaned. "None of us are now. Valour, meet this guy. I don't know his name. He's a Chosen of the Light, a champion of the Silver Premise."

"Oh." She glanced at the boy, unimpressed, and all she could say was, "Why does he smell like roast chicken?"

23. The Jewel of Perdition

Upon the west sea, weaving between the isles of the few, a great ship sailed. It was a military boat, piloted by some of the greatest sailors the Ring had in its ranks. The ship, known as the Serpent's Maw, was a vessel crafted for combat. It was one of the shining stars of the Ring's naval fleet, a dreadnought layered with protections both physical and magical. It had fared even with some of the more dangerous beasts that lurked in the depths.

The crew of the Maw numbered in the lower ends of fifty and, working together for as long as they had, considered one another family, brothers in arms. All it took to destroy this bond was a few whispers laced with a bit of magic.

Men once in unity now looked upon one another with scorn and distrust. One of the men slipped, an 'accident,' but it resulted in throwing a bucket of cleaning water over another.

The victim of the accident glared, but his anger wasn't so great he'd start something. Until a voice whispered in his ear.

"It was no accident. See how he talks with his fellows. See how he mocks you." A wind poked the man as he was speaking with a few others and he glanced over his shoulder. The man covered in soap reddened and stomped forth to yell and scream.

The man being yelled at blinked in shock, speechless at the sudden aggression. Until, "This is the one who got your friend kicked off the ship. Recall how he overreacted to a mere slip in formality and used it to his own advantage. He will use you to lift himself in the eyes of your superiors and reduce you as well."

The man flinched, then glared at him, puffing up his chest and went at him with screams and shouts of his own.

More whispers leaked into the ears of the witnesses. "See how he verbally assaults him. That will be you if you do not band together.

Retaliate! Do not let him get away with this!" And, "The upstart little brat is getting ideas. He is making a scene, drawing attention, he will get you all evicted from this ship, and you need this job, don't you?"

The ship started drifting as the sailors abandoned their posts to confront one another. Cutlasses were drawn and waved about, threats were roared against threats and the anger fed into the disorder that permeated the air.

Cereza Malachite, the brunette woman perched on the edge of the ship, breathed it all in with a loud sigh of ecstasy. "Now *this* is a smooth sail," she smirked at her cringey line, watching as the first punch was thrown. The whole crew stared as the blood from a broken nose landed on the decking and then, as if a starting whistle was blown, pandemonium reigned.

She hopped down, brushing the dust from the back of her trousers and straightening her buttoned shirt, before she waltzed through the carnage.

She lashed out a hand and broke a man's jaw. She didn't know who he was, but she did know he had done nothing to her. It didn't matter. Anyone who worked for the Ring did so because they had a reason to fear the Light, so as far as she was concerned, all of them were deserving.

She grabbed a man by his arm and he screamed as the limb turned green and his fingers curled up as the nerves died. She pushed him back and watched with a smirk as the rot spread, killing three more before she cancelled the spell.

"Well, this *has* been fun, but my prey is near." She frowned and then pouted as she contradicted herself. "Nay, the land my prey walks is near. Which means our time is at an end and I can write a conclusion most beautiful for our play."

She raised her hands and, with a smile of intense concentration, a fog wound itself around the hearts and minds of the people. Their wills folded and sight was shattered as sanity was prohibited, and a small shard of the Dark's power was called to lay a curse upon the Serpent's Maw.

"In the name of the power who venerates my work, let the powers of folly manifest. Defy peace, scorn respect, veto civility. Let every inch remind those of what awaits an unguarded self. Avreach garthak tobleriam lothrak!"

The sailors slaughtered each other and, with each death, the unwilling sacrifice of a person fuelled the spell, until the ship creaked and splintered under the weight of the anguish screamed by the souls of the dead.

Cereza laughed throughout, the powers of the Dark roiling within her as she tore the world around her apart. She strolled to the bow of the ship, stepped up onto the figurehead with perfect balance and, with a last smirk back at the massacre behind her, dived into the water.

The cold was a shock to her system and she gasped in delight at the sudden knives digging into her. Water rushed into her lungs and she felt the pain as she drowned, but she did not panic. In fact, she rejoiced.

With a well-practiced twist of her magic, her body exploded and the shadow of a beast far larger than a human swam through the sea at blistering speed.

As for the Serpent's Maw, it exploded after a fierce battle, where fire was liberally thrown near explosive powder. The pieces of the ship were cast adrift for anyone to find, be they a fisherman or a salvager, though all would regret the moment they touched an object cursed by the Dark.

24. The Negotiator

Anthony Carlachi awoke with a familiar voice in his ear. All Chosen of the Light had this sixth sense, a gift bestowed upon them to aid them in their battles, whatever they may be. A needed action in battle or a certain subject in a conversation, all of them knew the right thing to do.

And yet, he had never heard the voice scream so loudly that he must comply. He blinked awake, energy filled him and he returned to full consciousness within a few seconds.

Before him was an old man with an aura of light, tinged with the faint grey of doubt. Behind him, and Anthony had to swallow a yelp of fear, was a red-haired woman who glared at him with glowing red eyes.

Do not say anything to her.

He blinked. It had never so directly said to snub someone before. He shuffled in the chair and winced, the rattle of the chains binding him felt like a noose tightening around his neck.

Bastian. Medic. Banished.

The sense always knew everything about everyone who worshipped the Light. It was disturbing at times, but at others, it put him at ease. Like right now for instance; medics swore an oath to never harm!

She did not.

... And at others, it just couldn't help weighing in on how screwed he was.

"If you're done conversing with the sixth sense, we need to talk," Bastian said firmly.

That was alarming. Only the Council and the Chosen themselves were supposed to know about that! How in the world did he?!

"You infiltrated this city under false pretenses."

"What? No I didn't."

"You claimed to be here simply for a party, but you were seen speaking with both a known terrorist and a werewolf."

"But that was only—"

"And then you confronted the Lady Faralla, whom you knew had a cursed lineage. You knew that, as soon as she saw you, she would attack you and you would be forced to 'defend yourself,' allowing you to get away with her murder."

He let out an undignified squeak and protested.

"All of this would have allowed you to follow through on your deal with the wolf, putting the village of Timbura firmly in his hands, and a staunch ally and foothold in Brinia for the Silver Premise."

"What?! No! I was just here to deal with agents of the Ring!" he yelped desperately, glancing between the two, begging them to believe him. "We received word of Dark magics being used over here, and I was sent on the fastest ship we possess! I followed the trail to this place and sought to speak with those two and find out about their dealings!"

"Wow," the redhead scary girl drawled, muscles in her arms flexing as she crossed them. "Are you sure he's a negotiator? 'cos that was just pathetic."

Anthony blinked, his confusion and worry battling inside him.

They played you.

He blinked again. They played him? He looked at them closely, trying to perceive their true intentions, but seeing nothing but disappointment on behalf of the redhead and guilt on behalf of Bastian.

They threw you off. Then took advantage of your shock.

"..." His mentors would be ashamed of him. He knew better than to lose control of himself. He closed his eyes and breathed in deep, then opened them to glare forwards, locking himself behind a barrier.

"Ah, there it is," Bastian mumbled with a small smile. "The teachings of Val Nuthra, the speaker."

His eye twitched at the reference to his old master. His old master, who had a way of beating someone until they cried with just his words.

"I am Chosen of the Light, inheritor of the peace. I am the sword of justice and shield of the innocent."

"Which would be very impressive," Bastian said, "if you hadn't inherited those titles when you were chosen. Forgive me, but why were you anyway? I mean no offense, but at your age, I do not believe a lot of people would find your stature… enforcing of the peace you sought to bring."

His eye twitched. "It does not matter," he spat through gritted teeth. "You have me locked up like a common criminal, and I insist you release me."

"No," the redhead immediately said and he stared at her with his jaw dropped. "Seriously? Your first demand is denied and you freeze? What kind of negotiator are you?"

"He's not." Bastian suddenly had a revelation. "You're a deterrent, aren't you?" Anthony glared at him and Bastian nodded with satisfaction. "Basic training, then placed in a team sent to speak with others, your presence used to warn against violence."

He scratched his chin in thought. "But which one? The Silver Premise have forced a number of non-aggression pacts over the years. The Grey Legathrim of the giants, the Sillyian Accord with the Naga, but you're a champion of the Premise." He stared at him with narrowed eyes. "So there's only one they'll use their greatest weapon for. The Iron Claw treaty." He shook his head with disgust. "It is foolish to believe that anything they have could intimidate the United Species of the north."

"We've gotten way off track here."

"Ah, my apologies, Valour." He nodded to her and then refocused on Anthony. "You say you came here to deal with Ring agents. Why speak with those two?"

Be honest.

Anthony grimaced. "The magics used were of a specific sort. Necromancy, not enough that they would catch the fury of the necromancers, but our mystics sensed the disturbance, and linked with our seers. They found out that the Ring were creating abominations."

***

Valour shook her head in disbelief. The story was ridiculous. She gestured Bastian over to speak with him in whispers. "Mystics? Necromancy? This is starting to sound like a bedtime story, and not even one of the good ones."

Bastian grimaced and she had a bad feeling that the tied-up Light Premise's insane rambling held more than a spot of truth.

"The mystics are sensors, trained to detect even the faintest murmurs of Dark magic. They use their powers to trigger specific visions in the seers and locate the wielders, who, more often than not, turned out to be of the Ring."

"Specific visions? But granny always said a seer's visions could not be specifically directed, only suggested towards something?"

"An ancient secret of the Premise, I'm afraid. None but the Council were ever made aware."

"And there's nothing in this book of yours? That guy who trained the Chosen, he had to have been important if he was trusted with *that* duty."

"Unfortunately not. Ornstein only knew of the Chosen, and was only ever interested in uncovering the secrets of their powers."

Valour pinched her nose with a sigh, "Okay, what about this necromancy stuff?"

Bastian hesitated. "*That*, could be a problem. Necromancers are wizards who study the blackest path. Soul magic, death magic, they not only covet death, but worship it. To bring someone back? Well, not only would you be bringing a shade or something equally as foul, but you would be denying the 'greatest gift' to a resting soul."

"So they're insane."

"Of course not," he chided, looking disappointed with her. "Do not judge someone on their hobbies. It only becomes a problem or weird if they allow themselves too much indulgence. If they did, we would have many serial killers on our hands, and an open war waged on an entire branch of magic."

"Right," Valour muttered, completely unconvinced. "So what's our measure of him?"

Bastian glanced at the guy, who was glaring back with all the impotent anger he could muster.

"A ride along," he muttered, turning back to her with disappointment. "Someone who relies on the legacy of his mantle, and depends on a crutch made of the fear of others."

"I can hear you!" Anthony snarled.

They looked at him for a second and then went back to ignoring him. "What's our next move here?"

"We set him free. The local police have no reason to hold him."

"You mean Vivian's father has no reason?"

"Ah yes," he murmured with a small chuckle, "I had forgotten what power nobility yields." And then he frowned. "Quite worrying, but since it works in our favour, I shan't protest too loudly."

Valour rolled her eyes and then strode over to cut Anthony free of his bonds. "You heard the man, you're free to go."

Anthony rubbed his red wrists, then stood straighter to start speaking, but the other two had already left. He stood staring at the door as it slowly creaked shut and then hurried after them.

Do not annoy them.

Annoy them? He scowled. He was only going to speak with them, very loudly and very harshly.

Valour groaned as the smell approached them.

"Hey! You can't just lock me up for no reason and expect me to be okay with it!"

"We knew there'd be problems," Bastian grumbled, determinedly not looking back. "We just hoped we could outrun them."

"You can't outrun me!" he growled.

"Evidently."

"Also, you just called yourself a problem. I think you should seek psychiatric assistance."

"What does a psychic have to do with anything?!" he demanded. "My thoughts are private; I will not have some stranger come in and poke around my head!"

Bastian sighed as Valour chuckled. "Well, he's half right."

"And half wrong, but this time, it's a glass half empty situation."

"That's a pessimist optimist thing, not a wrong or right thing."

"Completely the same. There's the right way of looking at things, and then there's everyone else."

Valour laughed.

***

"And what is this supposed to be?" Alura grimaced, staring at the man she had hated with every fibre of her being, and yet she couldn't right now. She felt more pity and a bit of disgust.

"He kept following us, and wouldn't leave us alone, so we improvised," Valour beamed, and the Lady of the house could not bring herself to disapprove, as the young girl looked so proud of herself.

"Well, it is certainly effective. I do not feel the need to rip his head from his spine, so there is improvement."

They had covered up every symbol of the Premise that was on his clothes, since he had refused to change from his 'uniform,' and, to top it off, they had put a bag over his head.

Alura sighed, shifting uneasily in her bed, the doctor beside her chiding her gently as he checked her wound, before rebandaging it.

"How is she?" Vivian asked him.

"I'm fine!" she whined.

"Exhaustion. The curse venom in the wound was stronger than normal, but too weak to infect her. The wound will scar and she lost quite a bit of blood, so bed rest for at least a week."

"A what?!"

"After that, no strenuous exercise with that arm, no sudden movements in the neck and nothing else that could potentially reopen the wound before it can properly seal."

Vivian breathed a sigh of relief, "Thank you." The doctor bowed his head and left.

Vivian sat by her stepmother's side and the room lulled into an uncomfortable silence. A few seconds later, Valour twitched with the powerful urge to break the tense silence, when the door was opened.

"And this is where one of your saviours lay, grievously injured, yet healing valiantly." Raven strolled in, followed by the visibly nervous vampire they had come here to save.

"You know, for a recently rescued prisoner, you look quite spry, child," Alura drawled out, jealously.

"I am vampire, madam." He bowed his head. "I heal fast, when fed properly." He glanced around the room, eyeing everyone, brightening as he saw Valour. "Your doctors were very well informed, and I was provided with expired blood packet. Useless to humans, perfect for I."

Bastian spoke up from where he sat next to the window. "I have a few questions for you, Dream Strider."

"Please, call me Alec," he smiled at him reassuringly.

"Alec, then. Tell me, what coven are you from?"

"The Senway coven," he smiled fondly.

"I see. Given what I know of them," he nodded to Valour and Vivian, who had told him all they knew, "the Lady Rosalina cares a great deal for her coven."

"She does," he smiled happily. "If it is not an emergency, she decides whether or not anyone interested would be turned. She treats all of us like we were her own."

"Hmm." Bastian leaned back in his chair, taking in the wider picture of the vampire. "So why did you not reach out to her, then?"

Alec smiled politely, as if softening him up. "I am a Dream Strider. I send messages to people I have formed connections with. You know this, no? Well, unfortunately, my power only works by sending images to people when they dream. It is an unfortunate fact of vampire biology, but my people do not sleep."

"Ah yes," Bastian mumbled, grimacing at himself for having forgotten that fact. "Incidentally, the man who held you captive and the seer who used your ability. They are not the same person, are they?"

"No, sir."

"Called it." Raven mumbled from the doorway.

"The man was named Gordova and he was deemed unimportant enough to guard me as everyone left."

"They left?" Vivian frowned. "But why would they leave you? Why not bring you along or just kill you?"

"To answer your last question first, they could not kill me without risking the wrath of Lady Rosalina. She would have declared open war and torn the country apart looking for them."

"Really?" Alura raised a brow. "War, just for the life of one person? She would risk everything."

"What would you do to save or avenge your daughter?"

Alura slouched, "Okay, fair enough."

"But my Lady is one of the Old Blood. She would lose of course. One person, even a vampire of her stature, could not beat an entire country. But Brinia would not win either. Thousands dead, farms destroyed and crops ruined. The lands she struck would grow barren and the bloodshed would feed an army of vampires that would be freed from her rules, the second she fell."

"He is right," Alura mused. "Manipulation and conjuration is a vampire's speciality, and the Old Bloods have more tricks up their sleeves. The Royal City has wizards, but they are not trained to fight against such a being."

"They are not trained to fight at all." Vivian's father, Jonathon, swept into the room, hastening to Alura's bedside. "You lost? This badly?" he said, very alarmed as he reached for her shoulder, hovering over the bandages.

"I didn't lose," she grumbled. "I technically wasn't fighting him." She glared at Anthony and Jonathon followed her gaze, narrowing his eyes at the man doing a rather impressive impression of a stone statue.

"This is Anthony Carlachi, a Chosen from the Silver Premise," Valour mumbled to him and his eyes lit up in understanding.

"We're going to use him for our next step," Bastian declared. "He claims to be able to follow the trail left by the ex-Ring members."

"We don't know if they're retired," Anthony chimed in. "They could be spies planted here to carry on the work of the great shadow."

There was an awkward pause. "Who's the great shadow?" Valour asked.

"The strongest Dark wizard in the world," he uttered grimly. "The King of the Ring."

"Sounds like a wrestler," Raven and Valour said simultaneously, then both barked a laugh as they realised.

"This is a matter most serious!" the man with a bag over his head shouted petulantly, which made the two laugh harder.

"Anyway," Bastian muttered with a shake of his head, "we follow the trail, we find the ex-members of the Ring, we find the evil seer. Agreed?"

There was a chorus of agreement and they all turned to Anthony for him to start telling them about the trail, only to realise that the man couldn't see them and so stood there, bag on his head and looking like their current last hope was a rather foolish one.

25. Silver

It was on the fifth day of their travel south that Anthony felt a great cold wash over him, like someone had dropped an ice cube on his head and the ice-cold water travelled down his body.

They had passed Senway two days ago. Alec had stopped by to speak with his coven, announce to them all his safety and they could call on him should they ever need his help.

From Senway, they moved south-west towards the coast, passing through fields and plains, but no villages. The trail seemed to avoid populated areas and that's when Raven declared, "So we're not following a trail of magic, we're following the people who cast the spells."

He seemed annoyed and, when asked why, had no problems talking. "These guys were probably hired for a mission, and that mission was complete when the magic was cast. They likely split off and they're onto the next client. Probably don't even remember or care about the previous."

"You know a lot about how they operate," Anthony said, glaring at him.

"Obviously. I'm a bloody detective—"

"*Was* a detective."

"Shut up, Bastian. I *was* a detective. It was my job to put myself in the shoes of the suspect and retrace their steps until I found enough evidence to get them charged by the guards."

"Well, what did you think we were doing?"

"I thought we were tracing the spell."

Anthony burst out laughing. "Ha! And I suppose you also believe in the fairies that come to clean your house, should you be good?"

Raven frowned at him. "Those aren't fairies you're talking about, and they don't clean. They hide your things and feed on the frustration and anger you give off when you can't find anything."

"You cannot trace a spell to its origin," he said simply, making this statement and then marching purposefully, continuing the path he declared the right one.

Bastian stepped close to whisper to Raven, "Either the education standards at the Premise have failed in the past 20 years or that one's a special kind of bad student."

"I honestly don't care, but if he looks at me with that smug smirk again, I'm gonna set his trousers on fire and watch him run screaming."

On the fifth day, when Anthony felt that terrible omen, he asked the sense for answers, but the voice was silent. He looked around and had a terrible feeling, like something was creeping up behind him. He shook it off and banished the chills to the back of his mind, looking back at them with a forced grin.

"We are almost there," he proudly declared.

And on the sixth day, they arrived at their destination. Before them was a city, built before a mighty cliff. A monument to ancient design, the buildings were made of sandstone laced throughout solid white marble.

The city was not built for warfare but rather a temple of worship, to the older tower standing on the very summit of the cliff they shied away from.

"Why are we at Uru Almesh?" Raven asked Anthony, glancing over at the tower on the cliff.

"Because this is where the trail leads," Anthony said, walking towards the city.

"Vivian?" Valour gently nudged the distracted girl and she looked at her with wide eyes.

"Sorry, yes?"

"I was just wondering..." She glanced at the tower, "What is that thing over there?"

Vivian glanced at it and smiled softly. "That, is the ancient lighthouse of Ovryn. Built by the sages of the Day Court, and gifted to the race of men when they first parlayed in the early days. A gift of peace, and an offer of more, but things never got that far." Her face clouded over.

Valour was about to ask but refrained as she really didn't want that anger facing her, so she nodded with a "Thank you," and went back to sightseeing.

The group reached the city an hour after and were stunned to see the amount of sickness that infested the city. There was vomit in the streets being cleaned up by people in every bit of protective gear you could imagine, blood splatters were being washed off walls with sponges and there was coughing and crying heard all over.

"What is happening here?" Vivian murmured, looking around blankly.

"The work of the Dark," Anthony murmured grimly. "A reminder of the evil we face and the monsters we must vanquish."

Valour shook her head but Bastian was the one to speak up. "How do we know it is the Ring?" he argued. "For all we know, the people could be genuinely sick, and need actual medical help."

Anthony shook his head regretfully. "Your doubt clouds your mind. Your heart seeks not the defeat of our enemy." Bastian blinked, flinching as though the Chosen had slapped him across the face. "I guarantee, when the magic we have come here to slay is destroyed, everything will return to normal."

"Very well," Bastian agreed, and when Anthony started walking, Bastian was right on his heels.

Valour exchanged a worried look with Vivian and they both looked to Raven.

"This is…" he hesitated, glancing at them both helplessly. "I think he's gonna need our support at the end of this, wherever it leads to. There's nothing more we can do, simply follow until the end."

They followed him as Anthony navigated the streets with the ease of someone who'd lived there his whole life, offering smiles to those he passed, ignoring the outstretched hands and the suffering faces of the innocent.

Valour scowled, quickening her pace so that she was aligned with him. "Don't you have something that can help these people? I heard the Light had some of the greatest healers alive. Surely whatever chose you gave you something?"

He glared at her out of the corner of his eye. "Of course, the Great Power of the Light granted me an ability to soothe the minds of the innocent, but I cannot."

"Cannot, or will not?"

"Cannot. None of these people are truly innocent."

Valour almost punched him, snarling. "There are children here! Are you saying they are not innocent? That they deserve this malediction?!"

He glanced at her and she saw the doubt, before it cleared up. "I can see their auras. None of the people we have seen are faithful to the Light. Therefore, they cannot truly be called innocent." He sped up and Valour slowed as she stared wide-eyed.

"What's wrong?" Vivian hissed.

"H-he can't heal them because these people do not worship the Light. They are injured, dying and he can't help them because the power that gave him that gift, designed it with a catch."

Valour followed along dumbfounded. She had seen the cracks in his façade and hoped that the reason he was being so quick was because this was the only way he could truly help them.

***

Bastian grimaced as they came upon a normal house. It was just like all the others, with the exception of no sickness being present in the streets outside.

"This is the place," Anthony declared grimly. "It's drowning in darkness. I can see the Light being suffocated—"

"Quit the dramatics, and hurry up with whatever you're doing," Valour hissed at him. Anthony looked at Bastian expectantly, but he just raised a brow.

If the boy was intent on antagonising Valour, he certainly wasn't going to step in. She'd snap his old bones like twigs and he wasn't too eager on helping the boy either. He'd heard the description of his 'healing prowess' and was displeased to say the least.

Anthony shook his head and had the gall to look disappointed in him. The Chosen raised a foot and kicked the door open, storming in.

Bastian followed and froze.

There were three people on mats, pale and sweating, obviously sick and in the later stages of their illness. Two women and one man, above them were five frightened people, startled by the violent entry.

Fires blazed to life and Anthony laughed, "Simple flames? I expected more from the Ring!" His hands began to glow.

"Stop!" Raven roared, dashing forwards to grab Anthony by the arm and tug him back. "What the hell are you doing?! There are sick here. If you fight, their lives are at risk!"

Anthony stared at him, "Have you forgotten what we came here to do?"

"Look around, idiot! Do you think any of these people are capable of causing the sickness?!"

Anthony ripped his arm away and stepped forwards to snarl in Raven's face. "We came here to end the ones who cast the necromancy curse! Guess what? I can smell the foul magic, and they all reek of it!"

"Smells like beef to me," Valour mumbled, and Vivian nudged her with her elbow.

"We accepted a job where we had to use a spell, like the one he describes," said one of the men, a black-haired man with cautious brown eyes. He extinguished the fire, looked carefully at Anthony and then spoke to Raven. "We needed the money. Our friends fell sick and we didn't have enough to pay for medicine. The guards do what they can and the priests of the city pray for them, but it doesn't help."

Raven nodded and then stepped in front of Anthony. "I need to know who hired you. He's a terrorist and he's planning something that will kill a *lot* of people. Please, I know you left the Ring. You wouldn't be here and you wouldn't be caring if you hadn't."

The man scoffed, "You're saying that the Ring does not care for other people? That's sounding like Premise propaganda." He glared at Anthony, who stared hatefully back.

"I'm saying that care is a weakness that could be exploited. You know better than to show it there, but here? We can help. My friend over there is a healer."

Bastian strode past the two, ignoring Anthony's look of betrayal. "I took an oath to help those who need it. Seeing as there is no easy solution, it's time for the doctor to step in."

The man wavered, one of the people laying on the mats coughed and his resolve firmed. He nodded to Bastian and walked over to Raven.

"The man you are looking for, his name is Seren. He gave us nothing, but I recognised him. He was a prisoner at the Ravens Eyrie. His base, the one we were in anyway, was to the west, hidden outside of Alkanor."

"Right," Raven grumbled, running his hand over his eyes. "Because he's insane enough to build a base, beneath the very prison he escaped."

"Then we must leave. Immediately." Anthony strode away, then paused as no one moved to follow him. "What are you all waiting for?"

Raven pointed a thumb at Bastian. "We're waiting to see what we can do to help."

"Our mission here was to silence the Dark! You will not allow that and so we must move on. Their deaths are unfortunate." His glare at the ex-Ring said something very different, "But we must stop the greater evil. We cannot waste time!"

"No," Raven said, disgusted at his callousness. "If we save them, we can help the city. Give the information to the guard and they can heal everyone. We're not wasting time. Time used to save a life is not, nor will it ever be, considered a 'waste.'"

Vivian stepped closer to the spokesman of the ex-Ring. "When did the fire at the top of the lighthouse die out?" she asked.

He looked at her surprised and confused, but answered, "Recently. I do not know the exact date, but when the fire blew out, there was great sadness. The lighthouse represented a lot of things and it was a blow to the hearts of many when it went out."

"You're a disgrace to that symbol and everything it stands for! The purpose of the Light is to help, to protect those who need it!"

"Do *not* speak to me of the Light's purpose, *outsider*! The Light descended upon this land and created the Chosen, to fight against the Dark!"

"Indeed," Bastian said, cutting through the arguments. "And that is why the Silver Premise was created. To do what the Chosen would not. You were a member before you were chosen. Tell me, boy, when did you lose yourself? When did you cast aside your own identity, to become an unfeeling weapon?"

The words spoken not with malice but pity and sorrow stunned Anthony to the core. He clenched his mouth shut and glared at the ground. He huffed and spun on his heel to march towards the door.

"I take it you have a plan, then?" he spat over his shoulder.

"I do," Vivian said, folding her arms and chewing her lip, as she thanked the brown-haired man. "We need to relight the tower. I have a theory, but it isn't concrete."

Raven looked at her intently and then nodded sharply. "The idea has merit. You know the story?" She nodded. "Can you relight it?" She nodded again, firmer. "Then go. Take Valour and Anthony. I'll stay here with Bastian and keep them covered."

Vivian nodded and they left the house quickly.

"Are you sure that was a wise choice?" Bastian asked him, still checking the sick people.

"It's the wisest one. Valour can watch her back while she does what she needs to do, and the Light idiot is away from us. He can either catch his breath, or he can focus on the mission. Here, he'll just keep boiling 'til he explodes."

"That or you'll punch him."

"Oh, I'd do more than that."

***

"There's a second half to the story, but I did not think it relevant until now," Vivian grimaced as she led the way down the road. "It is said, that Uru Almesh was one of the last places the Day Court declared peace with. Whilst here, they were attacked. An unknown race took offence, that the humans would parlay with the Day, and not them. So they laid a great curse on the city. The Day Court acted quickly, and built this great tower, an artefact that countered the curse and prevented humans from feeling the effects."

"So, this sickness is due to a curse? And it's only taking effect because the fire went out?"

"Maybe," Vivian said doubtfully. "Like I said before, this is a theory. But for the sickness to take effect around the time the fire went out? And not to mention." She glanced back coldly at the slouching negotiator. "You can see it too, can't you?"

"I can," he admitted. "There's a magic I've never seen before, staining the buildings, rising from the foundations. I can't really understand it," he murmured, studying the buildings intensely.

"Don't look too close," Vivian dryly warned. "It'll drive you insane. Oélthrinír magic is different from our own, different even than the power given to you."

At the base of the tower, Vivian walked up to a blank section of the wall. Valour frowned as she seemed to be reading something that wasn't there.

"How are we getting in?"

Vivian glanced back at her surprised and then smirked. "Luckily we can." She glanced at the sun, high in the centre of the sky. "I just need to read the rest of this, and then I'll open the door."

So she was reading something, Valour mused. Something that only someone with Oélthrinír blood could see. Interesting.

"Oepelethni tirheer detoiorrh," Vivian spoke loudly and clearly.

Valour flinched as it was like the sun was suddenly shining through gaps in the stone. The rays highlighted the shape of double doors and the stone slowly opened with a grinding sound of rocks against rocks.

She closed her eyes, fearing a blinding light would be there, but a gentle laugh filled her with hope. "It's okay, it's not what you think," Vivian said, softly giggling.

Valour opened her eyes, small cracks at a time, before exposing them fully, staring at the gleaming spiral staircase through the doors.

She grinned abashed at Vivian, who beckoned her to follow, walking in and climbing the stairs. Valour's grin fell into a grimace. She looked at the stairs and then up at the very top of the enormous tower.

She slapped her cheeks, psyched herself up and then started jogging up the stairs, taking them two steps at a time.

A minute later, she stood at the very top, staring out of the window bug-eyed at the distant floor. "How the hell?!"

"Magic," Vivian grinned, then paused and wiggled her fingers, "Oélthrinír magic." She smiled down at her hands sadly. "Come on. No time for looking back, we have a job to do."

The staircase had opened up into a beautiful observatory, the walls and ceiling were made of a smooth, crystalline-like glass. In the very centre of the room was a great steel brazier. Upon the metal were inscribed various symbols and words. Valour couldn't read or comprehend any of them.

"Alright, I've got it," Vivian muttered.

Valour looked at her, concerned. The woman had been so confident and happy when she saw it, but now, she was... afraid.

"Valour, you see that lever over there?"

Valour gave her a weird look, because when she'd surveyed the room seconds earlier, there had been no lever attached to a pedestal right next to the staircase.

Oh.

Huh.

She ran over to it and grabbed it, but didn't pull it, looking back at Vivian for confirmation. "Pull it when I say so, but as soon as I light the brazier, you must pull it again straight away. No matter what, understand?"

She really didn't, but she didn't need to. The instructions were clear; pull the lever twice.

"Okay, I'm ready. Do it now!"

Valour pulled the lever and everything turned dark. Darkness moved across the glass ceiling and it was as if the room had been plunged into the night. Only there was no moon to give them light. Seconds later, the sunlight was allowed through the glass walls, which partially lit up the room.

Valour blinked the spots out of her vision and glanced towards the walls. Seeing her reflection in the mirror, she grimaced at the results of roughing it in the countryside and her eyes widened.

She shifted, her eyes gleamed and she whirled around to slam a foot into the space beside her. She felt her kick connect, there was a loud crunch and something flew across the room.

A wave of silver light flung out from where Vivian stood, but Valour didn't turn away. The creature stood up, a man made entirely of stone. Faceless, featureless, it 'stared' at her with half of its body burned black, any clothes that could have been on it long since turned to ash.

There were large cracks along its stomach from where she kicked it.

"A golem," Anthony gasped in horror, but she didn't care.

The boy was useless in a fight. She'd only seen him produce shields and a single blow to the back of his head had rendered him unconscious piteously easily and early.

Plus, any information he could give her would likely be heavily biased, and wrong information was a death sentence.

The golem charged and she met it head on. She caught a punch and threw one of her own, but it caught her fist as easily as she did. She tensed her body and pushed, but the creature matched her strength.

She grimaced. Judging by the cracks, the thing was a glass cannon like she was. Not a good matchup, especially when its strength seemed to be comparable with her own. She threw her head forwards at the same it did.

She felt the skin on her forehead bruise and heard the cracks on its head web across the stone. Yet, while her eyes swam and her mind befuddled, this creature that had no brain to rattle pushed her back.

She quickly glanced at Anthony, who, for some odd reason, was enamoured with something, and glanced back as a rock fist hit her jaw with the force of steel. She felt a crack and pain exploded. She threw a blind punch and an arm smacked her elbow, before her shoulder was grabbed and she was thrown across the room.

The reason Anthony was so 'enamoured' was the lady in white, shining like the sun, orbited by eight gleaming stars.

He saw even more stars when the golem punched him in the jaw so hard that he spun through the air. He landed and coughed out blood, a small bit of white dinking off the floor before him.

The golem turned to the last person standing, Vivian, but did nothing. It simply 'stared' at her as she smiled down at it, as if she were examining a particularly interesting pebble.

Before she could bring herself to care about anything, she had to fix herself first. The clothes had to go, the armour was weak and the rough cotton was insufficient. She waved her hands and, with a few murmured words, her clothes lengthened and softened, the shirt and trousers rewoven into a long silken dress of white. Her armour melted and hardened, the steel morphing into a hardened metal, reminiscent of the irons of the Day Court.

A chest plate and two sleeves, a silver that shone like the lakes of Ereglos, the land of the Silver Premise where the waters appeared as though they were the very essence of argent itself.

She pouted when she had no jewels to decorate it with, but even one as great as herself could not forge a masterpiece when the materials were so limited.

At last, she deigned herself good enough to present. She smiled down at the golem, this pitiful little thing, a mar on life and an insult to creativity.

Whoever gave life to this mound of rocks clearly did not hold even a speck of imagination. She held out a hand, like a lady would when greeting someone, as though she expected it to lay a kiss upon her knuckle.

She would not say she was disappointed when it turned away from her. It was expected that the mindless being would not know proper etiquette, but she felt an annoyance at its creator for not bestowing their charge with the simplest of basic information.

She sifted through her repertoire of magic, wondering what punishment she would lay upon it. Should she petrify it? To watch the world go by, unable to move or speak would be a torturous one, but not something this being deserved.

Besides, with a lack of self, it would not have even felt the despair crushing its mind into a thousand pieces.

She felt a shift in the wind and a small, delighted smile crossed her lips as Valour slammed into the creature with a vicious snarl on her face. The seething warrior did not waste breath on threats, her intentions made clear when she stood between herself and the monster.

She frowned when she saw the warrior slouch, felt the hatred roar to life as she smelt the blood on her face. She strode forwards and wrapped her arms around her, smirking as Valour leaned back against her, and glared at the golem.

She grew angrier as it merely stared at her, not recognising her rage, not feeling emotion at all, when she realised how she could punish it and she smiled a truly cruel smile.

"I shall not curse you, oh pitiful one. Instead, I shall bless you. I grant upon you that which no other has, and upon this day, under this black night, I grant you knowledge. Know what you are, feel what you should, and recall my wrath should you ever seek to harm what is mine."

The golem burned, stumbled and fell, but before a moment could happen, Vivian lashed out and a wave of light smashed into it. The golem vanished.

Valour turned to her as she smirked in victory, looking up at her curiously, though her eyes burned with a light unfamiliar to her.

"Hold still my dear," she murmured, placing her hands on her face. She smiled happily as Valour did not flinch or turn away, merely gazing upon her in wonder, as she should. The wound sealed shut with a hiss and she nodded firmly.

"You have given yourself to your instincts. That is why I shall refrain from showing you my wrath," she pouted. The other woman really should be praising her. Complimenting her beauty, her power and her strong sense of justice.

She turned to the final member of their little party and felt her eye twitch. She raised her hand and a small jolt ran through him. He leapt to his feet with a screech, spinning around in shock, before glaring at her.

"Did you just shock me?!"

"More skilled in observation, than you are in being useful," she murmured. "You left my warrior to fight alone and, as a result, she was injured. Explain yourself. Should I be satisfied, your punishment may be mitigated."

"Wha—? Punishment?! You blinded me!" he accused. She raised a brow and waved her hand, bidding him elaborate. "This! The whole bright light and the eight stars! The latter, quite unnatural!"

She frowned. She knew of the eight, though stars they were not. A source of her hubris, she grudgingly admitted.

"You were distracted by the lights," she stated. He nodded and she fought the strong urge to roll her eyes and smite him to the ground. "I shall not harm you, for who knows what the Light shall do in return."

She grimaced. Though she could not die, there were fates far worse than death that could be inflicted upon her. And angering one of the great powers enough that it sought her eternal suffering was not a task she dared undertake.

She waved her hand and his tooth shot from the floor and back into his mouth. He screamed in pain as it fixed itself, the nerves burning as they reconnected.

"Train yourself. Do not allow distraction to hinder your blade." She narrowed her eyes, "Or I shall lose my caution of the powers over all."

With that, she ignored him and turned to the brazier. "Interesting," she dully lied. "A counter-curse woven into the metal and powered by the 'everlasting' flame of the Day. Extinguished by our lost friend, I suppose I should reignite it."

She held up both hands and then hesitated. A wide smile and a mischievous glint flickered in her eyes. "I suppose, this *is* a great burden onto myself. I could always... reward myself a bit."

She spoke a single sentence, a list of words from the language of the Oélthrinír, and grinned as the brazier glowed red from the heat of the *silver* flame that roared to life. The smoke that rose was a greying white, like an artist's paper, and, on this paper, her own visage formed.

"Perfect."

26. The Ravens Eyrie

"I told you to pull it, as soon as I was done."

Vivian's face burned in embarrassment and shame as she descended the stairs. Valour just beamed at her. Her hair was recently brushed and embroidered with bright flowers.

"But you were so nice! And funny as well. Some of the jokes you made were a little dark, but I thought you were hilarious! And quite considerate as well." She smiled prettily, rubbing a thumb on her forehead.

"That's the thing!" Vivian gritted. "She's usually not! She's mean, vain, judgy and she always does this!" She waved a hand over the dress and new armour. "She's just so… so… argh!"

"You think of her as a separate person?" Valour asked.

"Of course! She's not me, she's like a completely different person. Don't you think of that battle mode of yours as a different being?"

Valour blinked, "Of course not. It's just me doing what comes naturally. It's like you moving without thinking in fights. What's that called again?"

"A reflex," she murmured. "You're saying my other self is a reflex?"

"I'm saying that she is you, but the sudden influx of power makes your mind shift, changes your body and mind into Oélthrinír, in order to help you deal with it. So, instead of thinking with your human blood, you're thinking with the Oélthrinír."

Vivian looked at her, surprised. "That was… incredibly insightful. Where did you learn something like that?"

Valour blushed bashfully. "I read a book about it; 'Tears of a River Selkie.' I like fantasy books."

***

Bastian and Raven met them at the door with smiles. "You were right, kid," Raven said immediately. He eyed the dress with confusion, but it wasn't important at the moment. "We saw the fire, and the tower glowed for a bit. Then everyone started waking up."

"I can confirm that those inside are symptomless."

"Congratulations," Anthony spoke up from the back. "We have saved the lives of our enemies. Are we going now?"

"Indeed," Bastian said, ignoring his grumpiness. "We head for Alkanor, and the Ravens Eyrie."

"What are those places?" Valour asked as they started walking.

"When magic first started to evolve from harmless entertainment into a weapon of war, the King of that ancient time knew that a stronger prison needed to be built, for stronger prisoners. The Ravens Eyrie was devised as *the* single greatest prison to ever be constructed on this island. Made of both Dark and Light magics, a true 'neutral' location."

Raven dropped back to walk with the sullen Vivian, an amused little smile on his face. "So, uh, what happened up there?"

"We encountered a golem," she said plainly. "I believe it was the being that extinguished the lighthouse."

"What?!" Raven was expecting a somewhat embarrassing story regarding the dress, not this. "Are you sure?"

"Not completely," she grimaced. "But it makes sense. The necromancy, the lieutenant, this creature, it all adds up to something disturbing."

"All said, we got rather lucky on this one," he commented lightly.

"Lucky?" She glanced around at the people, all in various stages of grief. Hysterical sobbing, angry cries and mournful prayers. There were carts covered in tarpaulin pulled by stone-faced guards and a keening wail rang out as a hand fell out from underneath. "I would hardly call this lucky."

"The curse would have killed everyone in this city, then who knows what could happen, where it could spread to, if not for you."

"You're saying it was an act of fate?"

"I'm saying thank gods you're here, and good job. You saved a lot of lives today."

"Oh, thanks," she murmured, suddenly bashful.

He just smiled and patted her shoulder.

***

A few hours later.

Alkanor was not a true village, in that it was not a residence for people to make their homes in. Originally built as a first line of defence, it soon became a garrison for soldiers, be they of the island's army or the guards posted on the Eyrie itself. But all of this was irrelevant. Why?

"It's completely abandoned," Raven whispered in disbelief.

"The prison's completely destroyed," Bastian muttered, eyes wide.

It was hard to say what the prison had looked like now that it was merely a great mound of rubble.

Raven started striding quickly towards Alkanor and the others followed, staring around. There were no signs of battle or of a sudden departure. It was all strange. All wrong.

The building Raven came to was an office. The door was locked, so he kicked it down. He hurried in without a look back and made his way to the hallway past the reception desk. He opened the first door and then ignored the room. The same with the second.

The third, he entered. It was an office, a large space with a nice desk and chair, a filing cabinet in one corner and a safe in the other. Raven held his hand over the safe's lock and murmured a spell. With a clang, the door sprang open.

"Damn it," he hissed, seeing it empty. He went to the next filing cabinet as the others walked in, looking at him confused. He opened the drawers and then slammed the empty cabinet shut. "Basic practice," he explained as he passed them out of the door. "Always leave behind copies of documents in a secure location, for the eventual case when you return."

"Three things," Valour said. "How do you know that, why would they come back to this place and why would important documents be in a place anyone could access as easily as you just did?"

He grimaced, turning in the hallway to face her. "Not important. This place has immense historical significance and is a strong military asset. And I apologise. I just had a bit of a moment."

"Might there be an archive of some sort?" Bastian asked.

"There is," he agreed. "Unfortunately, it'll be concealed in such a way that we won't be able to find it, let alone access it."

"I know where it is," Anthony piped up with a smirk. Raven glanced at him and then ignored him.

"We'll just have to go up to the prison itself, see what we can discover, if anything."

"Hey! I can feel its presence!"

Raven sighed, "You can't feel the presence of it. It's under concealment spells, military-grade concealment spells. We try one of the bigger revelation spells, anything within five miles is gonna see the big flare we send up."

"I don't have to use spells. I can sense the magic that powers the shroud."

"Again," Raven said, looking annoyed, "that's impossible. The purpose of concealing spells is to hide *everything* the user wishes to target. Location, magic, everything."

Anthony huffed loudly and glared at him, "Will you just trust me on this one?!"

"No."

"Raven," Valour mumbled to him, "it doesn't hurt to give him a chance. If he's wrong, we only lose what, five minutes?"

"Less than," Anthony said. "The doorway is right over there." He pointed at the end of the hall. He walked over and started tapping specific points and, as he did so, symbols lit up on the wall and a door started appearing in stuttered thick lines.

"Raven, this is impossible," Bastian whispered, leaning in as they stared at the Chosen working. "It's one thing to know where the door is, but it's quite another to *guess* the password to get in."

"Look at him," Raven whispered back. "I don't think he even understands the magnitude of what he's doing."

And as they watched, it seemed like Anthony was just playing some kind of game, looking at invisible spots on the wall and deciding how hard to hit them. But every time his skin met the stone, a web of light spread out from the impact site.

Moments later, a fully fledged door stood out and Anthony pushed it inwards, revealing a long staircase. He folded one arm behind his back and pushed the other out, like a proud curator showing off a shiny piece in his museum.

Raven walked past without acknowledging him and his smile stuttered, but he followed him in.

The room was at least twice as large as the office building, filled with rows like a library, but instead of books, there were boxes filled with papers.

"Bastian, take the girls and head up to the prison. See what you can find out about the fall. I'll stay here with the kid and get started on looking for what I need. Agreed?"

Bastian's gaze flickered to Anthony, then he nodded. The three left and Raven turned his full attention to Anthony Carlachi.

"We're looking for recent documents, we don't know where and we don't know the filing system. Quicker we start, quicker we finish."

He moved over to a shelf and feigned looking at the boxes. "I'm curious. What aspect are you aligned with?" he asked, glancing at him as he stared at the boxes before moving on, as though there were labels on them.

"Peace. That's why I was moved to the tutelage of Master Val Nuthra," he murmured absently, as Raven narrowed his eyes.

Of the Light and Dark, there were aspects. The full blessing was far too much for any mortal to bear, quickly crushing them under the weight of their own gifted strength. And so, the blessing was divided and the Chosen were considered, their most prominent traits used as a basis for the blessing.

In all the history of the Chosen, none of them had powers that allowed one to see through concealment, nor did they have anything that would allow one to accurately guess a password on a magical lock.

And Raven watched the symbols as he pressed them, a truly random password that no one would ever guess, save the one who set it.

So, how?

"Found it!"

Anthony put a box on the ground, lifted the lid off and threw it aside, pulling out papers. Raven walked over to look at them and, sure enough. He glanced around but none of the other boxes were opened.

Anthony had known that he was holding the right box, without opening it, without checking to see if his sudden announcement was even correct.

How?

***

Three minutes later.

Bastian placed his hand on the fractured doorway, a single pillar the only part standing, the rest fallen into dust and rocks. He flinched, pulling his hand away as though it were burnt and stared at it in shock and confusion.

"What's wrong?" Valour asked worriedly, glancing between him and the rubble.

"The wards were broken," he murmured. "No, not just broken. Torn apart by an explosion, not of magic or chemistry, but of sheer presence. The Light and Dark that were already present within this place, expanded."

"Oh, right, you told me about this," Valour mumbled, pinching her brow as she fought to remember. "When the forces of Light and Dark collide, like the Chosen or powerful sorcerers, places of power react. They strengthen or weaken regarding the outcome and can even affect the surroundings."

"Very well remembered," he muttered. "In this place, the Dark won, and destruction has reigned. Neutral ground." He shook his head in disgust. "Placing both in the same place is just waiting for something like this to come. And yet, I never anticipated that *this* building would fall."

Valour turned as footsteps approached and she froze as Seren ascended the final step, looking at the former prison nostalgically.

"None of us did." The other two turned around in shock and stood guarded as they saw him. "Some prisoners lived here for half of their lives. Of course, any survivors that were found were put to the sword. Nowhere else to put them, all their cuffs and chains destroyed, nor the manpower or resources to heal them should they be injured."

He looked at Valour, a tick in his brow as he showed his annoyance. "You're not supposed to be here. I must confess, I did not expect the negotiator. He was supposed to still be doing damage control with the United. Now, when *she* gets here, she'll be distracted. Thank you for that." He muttered the last part sarcastically.

"She?" Bastian asked warily.

"The Shattering Flame." Bastian paled and Seren chuckled. "Ah yes, I must confess it was one of my better ideas, to tell her old Felenot had secretly left the safety of Ereglos and come here. She was *supposed* to tear this country apart looking for the Chosen of the Light, but now she'll likely come for all of you."

"And the Premise would hear, and send several Chosen after her, and they would battle," Bastian said with a fierce scowl. "The King would have no choice but to declare war on these two groups of invaders, and when they died, the Ring and the Premise would both retaliate. Of course, their forces would spot each other, and try to kill them. An escalating war."

"Indeed," he smiled approvingly, which then sank into a dark frown. "Which begs the question, why is he here?"

"He was sent after Ring agents who performed a necromantic spell," Bastian said.

"Ah," Seren deadpanned. "Foiled by my own sword. Typical. Well, lesson learned. Don't have so many plans running at once, as they will interfere with each other."

"What is your end plan? The Final Moment?"

"Please. That's just a means to an end."

"The end of time itself, is a means to an end?!"

"Literally," he smirked. "I was a prisoner here, you know. I was a powerful seer, but I fell into the great trap. I wanted more. More visions, more accuracy, I wanted the future in the palm of my hand. And for that, I needed silence. Absolute. No people, no voices, no animals, no wind. Just, silence."

"Solitary confinement. Understandable. I've longed for the same myself."

Valour tensed up, grabbing Vivian's arm. She heard the footsteps, the stiff grinding of uneven limbs, there were golems here. And whatever cloaked that one was doing the same again.

"But then the moment came. Somewhere, a Chosen of the Dark slaughtered a Chosen of the Light. The Dark rose around the world, crying out its victory, and, in places of power, conflict rose in the hearts of all. The wardens opened the doors and powered down the spells. The inmates were set loose to fight, and fight they did. Freedom was a distant thought and the battle that raged, brought down the Ravens Eyrie."

"And what about you?"

"I, was in the midst of my meditation when the power surged. I was forcing a vision past the magic binding wards, seeking to peer into the streams of time itself, when darkness forced itself upon me. My power flared, the strongest it has ever been, and then it broke."

He looked down at his hand with a trembling lip and his eyes reddened as though he were about to cry. "Everything that I was, everything that I had worked for, gone in an instant. But a mercy was granted to me." He looked up and scared them all with the fanatical glint in his eyes. "A mercy, a vision. I saw the end of the world, and it was beautiful. I saw the ruin, I saw the light, and I saw the eclipse. Everything."

"He is insane," Vivian said firmly. "What did you create with the necromancy spells? No one would risk the wrath of the necromancers for a single puny golem, so what else is there?"

Seren glanced at her and then stared straight at Valour. "I needed them, in order to face you, you know." He smiled sardonically at her confusion. "You defeated a werewolf, in both his cursed form and his regular form, when both are so far beyond human it is insane. I needed a weapon, that would equal you. So I made six. I don't know what you did with number one, but his five brothers aren't happy with you."

Valour tensed as the footsteps slowly closed in around them. She glanced back at Vivian and Bastian, then up at the sky. The sun was falling but night was still far away and there were few clouds left in the sky.

"The lighthouse at Uru Almesh!" Valour blurted out, trying to buy more time. "That was you, wasn't it? Why?"

Seren smirked at her chidingly, knowing what she was doing but perfectly willing to follow along. "I was hoping for something a little more fast acting, at the most something instant, but alas. I did a bit more research, and for a country steeped in magic, there are surprisingly little doomsday artefacts in Brinia," he scowled.

"Oh, and you should have stayed in Timbura, little Miss," Seren spoke to Vivian. "Your stunts with the Oélthrinír magic have consequences you cannot begin to imagine."

"Excuse me?" she frowned at him. "I have been using that all my life—"

"In Timbura, where you could not be found. The second you stood under the covered moon, *they* saw you, and do not doubt that they will come for you."

"What? Who is *they*?"

"Why, everyone." He looked truly bewildered, as if the notion that she didn't know truly never occurred to him as a possibility. "The Royal City does not tolerate half-breeds, unstable weapons of mass destruction that you are. Going around twisting the laws of the world and the people to your own pleasure, and then there are your mother's enemies."

"Wait, *you* know my mother?!" she said aghast, almost sickened that her mum might be *friends* with this man.

"Not really." She sighed in relief. "But she was at the forefront of quite the scandal. I would be surprised if anyone important did not know of her. When she was banished back to the Day Court, she injured quite a few Oélthrinír. Someone of her blood, would be quite powerful indeed," he smirked at her.

Vivian had questions, many questions, the number bordering on the thousands, but that one word stole her breath. That one word locked her jaw and snatched the words from the tip of her tongue. Banished. She didn't leave by choice. She was forced to go.

Valour's gaze flickered. More footsteps, but she sighed in relief as Raven walked into view. She frowned, suddenly panicking as she realised he didn't know about the invisible enemies. She looked at him and tried signalling with her eyes, but he just looked confused and slightly worried. Probably wondering if she was having a stroke.

"And you must be Raven?" Seren smirked, still facing them. "Though I must ask, what kind of name is—" He turned to face Raven and then a look of absolute *panic* erupted over his face. He snapped his fingers, stumbling back, and Valour felt the presences brush past her as they surrounded him. "W-what?! You're alive?"

"Oh. It's you," Raven muttered, face twisted as if thinking, 'Of course it is.' "I," he huffed, "I honest to god did not think you'd change your name."

"Hypocrite," he hissed.

"Yup. I, really do not know what to say right now."

"You died! No one could have survived that fall!"

"And you would not believe the amount of finagling I had to do. What, you think I would have willingly jumped if I didn't guarantee I'd live?"

"You have a habit of faking your death, don't you?" Bastian muttered, rolling his eyes.

"Oh, sod off," Raven grimaced. "I take it Barney is helping you on this?"

"You know he hates being called that," Seren smirked in amusement, even as he glared hatefully at Raven.

"You did take advantage of the little psychopath often. So, insanity, huh? That's a new one, even for you. What, was the criminal mastermind gig not enough?"

"I'll admit, the 'gig' lost its allure to me early on," he murmured. "Too many idiots depending on me for everything. What about you? Have you lost interest in your little morality train yet?"

"No. Doubt I ever will. Too much to make up for, not enough time to do it. Might as well keep at it for as long as I can."

"Indeed." Seren glanced at them and his eyes widened. "I remember this."

"What?" Raven was instantly on guard.

"Yes," he murmured, scrunching his eyes up. "I was right... there." He grinned at a certain spot to his right. "Hello little me. This is where I gained the inspiration, you know." He snapped his fingers and the air wavered as the golems revealed themselves.

"Necromancy. It's a funny little thing, and gets me strong enough weapons to do this." He snapped his fingers again and the golems lunged.

Valour darted forwards to meet them mid charge, but two slipped away. She slammed against one and the other two struck out at her. The blows landed on her ribs and she gasped out in pain, then her arms buckled as the first one powered through her weakened guard.

Raven heard her cry out and ran for her, but was beset upon. The golem lashed out and he blocked the blow, wincing as a bruise blossomed along his arm. He lashed out and held back a yelp as punching stone went about as well as you'd expect.

Vivian drew her blade and cut down from high left, but it ducked under. She stepped back and slashed horizontal, but it stepped back. She held her sword up to guard a blow that never came. It just stared at her, waiting for her to strike again.

Valour let go and rolled back, quickly getting up as the other two attacked her in unison. She tried to focus on one but, as soon as she attacked, she would be charged by the other and she'd have to jump back. A kick slammed into her leg and she staggered, refusing to fall, but a jab rocked her head back and she stumbled.

Raven retreated and his hands started sparking, but the golem stayed close, reaching for his wrists. Lightning flew into the air as Raven tried to direct it down, but the golem kept forcing his arms back. He let out a cry of frustration, forcing all his strength forwards, but was outmatched. He ducked under to its right, twisting his body and its arms, but it refused to let go, even as its limbs cracked.

Vivian swung her blade but, each time she did so, her golem ducked or dodged it. But even when she overextended or left a trap opening, it did not react. It didn't seek to punish her mistakes; it didn't try to hurt her. She gritted her teeth in agitation when she heard the desperate and pain-filled cries of her friends and threw herself at it with a roar, angry as it did not take her seriously.

Valour swung her left arm out randomly. She hit something and almost cheered in relief, but two arms locked around her own and her stomach sank. She tried to throw a punch with her right, but that arm was grabbed as well. Her legs were kicked out and, as she fell to her knees, two arms wrapped around her neck and she stopped dead, eyes dilating as her blood froze.

"Stop!"

Raven raised his arms and spun again, forcing the golem to spin as well, and then he threw all his weight down and towards its legs, flipping it over his back and smacking it into the ground, yet it still didn't relinquish its grip. But he didn't care about that now, not when he was standing over it awkwardly, with both palms facing it. He smirked and the stone creature was smashed apart by searing bolts. He grimaced, rubbing his back in pain, then, "Stop!"

Vivian almost growled ferally as it continued to mock her. Bastian moved an inch, a warning cry on his lips, and the golem tried to lunge for him. Vivian snarled as she leapt into its path, almost howling as it paused, and resumed its passive approach towards her. She was so close to throwing her sword down and hurling herself at it like a drunken brawler in a bar fight when she looked past it and froze. "Stop!"

On that hill, nothing moved. Not the people, not the wind, not even time it seemed. At the apex of the stairs stood two familiar faces, and yet neither of them were anticipated. Lady Rosalina, the Old Blood leader of the Senway coven, and Alec, the Dream Strider.

27. Showdown

"Oh dear," Seren muttered, face paling. "I have been anticipating your arrival my Lady, but alas, it is still a surprise."

"I do not doubt it," she said coldly.

"I don't suppose you will allow me to leave, if I promise to release the girl unharmed?"

Rosalina glanced at the scared Valour, a sad and regretful apology on her face. "I'm sorry, but I cannot allow him to leave."

"I thought not," he grumbled. "And what about him?" Seren pointed back behind himself, where Plato, the lieutenant, had an arm wrapped around Anthony's throat, the other gripping his wrist.

"I do not know who that is. You will have to do better, if you wish to bargain with your life." She looked at Plato with disappointment. "As for you. I know your pack would be quite ashamed of you." The werewolf growled and she turned her nose up at him like he was something foul.

"Oh, don't blame him, that's all Savage's fault," Seren said calmly, edging over to the golems and Valour. "He swayed him to our side by promising to protect his pack from the unjust persecution of the King's army. You know how they are, humans and everything different."

"I do," she said coldly. "I understand a desperate hope. I understand a last gambit. But to parlay with murderers and cultists, is something I shall never condone."

"Cultists? Hardly."

"You worship the end of the world, you covet destruction and you have brought plague upon this land for no goal except the end. You worship death more than any necromancer. You have taken others under your wing and use them to further your goals. You are the leader of a cult."

"Then, from one leader to another," he smirked before gritting out, "stay out of my way. I can deal with you, but I would prefer not to. I have plans that include you, and I would hate to go back to the drawing board."

At that the Old Blood snarled, baring her fangs and her eyes blazed in outrage. "*You* have plans for *me*?! I am thousands of years your senior and yet you think you have the intelligence to manipulate me?!"

"Age does not beget wisdom, my Lady," he said. "And even then, the young must eventually become the wise. And they do this by questioning the wisdom of the old. I am beyond what you are, simply because you have stagnated, hiding away in your tunnels as your brothers and sisters slaughtered each other, seeking a throne that was never theirs to take."

"Watch your words, boy," she cautioned calmly. It seemed her anger had grown so great that her features had slumped into apathy. Yet her body was so tensed you could turn a boulder to powder between her muscles. "You know nothing of my struggle and I would advise you to pick your battles."

"Very well," he smirked. "I pick this one." And he turned to Alec with a big smile. "Hello Strider, how are you feeling? I must admit I miss our little chats, though, not as much as Savage misses you."

Alec smiled weakly. "Unfortunately, I cannot say the same. And yet, my tormentor and I are connected, by a bond of contempt and pain. I shall find him after this, I assure you. Our talk will be just as *detailed* as my Lady and yours."

"Will it now," he mumbled. "I must say, I did not expect to see *you* here." He glanced up at the sun, shading his eyes as he narrowed his eyelids. "How is this possible, may I ask?"

"By the grace of my Lady, I have come to the aid of my rescuers."

"Have you? My, that is a surprise, given how she seems so ready to betray them." He paused and then looked at her with a knowing smile. "Or is she?" Rosalina narrowed her eyes at him. "You know this girl. What she is. You know what her death would bring," he smirked. "I would order her dead right now, but I wish to be alive to see my victory. So, another day?"

"..." Rosalina glared at him. "The next time we meet, I will ensure she is in no danger. Then, our *discussion* can begin."

Seren smirked. Strolling away, he nodded to Plato, who threw Anthony away from him. "The next time we meet, I will have everything I need for you. And when that fails, I shall have other things to ensure my escape." He nodded to everyone there. "Farewell for now, my friends. I know we shall meet again some day, and when we do, I know we shall come to blows. But in the meantime, I do wish you a joyous life. That will make the end all the greater." With a bow, he left, Vivian's golem leaving with him.

There they stood for twenty long, agonising minutes, until the golems around Valour released their grips. She fell choking, scrambling away, and the Golems lunged at Rosalina.

Alec flew forwards, a snarl on his face as a ball of white lightning appeared in his hand and he slammed it into one of the golems. Its chest and back exploded, but even as it died, its two 'brothers' sprinted past.

Rapidly, they approached Rosalina, but she vanished. They stumbled to a stop and then turned as one. She stood behind them, hands extended, and her nails lengthened and sharpened like daggers.

As they turned, they kept turning and their upper halves slid off, showing that the golems were bisected at the waist. The lower bodies fell, but the golems' torsos were still scrabbling towards her, still seeking to attack.

Red energy glimmered between her fingers and she flicked her right hand back over her shoulder. The golems were enveloped and their bodies seized, cracks running through as their joints weakened. With a creaking groan, their bodies fell apart as all the energy within them was siphoned away.

"Damn," she muttered, and vanished in a sudden burst of speed.

"Are you all alright?" Alec asked them.

Raven glanced back as Bastian and Vivian braced Valour and checked her over. "We will be. Give us a few minutes, and we'll join you in the chase."

"I'm ready now." Valour stood, waving off their protests. She glared forwards, clenching her fists and grinding her teeth. "Let's catch up to them."

"Indeed we shall." Rosalina blurred into view, a small thump sounding as she hit the ground. "He escaped me, but this Savage shall not."

"Escaped?" Alec muttered in shock. "But how? A human should not be able to outrun you."

"He did not," she said. "I tracked him to a spot where his scent just vanished. He is lost to us for now, but the other isn't. Alec, find him."

"Yes, my Lady." He closed his eyes and then, a few heartbeats later, snapped them open. "He is still here!" With a snarl of rage, he sprinted towards the steps and leapt down them, as many as he could without falling.

"Bastian, take up the flank! Valour, stay with us, pick up his scent!" Raven shouted.

***

The trail stopped at an abandoned building outside of Alkanor. The entire area and the first layer of trees around it reeked of illusion magics. Surrounding the base, there was a large stone wall and an iron gate with the doors wide open. There were boxes full of armour and weapons, but little else. Alec and Rosalina charged in. The first vampire passed through the gate with ease, but as soon as the Old Blood stepped past the doorway, a large rune carved into the ground lit up and the coven leader was enveloped in a great explosion.

"My Lady!" Alec cried out in alarm and terror. He heard scratches and thumps as humans threw off tarpaulin atop the walls above him. Some wielded bows and arrows and the rest bore aloft great mirrors matching their own size.

In an instant, he realised. In his anger, he had rushed right into a trap. The scents of humans diluted they may be, but they covered every inch of the stone around him.

There was low clapping and the doors to the main building creaked open. Out stepped Savage with a twisted little smirk. "Well, well. I owe the old man two silvers; you know, I didn't think you'd be dumb enough to come! I thought you'd regroup, set out a plan, maybe get yourself some weapons and armour, but no. You ran right over like a bat out of hell."

There was a squeaking paired with a rumble as several humans dragged out a large, covered object atop a four-wheeled cart.

Savage looked past him out of the gate, squinting as the smoke slowly cleared up. "You left half your team behind?" He tutted, mockingly disapproving of him. "They might have saved you." He snapped his fingers and one of the men pulled the cover off.

A glass sphere full of light appeared and Alec hissed in pain as his skin started smoking. "Didn't even need to bring out the big guns for the missy back there. I'm a little disappointed."

The men held up the mirrors and the light struck them. Little words and sigils slowly glowed on the wooden frames and the glass started radiating.

"What the hell?!" Valour skidded to a halt next to Rosalina's form. The Old Blood was frozen in place, her eyes fogged over like she was unconscious, but vampires could not fall asleep. She felt her skin start to heat up. She glanced around and then saw Alec. She darted forwards, the earth breaking beneath her step.

Rosalina stirred, staring forwards as Valour rushed to save Alec. The others arrived and were forced to stop as well, backing away from the heat as the levels grew to scorching.

Valour reached out. Alec turned to her with a look of surprise and a relieved smile. He reached out and she grabbed his wrist, his skin turning to dust in her grip. His smile stuck, even as the light faded from his eyes.

A shockwave blasted out as the dust exploded under the rays enhanced by the mirrors and she flew back like a rag doll.

"Mission accomplished," Savage muttered. He glanced back at the light orb with a remorseful sigh, not looking away as his sight was filled with black spots. "Been waiting to use this bad boy since we finished development, before we even captured the brat. Seems a shame to leave it behind."

He pondered for a few moments and then shrugged. "Oh well." He raised his hands and clapped them together loudly. Valour's ears twitched from where she landed, two familiar *Bamf*s rapidly occurring.

"NO!"

Rosalina screamed. She leapt to her feet and then stumbled, falling to her knees. She looked down and hissed as she saw the rapidly healing wounds on her left leg and the skin regenerating over the stump of her right.

She flexed her power and the earth surged up, hardening into a temporary replacement, and she burst forwards, the dust and smoke vanishing beneath the sudden gust of her movement.

"No, no, no, no…" She looked around desperately, tears that would never fall welling up, before evaporating as the air around her began to shimmer.

"Valour?" She glanced up as Vivian knelt down hurriedly by her head, grasping her cheeks and looking at her intently in the eyes. She would have blushed, might have blushed, she didn't know. Everything was a bit numb. "I'm gonna need you to keep looking at me, okay? Look at me. Your clothes burned away, but the heat didn't damage your skin." Vivian glanced at Valour's stomach and paled.

"Large bruise," Bastian muttered, falling to a crouch beside her. "Possible broken ribs, an explosion of that magnitude would have hurt a lot. Oh dear, why is it always you?"

"'Cos I can handle it…" she croaked with a snarky grin. Or at least she hoped so; a grimace really would have hurt the purpose.

Raven went straight for the stairs leading up the wall. He wasn't wasting time; the others could help Valour, he couldn't. He reached the first man, still getting up from the shockwave, and smacked him across the back of the head, rabbit punching him and sending him straight to the floor. Alive or dead, he didn't care right now, just that he was out of the fight.

The next man directed a mirror at him, but it was out of the light now, so all it showed was him. And he almost hesitated. The image was a frightfully familiar one. He had a darkness in his eyes that was more than anger, more than vengeance. It was something he'd lost himself in once, and he wasn't looking forwards to it again.

He punched the glass, smashing his reflection, grabbed the mirror and threw it off. The man foolishly refused to let go and, with a cry of alarm, he hit the ground hard. Alive, but heavily injured.

The rest of them were ready for him and he held back, wary of fighting them all, even in this single-file line they were in, when a low growl triggered fear in him. And not just him; his enemies cringed as well.

A blur whooshed past and the first man's throat erupted in a gush of red, a whine escaping his mouth, though he clearly wished to scream.

The others met similar fates. Skin was ripped open and blood poured, the walls were cleared in less than a minute. Fifteen men dead in the amount of time it took to drink a glass of water.

Rosalina appeared before him and he tensed. Her lower jaw was caked in blood and her eyes were pitch black. "Our mission here is a catastrophic failure," she said stiffly. "We failed to kill either of them. We lost one of ours. We have no leads. I shall return to Senway and inform my children of their brother's fate."

"Be careful with what you decide next," Raven murmured, carefully cautioning her. "Remember what he said back there. He has plans. If you need help against him, or if you discover anything about him, you can come to us."

She nodded. "I thank you, but I shall make no move for a while. I shall grieve, and I shall attempt to temper my rage." She glanced over at Valour. Bastian was running his hands over her stomach, hands glowing. "She tried to save him. That is more than I can say for most. Thank her for me, will you?" He nodded and she vanished without a further word.

28. The Next Step

Vivian stared at the scorch mark on the courtyard floor. She was still holding Valour's head, still sitting next to Bastian as he waved his hands over her body, infusing her with the light that issued from his palms.

She was lost in her own mind, twisting and turning through her thoughts like some kind of demented labyrinth. She couldn't get it out of her head, the last moments, *his* last moments.

She wouldn't claim to be his friend. They had hardly even exchanged a word, but he was a good person. And she would've liked to have known him better. But that look on his face, the twisted expression of rage and pain, it was more familiar than she'd like to admit.

She felt it even now, the demon in the pit of her stomach, clawing at her guts and howling to be unleashed upon the world. She side-eyed Anthony, who was staring at one of the mirrors with interest. Anthony, the Chosen of the Light who'd distracted her stepmother and caused her to be wounded by the werewolf.

She felt her eyes narrow and her blood boil, but she closed them and forced it down.

She looked down at Valour and lightly slapped her cheek to keep her awake and focused. Her eyes were foggy and she whined a little in protest, but blinked furiously and then kept them wide open.

"There's nothing," Raven hissed, storming through the doors of the base and stopping next to them. He gave Valour a worried look, but put a smile on as she beamed up at him, like she was on painkillers and feeling a little loopy.

"But how?" Bastian murmured with a frown, asking the question even as he kept most of his attention on Valour. "He was there to distract us from the evacuation, obviously, but how did he do it so fast?"

"Obviously he left a few things behind," Raven muttered, "and Savage managed to pull a fast one and dip out on us, but I have no idea."

"Bamf," Valour mumbled, then giggled.

"Er, what?"

"Don't mind her, she's a little delirious. Two broken ribs; I had to dull her pain receptors a bit, the bones weren't healing right. Enhanced healing factor is a drawback of this. I needed to rebreak them and encourage proper position."

"Teleporting kitty cat. Bamf!" she giggled again.

Raven chuckled a little, but Vivian paled. Teleporting cat. That sounded very similar to a certain entry from that book 'Cats, Big and Small' she'd gotten two birthdays ago.

Ahem, "Valour?" she asked, deliberately keeping her tone light. The girl hummed and glanced up at her with wide eyes. "The teleporting kitty cat... by any chance, would it be a panther of above average size, with naturally grown armour made of devoured minerals?"

The redhead stared up at her blankly and then beamed. "Teleporting kitty cat panther," with a proud nod.

"Umbral Kynosar Sabra," she muttered in awe. "Armoured vanishing black cat."

"How do you know that?"

"Hmm?" she blanched as they both stared at her in confusion. Even Valour was copying them, furrowing her brow playfully. "No reason. No reason at all. Don't worry about it."

No way in hell was she disclosing her fascination and love of cats, especially to the man who could transform into that beautiful specimen of a Havana Brown. No way.

"This is all well and good," Anthony frowned, "but we need to figure out our next move. This place is a bust, and we are none the wiser as to our next goal."

"Not to mention the one hunting you," Bastian said.

"Wait, what? Who is hunting me?" He actually chuckled, looking amused and Vivian couldn't blame him. Someone looking for a fight with a Chosen? Even though this one wasn't very impressive, a bit of a wimp actually, the reputation alone should have been a clear deterrent.

"The Shattering Flame, the Jewel of Perdition, take your pick. Cereza Malachite is on Brinia, and is coming for you."

Anthony swayed and Vivian alarmingly thought he had passed out. His mouth flopped open and she reassessed. He wasn't unconscious, just on the verge of it.

"W-what...?" he actually *whimpered*. "B-but she isn't... why is she...? By the withering scales, I-I have to get off this island!" He scrambled back, tripping in his haste, and then scrambled up, trying to look everywhere like a frightened rabbit.

"Calm down." Raven rolled his eyes. "It's too late, she's not gonna let you leave, and even if you did, she'd follow you." He blinked and then smirked as an idea lit his eyes up. "Never mind. By all means, we'll give you all our aid in helping you off this forsaken rock. No need to come back, all of us are lost hopes, no need to send anyone else."

"You think this is a game?!" he demanded hysterically.

"No," Raven said, all traces of humour vanishing as he glared at him. "I think, your presence is putting our home in danger. I know that kid, and the second she got within range, she would've noticed she'd been lied to, and she doesn't take too kindly to deception."

"Bastian," Vivian mumbled, "who is this Cereza they are speaking of?"

He sighed morosely. "A tragic story for another time. For now, I shall tell you what she is and what she can do. Cereza Malachite is a Chosen of the

Dark. From what I heard, all aspects of the Dark fought with each other, each one wishing to bless her. Eventually, discord won out, with a promise to the others that they could show favour upon her.

"She won this great honour by, when she was a normal wizard, unblessed, single-handedly destroying the strongest fortress of the Premise. The one that held Arendim back, protecting the half of Ereglos he had yet to conquer."

"Arendim?"

"General. Did I not tell you his name? How silly of me. Anyway, Aruth Hanir, the Great Dividing, was the great fortress of the Premise, second oldest and strongest next to the capital. She wiped it out single-handedly."

"Really?" Raven asked with an amused smile. "How'd she do that?" He ignored Anthony, tuning in to the conversation.

"She used a volcano."

"Wait, what?" He blinked. "But there's no volcano near Hanir. It was built on the plains of Harnore. There's no mountain around for leagues. Where'd she find a volcano so powerful it'd reach that? Did she sink half the continent with it? What the hell?!"

"No. That would be the pride of the Premise coming into play," he sighed, rubbing his head to stave off a migraine. "One of the plans of the Ring. They spent ten years building a ritual, sacrificed the lives of fifty people and created a mountain golem. They sent it against Hanir, and somehow the fortress killed it."

"They killed... how the hell did they do that?!" Bastian shrugged, so they both turned to Anthony, who was smirking cockily.

"They combined the powers of two powerful relics in the armoury, and created a weapon that could kill the beast," he proclaimed.

Raven and Bastian shared a secretive glance. Vivian swore she could see doubt and something else. A slow realisation? Mounting horror? It was unclear, but whatever it was, it gave her an uneasy feeling.

"When it died, the corpse was transformed into a volcano by the mass of dark magic inside it. Considered dormant, it was left alone next to the fortress," Bastian resumed slowly. "And she took advantage of it. She somehow triggered an eruption, and the great magical defences did nothing against the tide of lava. The greatest hope of the Premise, the last line of defence, the titan that withstood the storm, vanished beneath a sea of red fire."

"Wait, wait." Vivian slowly shook her head. "How did... they had a volcano in their back garden and did not think it wise to build defences in case it should erupt?" Bastian shrugged, so they both turned to Anthony.

"It was dormant," he said, with a small, embarrassed blush.

"So this woman is coming after us." Vivian paused and then corrected herself. "Coming after Anthony."

"Indeed," Bastian said. "We must now act swiftly. Seren shall be anticipating the most logical move we can make."

"Finding a hole and plying on as many defences as possible," Raven muttered. "And then sending a prayer to the powers, hoping they'll get her to ignore us until we're finished with what we need to do."

"That would be ideal," Bastian nodded. "But instead, we shall do the opposite. Valour, we shall need your grandmother's assistance."

"No," she instantly murmured, frowning through the wooziness. "You know it hurts."

"I do," he muttered gently. "And if there was *any* other way, I swear, we would pursue it. But our time is limited. We have no leads. This is it, my dear."

Valour grimaced and glared, but eventually huffed. "Only if she agrees. And if she doesn't, you won't pressure her. Understand?" Her eyes sparked and Bastian smiled.

"Of course. That was never in question." He stepped aside and mumbled to Raven and Vivian. "That was the hard part. Now, for the stupid part."

29. Preparation

"Thank you, sir," Plato smiled as he accepted another of the strengthening potions from Seren.

"My pleasure," he drawled. "Now, are you sure there are no side effects we should note?"

"No. I am functioning at a hundred percent," he lied. Even as he spoke, he could feel the stomach acid bubbling up towards his throat.

"I see. Well, keep up the good work. I'm sending you to the Grey Woods. See if you can convince some of your brothers and sisters to come fight for us."

Plato grimaced. He didn't know what was worse, the feeling tearing his body apart or the idea of going back *home.* "As you wish, sir."

He left the room, actually feeling better. Every time he was sent *there*, it was just another holiday. A few days off, considering if his 'brothers and sisters' ever saw him again, they'd tear him limb from limb before planting his head on a spike. At best, he'll just hang around the edges. Go in a few metres, hide in some of the bushes, come out a few hours later and boom. Anyone spying would believe he'd actually gone in to negotiate.

Seren watched him go with a flicker of disappointment. "So it's not killing him," he murmured, "but weakening. Damn his constitution. I'm surprised none of them have actually killed him yet."

A man burst through the door, huffing and puffing. Seren was about to shout at him when something made him hesitate. The man was scared, as he should be, running into his room unannounced and without permission. But he wasn't scared of Seren.

"S-sir!" At least he obeyed proper formalities, straightening and saluting. "A member of our Iron Claw squad returned!"

"Oh, really?" Now that was surprising. It also explained why he had come here in a rush. "What do they have to say?"

"They tried a few times to break the Treaty but were laughed off. Three of them were killed, one was sent back as a message."

"Still alive?"

"Not for long, sir. He was alive just long enough to inform us the cart he was returned in was a bomb, then it exploded, taking out just shy of a dozen men."

Now *that* made more sense. "So what was the warning?"

He coughed nervously. "To stop our attempts. Though a faction, they are intrigued at the possibility of a renewed war, but they do not want to incur the wrath of *her* and her band."

"I see," he murmured. "Disappointing, but expected nonetheless. It was why I never put much faith in that idea after all."

"S-sir?" Seren hummed curiously. "Who is *her*, if I may?"

"Of course. I would never discourage curiosity. She is the reason the United Species agreed to the Treaty, and it is by her claws that the leaders of the anti-peace movement were killed. She and her band of fellow beasts patrol the borders of the different factioned countries, stopping violence from either side. She was on Ereglos last I heard and should not be here for another three years. This is quite concerning, and it is unfortunate, but we must stop the Claw plans."

"Very good, sir. I'll inform the others at once." He bowed but couldn't wipe the relief from his face.

"As you were. Oh, and if you ever enter my room without permission, or in such a raucous again, I shall beat you bloody and deliver you to Savage wrapped in a bow. Understand?" he asked calmly with a small smile.

"Y-yes, sir, my apologies, sir, it won't happen again!" He quickly fled.

***

Footsteps. A single pair. It's all she ever hears as she continues her journey. Because when the dust settles and the work is done, she goes home to wherever she happened to lay her sheathed sword that morning.

Of course, she will occasionally pass others on the road, exchange a nod and a greeting, but in the end, they too fade into the distance behind as she carries on. None shall walk in step with her ever again.

She had it once. And once it was taken away. So she swore that there would never be a second. Nothing to take and no one to dare attempt to take.

Cereza tilted her head back and breathed in deeply. The pleasant smell of the fresh air brought to her by the breeze filled her senses and her smile was swept away by the *taint*. And once again, her mood was brought low by the sharp reminder that she had been lied to.

For even though it is always the same, that foul stench, the strength of it is too weak to be the prey she yearns to fell. And she wonders, when did she become so desperate that a simple letter was all it took to rouse her rage?

The melody of discord, the blade of madness, the jewel, whatever other inane names they used to justify their failure to end her life. The reasons she gained those names, the history she carved with all her power, all of it swept away as the anger numbed her sanity.

"Beware, o' Light of the Dauntless," she murmured. "The black hounds of the reaper nip at thy heels. Although thou are not the wrath that justice hath wrought, a light thou are. A light this one has sworn to extinguish."

***

Savage cracked his knuckles, letting loose a loud yawn. The trembling secretary whimpered as he glared at her from across his desk. "Are we done yet?"

"N-no, sir. W-with the destruction, o-of the Wise Bears, t-there has become a power vacuum within Senway. W-what do you wish us to do?"

Savage hummed. That was the question. He'd used the Bears to reign in the place, to enforce the rules of courtesy. Even when they were brought low, their reputation and his own name were enough to keep the rabble in check.

There were small mercenary groups seeking fame, there were small-time criminals seeking riches and power, and there were crime-lord hopefuls seeking dark corners from where they could strike.

Usually, it sorted itself out. One would make connections to become stronger, only to be betrayed because either they weren't smart enough to hold a trump card or they had nothing with which to secure the loyalty of their soldiers.

Backstab after backstab, and the only work he'd have to do was send in a clean-up crew. Now, he didn't even have that. His grip was loosening and he blamed Seren. But it was hard to hold on to his anger.

"Do nothing."

"S-sir?!" she yelped.

"You heard me. Do nothing. Our long-term plans have made Senway obsolete. We no longer need it and, pretty soon, having it is going to be a hindrance."

"A-alright, sir, a-as you say."

He leaned his chair back, balancing it on two legs as he thought to earlier that day, when Seren had ordered him to kill the Strider vampire. He whined about it of course. He wasn't done with him yet, but a way to track him in the hands of an enemy? Not an option.

And so he killed him. Or ordered his death. It might as well have been the same thing. And thus, his clock had started. He wondered how long it would take for the coven leader to catch up with him. He wondered how long it would be before her fangs were buried in his neck.

He rubbed his throat and grinned. He wondered just how the pain might feel when those ivory daggers pierced his skin. Would he scream? Would he cry? Would he beg, would he plead, would he attempt to barter?

When that fear of his own demise flooded his body, what would his final reaction be?

***

"You asked her knowing she wouldn't say no, in her current state of mind," Raven accused Bastian. They were walking the path they came from, back north towards Solitude. "Some might say that's blatant manipulation."

"And *you* wish to talk me about manipulation?" Bastian retorted.

"I do. I expect it from myself. I know that I'm a terrible person. But you? You know you could have asked her when she was lucid, explained your reasoning and she would have agreed anyway."

"Maybe," he replied. "And maybe she wouldn't. I could not take that chance."

"Or maybe, you don't wish for her to begin seeing you, as you currently perceive yourself."

"And what would that be?"

"As someone to be doubted," Raven sighed as Bastian turned away from him. "You see the actions of the Chosen and you suddenly doubt everything the Premise ever taught you."

"To be kind, to be helpful, I swear to do no harm and to heal all those who are in need of healing," he grumbled. "And then we see him, the Chosen. The epitome of all we should strive for. And he is only able to help those who swear fealty to the Light? And he is willing to abandon those in need, in order to harm his enemies? I am... conflicted."

"It's fine. You know I'm the one to come to when doubt is the word of the day. Trust me, everythin' you're goin' through? It's natural. The ones who stole you away, raised you from a kitten into the man you were, tried to kill you, sent you away and now the veil is ripped apart, and not gently. It's understandable. If you need time, then take it."

"Unfortunately, time is a luxury we do not have. Even the lords of magic know better than to ask for time. But I cannot help feeling the pull from both sides. That boy, is empathising everything a Chosen of the Light 'should be,' because he does not feel as though he has earned it."

"Yeah." They glanced over their shoulders at Anthony, who was taking his turn carrying Valour's unconscious body, speaking lightly with Vivian to take his mind away from the burden. "Are we sure she's safe to travel?" Raven asked.

Bastian glanced at him with a small smirk. "Well, well, worried are we? Well, don't be. The medic has declared her fit for travel, but naught much else. But there has been one question nibbling at the back of my mind." Raven looked at him curiously and then motioned to carry on with his hand. "How do you know our enemies?"

"Oh gods' damn it," he huffed, eye twitching as an old annoyance rose up. "Look, I was younger, and just startin' out this whole saving people thing. I'd heard of this crime syndicate poppin' up, and I went to investigate." He scratched his nose to hide his blush. "I, uh, may have demanded them to their faces to cease their activities, forgettin' the fact most of my arsenal was unavailable to me at the time."

"Oh my gods." Bastian looked at him as though he was offering two handfuls of pure gold. "You… you actually did that? Oh my gods, this is the best story I have ever heard in my life."

"You haven't heard it all yet," Raven muttered, and felt his reluctance slip away at the joy on the other man's face. When had it come to this, he wondered. When had he become someone willing to endure embarrassment to cheer someone up?

"I was laughed out of the base, not even deemed a threat. So, I plotted revenge. I did some recon, found out their base was atop a mountain, then I pissed off a few mountain trolls and led them right to the front doors."

"Mountain trolls are territorial," Bastian recalled. "At the mere sight of someone setting up any kind of building inside their territory, they go ballistic."

"Yep," he smirked. Then the smirk fell into a grimace as he told the next part. "I got cocky. Wanted to see their faces and mock them as everythin' came crashin' down around them. I did, but then everythin' started fallin' down and I needed to make an emergency exit. So, I jumped out of a newly created hole in the wall, not realising it led to a drop."

"You told them you planned every variable; you knew it was safe," he grinned.

"I lied through my back teeth," he declared. "It was pure luck the drop wasn't far enough to kill me, though I did break my arm and a few ribs. The first from rollin' down it, got a load of bruises from that one, and the latter from the boulder I used to halt my descent." He cast a playful glare back at Valour. "Unfortunately, I don't have that one's regeneration power, so I had to sit still and eat my pills for a few weeks."

Bastian chuckled and they fell into a comfortable quietness. They strolled along the dirt path and eventually Bastian had to break the silence.

"What can you tell me about them?"

"Savage was Seren's protégé. Little bugger always nipped at his heels. He was sadistic, and Seren fed that urge like a drug, letting him get away with everythin'. Taught him everythin' the little psychopath knows. Made sure that, even if he fell, Savage would still be able to carry on his legacy. They're both smart. The reason we got away with most everythin' we did, was because they didn't take us seriously. If we manage the victory we want, that'll change quite quickly."

***

Four days later.

Taking various shortcuts, dangerous little paths that flirted with the boundary of sensibility quite often, they made it to Solitude with no fights and only a few close encounters. Valour had woken on the second day, but was only able to properly walk unassisted on the final stretch of the fourth.

They met Lydia outside her house. Valour asked her where she had been staying, but the woman just smirked at her and refused to answer.

When Bastian explained what they needed, she accepted it easily, to Valour's dismay. They entered the house and Valour dragged her new chair from by the fireplace over to her grandmother so she could hold her hand.

"Aren't you a dear," she murmured, patting the offered limb gratefully. Lydia closed her eyes and focused.

Her face started turning red, and not the healthy kind, though it wasn't painful looking, merely as if she'd been out in the sun a little too long. She gasped and her eyes snapped open. She furrowed her brow with an annoyed hiss and closed her eyes again.

A line of blue slowly appeared on her face and her cheeks tinged purple. She snapped her eyes open once more and started coughing, holding her head in pain.

"What did you see?" Bastian sent an apologetic look to Valour as the woman growled at him. "I am sorry, but we need to know."

Lydia stared at the wall, eyes darting around as she recalled her visions with worry. "I... I don't believe they have anything to do with what you're doing," she muttered, looking worried as her gaze went to the floor, fogging over as she thought harder.

"Damn it," Bastian hissed. "I knew you couldn't choose, but I still hoped." He looked at Valour, "Once more, I apologise. This was indeed a long shot, but I had still hoped..."

"Usually I can give them a nudge, and they can go the direction I want them to," Lydia admitted, "but this shouldn't be possible," she murmured.

"What shouldn't?" Valour asked her gently.

"There is one, can't call it a rule, but it's the closest thing. The future is ever shifting, and the only certainty is the end. No vision is the same, and yet." She started chewing on her thumbnail, "Why is it, that I just had the same three visions in a row?"

Bastian, and even Anthony, paused and looked at her like she was insane. "Three?"

"Indeed. I had my first vision two days ago, and then these two I just forced." She rubbed her head with a pained wince. "They were the exact same, down to the last detail. A city next to a tower, the top glowing with silver fire, and a light that shone brighter than the sun, in one of the middling districts."

Bastian frowned. It was obviously Uru Almesh, the silver-fired tower was a dead giveaway, but light? What kind of light, and why would three visions show it?

"That's obviously important, I won't lie," Raven said, "but not what we need." He glanced around at the others, seeing the exhaustion of carrying Valour on their shoulders, not to mention his own from carrying the redhead, and quickly made the decision. "We're done for the rest of today. Rest up, and we'll reconvene in the morning."

The others nodded reluctantly, but he could see the relief they tried to hide. "Alright, the injured takes the bed. We'll make do with what we have," Vivian declared, glaring at Valour when she tried to protest.

"Actually," Lydia said, strolling over to the door that led to the kitchen and throwing it open. "You'll be sleeping on these." She gestured to the three beds all laid out in corners of the room. "I figured this would happen, so I called in a few favours and had some guys move them in. I didn't know there'd be one more of you," she said, looking straight at Anthony, "so one of you will have to take the couch."

"I will," Raven immediately volunteered. "I need to think a few things through anyway."

***

An hour after sunset.

Raven blinked as someone lightly knocked on the door. He threw a glance at the others sleeping soundly in the kitchen and then got up to answer it. Opening the door, he was on edge as the man blinked pitch-black eyes at him. He was scowling, wrapped head to toe in black clothes with a large, hooded cloak thrown over the top and, without saying anything, handed him a letter and left.

"… and goodnight to you, sir," he muttered sarcastically.

On his way back to the sofa, he ran a hand over it, but nothing magical or physical popped out. He checked the front, but there was no name. He opened it with his thumb and held it open above the floor. A single sheet of paper fell out and he stepped away, but again nothing.

He sat down and picked it up at the corner, pinching it between finger and thumb. He opened it and started reading.

"Well, that was convenient."

***

When Valour woke up, she struggled with her breathing. It came in rasps and she held her ribs as a phantom pain slammed hammers into her abdomen. She weakly grabbed for a box of pills Bastian had assigned her and swallowed two of them.

"Whenever someone heals something serious, like broken bones, there will still be pain. Magic heals it quicker than biologically possible, so the body still believes itself to be in critical condition, and will… encourage, you to take it easy."

She sighed in relief as it faded to a dull throb, itchy but manageable, and slid off the bed. She briefly wondered, as she moved towards the stairs, why exactly it was her who was getting hurt all the time. Then she thought about the others being this hurt and shuddered. It was better this way.

She entered the living room to a debate and Vivian and Anthony eating bread on the sofa, staring at the intensely focused duo.

"What's going on?" Valour asked Vivian quietly, sitting down as the woman shuffled over to make room for her.

Vivian picked up the piece of bread on her lap and offered it to Valour. "Last night, Raven was given a letter from an envoy of Lady Rosalina. The werewolf Plato was spotted heading towards the Grey Woods."

"Why would she tell us instead of going after him herself?"

"Because by the time word got back to her, and she got within sight, he was already within the borders and dare not strike."

Valour frowned, "Okay, but why not just go inside?"

Vivian chuckled, then stopped when she saw Valour's sincere confusion. "Oh, forgive me, I did not realise you were not aware." She coughed to hide her embarrassment. "The Grey Woods are the territories of the werewolves. Seventy years ago, when Lycouse, the father of wolves, started expanding his pack, he took over the Grey Woods.

"A coven of vampires was sent to destroy the pack and reclaim the lost ground, but they were met by the warriors who were changed by the curse. More feral, their old personalities rewritten by the influence of Lycouse, and changed to be more territorial, combative and pack oriented. That began the ten-year War of the Red Moon, which ended when the king of the time, Halmadden, led his army and beat the two weakened forces down, and ordered them to agree to a ceasefire.

"Of course, at this time, if the war was restarted between their current forces, both sides would be wiped out. They are both weakened, suffering from a loss of numbers, but the pact also decrees that, should one side break the truce, the army of Brinia would destroy the aggressor."

"So she sent this letter to us, because no one would care if we went?"

"Precisely what I believe," she nodded.

Valour nodded absently, nibbling on the bread, and then looked past her as Anthony twitched. She furrowed her brow; he was looking really jumpy. The paleness and the gathering sweat on his face. Raven jabbed his finger at something on the table, making the slightest of sounds, and Anthony flinched.

She caught Vivian's eye and motioned towards him, raising her eyebrow. Vivian winced and mouthed back, "Hunter." Or something like that, she wasn't the best at lip-reading. Of course, she had no idea what she was talking about, but she just ahh'ed and turned back to the other two.

"We have no other choice then," Raven grimaced. "They'd smell and hear us the moment we try to sneak in and, if we try to fight through them, we'd end up having over a thousand angry Platos coming to knock our teeth in."

"Agreed. Diplomacy is the only choice," Bastian grimaced. "I do not like our chances. But, I do know how we can get an audience."

"Really? I think we just had the exact same idea." And, simultaneously, they both turned to Vivian.

30. Peace Is

Two days later.

The Grey Woods are in the south of Brinia, a large expanse of woodland that covered more than three thousand square miles, ending just shy of the beaches by the southern sea. The trees tower over the ten-metre mark, earning the forest its name by being as grey as fog.

Every single tree that bordered the inner forest was marked with three long jagged scratches, a declaration, a claim and a warning, all in one little symbol.

Valour pinched her nose with a sad little grimace. Even now, standing at least twenty metres away, she could feel the smell marking their borders like it was a physical shield.

"Maybe he's not even here any more?" she said hopefully, her voice a pitiful warble.

"Sorry, kid, but he's still in there," Raven murmured. "Got vampire eyes all over, we'd have gotten a letter saying he's moved, or Rosalina would've pulled 'em out after she tore him apart."

"Our entry point is there." Bastian pointed at a bit of the woods that looked no different from the rest of it, but she shrugged that off. "Valour, Anthony, please keep watch. If you see him alone, do not attack first. Agreed?"

Valour nodded glumly, a bit ashamed that she wasn't putting up a fight, but that scent was sending all her instincts into a spiral.

She waved goodbye as they started heading towards the forest and she turned away to find a good spot to sit.

***

Vivian's eye twitched again as they picked up yet another tail. They were hardly being subtle about it; she thinks that last one was the third time they had deliberately stepped on a twig.

The group walked for five minutes before a soft growl from their left had them moving right. Another two minutes and another growl had them moving right once more.

For ten minutes, they followed this pattern, herded until they entered a glade. Vivian took a second to admire the scenery, a nice little stream, some large rocks scattered about and the four men and women standing before her in leather briefs and vests.

Muscles and scars were put on obvious display, hair mussed wildly, they gave off the image of powerful savages, one of them even fiddling with an axe, running his finger up the edge to show off how sharp it was, licking the bead of blood as he glared at them.

Vivian stepped forwards, ignoring a low growl from the side as she likely trod on pack civility. Oh well, she cursed faintly in her mind, no redoes on this little mistake.

"Greetings. I am Vivian El Lock, heiress of the noble house of El Lock, daughter of the house of Faralla. I seek an audience with the alpha."

There were more growls, but the general look of the group she could see was of curiosity, so she held her breath as a silent debate was wagered.

It ended when a giant of a man stepped forwards. Tallest of his group, he also had the most scars, a prominent one being teeth marks dug into the angle where his neck met his shoulder. As he moved, she tensed as the sun hit his hair and turned the dull orange into a fire, his blue eyes burned and she felt herself tremble with shock, almost believing herself to be in her father's presence.

Wisdom, strength and, strangely enough, a protectiveness that showed as he placed himself between her group and his own, glaring down at her with his lip curling back.

"I am Thurian Malayne, alpha of the Grey Woods. You are trespassing."

She nodded but did not remove her gaze from his. Eye contact was essential; she could not afford to be seen as a lesser wolf. She'd been briefed on the way here. She was essentially portraying herself as the alpha of a new pack and, if she wanted the talks to go well, she could not show weakness.

"I am. Grave news brought me swiftly here, and I sought out an audience to determine the truth." She bit the inner part of her mouth, cursing herself as his eyes narrowed. "An oath breaker has been seen entering your forest. I came here to ask if you were harbouring him."

Thurian's eyes narrowed and his teeth were bared. "No new blood has entered my forest. My sentries have declared none have passed through. Your source is mistaken."

"They are not," she said back instantly. "More than one pair of eyes has seen the werewolf known as Plato—" The wolves howled and roared angrily, Raven stepped forwards quickly as a man charged towards them from the treeline, practically frothing at the mouth.

But Thurian intercepted him, snarling angrily. He grabbed the man by the throat, slammed him down and howled in his face. "You dare disrespect me like this?!" The man in his clawed hand realised his mistake and went limp, showing his neck.

Thurian snarled and slammed his fist into the man's face once, twice, three times, then picked him up by the grip he had on his throat and threw him across the ground towards where he came from.

After a sharp gesture, a man and a woman came forwards. Slinking low to the ground, they grabbed him by the shoulders and quickly dragged him away.

"You accuse us of harbouring the kin slayer, the oath breaker, the traitor," Thurian growled, turning his anger towards Vivian, who kept her back straight. "Have care with your next words."

"If you do not harbour him," Vivian said slowly, "then why would he be here?"

"He came before me only once," he snarled, "to attempt to entice us to his master's side. I refused, and enforced his banishment from our forest. We have seen no trace of him ever since. If what you say is true, then we shall increase our scrutiny." He glared at the group over his shoulder, "And I shall ensure the loyalty and competency of my pack."

"I see. I thank you for your generosity and hospitality, but your words have given me much to think about. So, by your leave, I would like to exit your forest and think upon what you have given us."

Thurian glanced at her out of the corner of his eye and nodded to her almost respectfully. "Go in peace, daughter of El Lock, daughter of Faralla. But before you do, in exchange for the information you have given us, I would give you some in exchange."

Vivian nodded slowly, "Anything given freely is welcome."

"Be wary of how you use your magics." She froze. "Unshielded and not properly hidden, it sends a signal to all who know how to see. The lakes are restless, the shadows dance, our omens speak of an arrival not seen since the ancient days. My elders believe they shall seek you out, and you must deal with them. Do so quickly, and do not allow them to approach my forest. Now leave."

Vivian nodded blankly and turned away, walking past Raven and Bastian to lead them back down the path they travelled.

Raven waited until they were out of sight, then lunged forwards to wrap her arm around his shoulder and his hands on her stomach and back. "Easy, easy," he gently soothed her. "You did so well back there."

She nodded absently, shivering uncontrollably as she stared unblinking at the ground. "I-I-I think I'm, having a panic attack," she gasped. All she could see was his hard gaze and the eyes of all the werewolves around her. The snarling, the growling, the violent intent, it was petrifying. Everything she refused to feel back there rushing back, and it was overpowering.

"I know, I know," he grimaced, "but it's over now. Come on, you're going to be alright. We're going to get you out of here, and you don't have to do something like that for the foreseeable future."

She nodded again and Raven sent a panicked look to Bastian, who nodded firmly. He got in front of Vivian, cupped her chin and started gently murmuring. "Okay little one, focus on my voice. That's it, now do me a favour, look around and tell me five things you can see."

***

Valour sighed loudly with exaggerated boredom as Anthony plucked another blade of grass.

"Do you have to do that?" she muttered.

"Is there anything else to do?" he asked with a bitter glare. "We're stuck on the most boring part of this mission, jack all around us." He turned a cold glare on the forest, "Not to mention how bad this place is."

Valour rolled her eyes. Honestly, she felt like he was playing up the whole 'Saturated in darkness!' bit to be more dramatic. "So what's life like back in Ereglos?"

He looked at her weirdly, "You care?"

"Of course." Not. She really didn't, but anything was better than hearing him pull grass from the earth and whinge about not getting the more interesting parts.

"Well, before I was a Chosen, I could visit wherever I wanted, and there is no shortage of beautiful sights." He smiled at the ground, "The lakes, the hills, even the parks, everything was beautiful. Of course, since our buildings radiated Light magics, everything was so saturated they may as well have been sources themselves.

"It makes everything appear ethereal, as though the aspects had descended to our plane and crafted everything with their own bare hands."

"You said before you became a Chosen," Valour noted. "Why would this have stopped you?"

"Because when I was, I became a target. I needed to be put on a fast-paced training schedule, and when I finished, I was assigned to Master Val Nuthra. From there, I travelled around Ereglos, and even went north to Terramae. In case you were wondering, that's the home of the Selkies."

"Selkies, huh?" She sat back with a whistle. "And how was talking with them?"

"Not as difficult as you might imagine." He smiled, scratching at the dirt. "They have a strange dialect, not one an ordinary human's vocal chords can speak, but I had an advantage."

"Does being a Chosen come with a change to your body?" Vivian asked curiously.

"Not always. But when a Chosen does something that impresses the power that blessed them, or does something that begets a reward, they occasionally give it. Of course, they usually stick to giving them something of equal value to the deed they did. Can't just go on a delivery quest, and suddenly be able to drop the sun on someone."

He smirked and Valour chuckled. "So what extra powers do you have?"

"Eh, just my gift with languages and barriers," he shrugged. "I haven't really done much yet, never really been in a situation where I could prove myself."

"Is that why you're here then?" He looked at her strangely, "Here in Brinia, I mean. The Premise sent you here to prove yourself, so you could pick up an extra skill?"

"No," he immediately denied. "To do something with the expectation of a reward isn't something that impresses anyone. It means you depend on them for everything, and aren't really worthy of their attention. It means you aren't the kind of person they believed you to be, and that could lead to them rescinding their blessing."

Valour hummed along and made interested noises when appropriate, but the truth is she had stopped listening as soon as he said no. When he had been in that chair in the interrogation room, he had told her his mission here was to kill the suspected Ring members.

And now he was telling her that his only skill was being an exceptional linguist, and pretty good at shielding himself? An ambassador, a trained negotiator, was sent to assassinate people who could cast a spell so strong it was felt an entire country over?

Yeah, something about that picture was *severely* wrong and messed up in the extreme.

She had to stifle a sudden giggle; this whole detective thing was actually pretty fun. She should ask Raven to give her a few pointers. Movement at the treeline caught her attention and she froze.

Plato walked out, looking around suspiciously. She grimaced. He had to know that they were there. But was he alone? It didn't matter. She had a moment, and she needed to take it.

"Anthony, come on!" she hissed, before blurring forwards, not checking to see if he was following.

And he was going to, but as Valour left, he felt something. Something cold, like a sharp chill on a winter night. He gulped as his limbs started trembling, his teeth chattering, his heart seizing.

"Well, well. I did not expect to find a whelp where I sought a hound. Tell me, pup, why are you here? And where is your master?"

***

'Do not attack first.' That was going to be a very hard order to obey. She zeroed in on him and then skidded to a stop. She cast a glance over her shoulder, cursing when she realised she'd left her backup behind in the dust.

"Well, this is a surprise," Plato grumbled. "If you're here, the rest of your pack can't be too far behind." He sniffed the air, then sighed. "Of course, the boundary covers it all up." He looked at her weirdly. "Why didn't you attack me just then?"

She said nothing, staring at him warily as he palmed a familiar bottle. She could knock it out of his hand, but that would be an aggressive action, and she could have an unknown number of enemies brought down on her head.

"Unless you put a foot forth without thought. You were ordered not to pick a fight with me." He wondered, then grinned when she stayed silent. "That must be it. Well, I have no intention of fighting you, so I think I'll just be on my way."

"Back at the Ravens Eyrie, when Seren was speaking of you—" He stopped in his tracks, turning curiously. "He said he threatened your pack to make you comply. You're with him, doing all of this, because you're trying to protect them, right?"

He smirked with lips peeled back, baring sharpened fangs that cut into his mouth. "Not quite."

Valour frowned for two reasons. One, his words. Two, the hand that clutched the bottle was starting to change. His nails were sharpening, hairs were growing, he was reacting just from the presence?

"See, I broke the one rule you never should. Werewolves are like common wolves, except dialled up to eleven. Me? I was always broken, hated the others, and when I had the chance? I killed one of my packmates."

"What? Why?" Her mind blurred, she needed a moment. Too much information at once. He was partially transforming, but the potion she'd seen him drink only enhanced his abilities, there was no physical change, and just from touching the glass?

"Killed him and threw his body into a lake to hide it. But, turns out I picked the one day where two others were bathing," he chuckled unrepentantly. "Oops. Need to kill the witnesses," he grinned. "Never liked their faces anyway." His smile dropped into a scowl. "Didn't see the alpha coming. He knocked me on my arse, but couldn't kill me without breaking his own rule. So I was banished instead. When I met Seren and he convinced me to join him, I was sceptical. But then he tried to blackmail me into staying by threatening to cause a losing war by breaking the truce."

He shrugged. "No idea how he was going to do that. In all honesty, never really cared anyway. So I agreed to his terms. Acted the part of cowed little dog, and kicked up my heels."

"So what you're saying is, if I start a fight with you, none of your allies will come running?" she asked.

At once, they both realised their mistakes. Valour swore and started to run at him, Plato lifted the glass towards his lips, but she was much faster than him and she could cross the gap in little to no—"AAGH?!"

Anthony?!

She froze.

Plato's lips curled victoriously as he downed the entire bottle.

Valour swore and turned back to him, then she was ripped off her feet and sent flying. She hit the ground hard and scrambled to her feet woozily. Everything was hazy and numb. She glanced around and quickly found Plato, but frowned.

It might just be her pounding head, her blurry vision or any manner of concussion, but since when did the werewolf have three arms? Her gaze sharpened. Horror-filled realisation broke through and she looked down at her numb left shoulder. The pain set in and she howled.

31. I Am Not

"That doesn't sound good," Cereza murmured absently, glancing towards the pain-filled scream. She looked back at the huffing and puffing boy on the ground and felt flickers of something familiar try to twist her gut. Regret? Pity? She wondered, trying to think back to the last time she felt such things.

Anthony flinched, looking between her and the source of the scream, and she was intrigued to see him conflicted. "You... are not like the others, are you?" His face reddened, but she didn't care. "The sound of one in pain would not draw their eye, were their enemy standing before them."

There was a long, drawn-out howl and Anthony twitched towards it. "You are on a precipice, youngling." She raised her hand and the shadows that caged them both in together faded away. "I will let you go, so long as you go to her—"

He sprinted off in Valour's direction and Cereza blinked. "Well, that was fast." She jogged after him, easily catching up but stayed a few paces behind him. The wolf lunged for the girl on the ground, but a spell caused his own shadow to yank him back and bind him on the floor.

"Valour!" the boy cried out. He ran over and grabbed her arm, lifting it up and ignoring her painful protests. He put his hands over it and pressured it, but the blood was leaking through his fingers.

"She won't last long," Cereza said, glancing at the girl's face as it grew paler. "You'll need to heal her. Don't really know why you haven't done that in the first place, but each to their own, I guess." She breathed in the emotions he bled, the discomfort and disquiet feeding her. The discord was enticing.

"I can't heal her!" he panicked. "My power only works on those faithful to the Premise!"

Cereza blinked. She was pretty sure she heard a cosmic-level facepalm in the distance and screeching laughter. "No. No, that isn't how that works."

"And what would a darkling know of the powers of the Light?!"

"More than you, apparently. Surprisingly. Also, darkling isn't an insult. It's not even a real word. Made-up words don't work as insults if you're the only one who knows what they mean."

He gritted his teeth. "Alright then, how do I help her?"

She needed to reassess the boy. First impressions didn't account for much, apparently. All it took was the right knife to scrape away the paint. "The Light does not care about faith. It sees someone in pain and thus seeks to heal it. Pain is a pathway to darkness and a motivation for power. Power is a drug that leads you ever down, and should you step off the white marble path, you shall eventually forge your own."

He stared at her with a growl, "Get to the point."

"Ah yes, forgive me, I forgot I started with one for a moment there. Simply use your power, but do not see her. Ignore what she is, ignore who she is. Focus on the specifics. She is a person in agony, and you must rescue her from the darkness. Heal her pain, and expunge the corruption before it takes root."

She watched his hands start to glow with an annoyed detachment. Why in all that's unholy and brutal was she the one to teach him this? As she watched on, the skin slowly knitting back together, an idea started to form. Her eye twitched.

Why did she let him go again? Why did she encourage him? Why did she teach him a trick he already should have known? An image started to overlap in her memory and she scowled.

"... Not a..."

She blinked. "Excuse me?"

"...I..."

She frowned. "That was no clearer than the last. If you have something to say, speak clearly."

He turned to look at her and something froze inside her. "I am not a weapon." His eyes were teary, filled with regret and sadness.

"... And why would you feel the need to question this?"

"From the moment I was chosen, everyone kept telling me, I was now the 'blade of hope that would sever the evil.' That I wasn't really a person any more, just a weapon they could point and unleash."

"..."

"But since I got here, I don't hear their lessons. I've been called out on it, actually." A smile, a small, sad little thing crossed his lips. "And it made me feel bad. I'm used to ignoring everything around me, all the misery and pain, and I got by thinking that I couldn't do anything about it. But now? I could have. I could have helped them, and it makes me feel pretty damn bad."

"... Well, crap." She didn't really know what else to say. This random kid just spilled his heart out, a wall that held back a *lot* of repressed trauma and sadness just broke, and because she was the only one conscious, Plato growled as his restraints stretched and she amended her thought. She was the only one conscious and not an insane blubbering moron, and because of that, she got the feels right in the face.

Anthony wiped the blood away from Valour's wound and sighed in relief. "She's gonna be fine." But he kept holding it, staring at it with a strange look of awe on his face.

"Okay kid, turn down the creepy. You did your thing, feel proud, but we've still got some stuff to sort out."

"... Like what?" She stared at him as he stood up, wondering if she'd got him pegged wrong after all; maybe he was an idiot. "You beat me. I can't win. You broke my strongest shield like it was paper, and then flipped me head over heels. I can't beat you."

"... That can't be it," she said bluntly. "You're a Chosen of the Light, a young one, why would they send you alone to a foreign country that hates what we are, alone, knowing that I or one like me would chase you?"

She paused and knew the same look that was on his face had just fallen over her own. "No," he said firmly. "That's not it!" She said nothing, ignoring his plight and discomfort, as she cursed herself for being so foolish.

"Again, my vengeance has blinded me," she hissed. She closed her eyes and tried to ignore the blinding spot of sun next to her.

"No," Anthony muttered. He tried to think. To remember. But there was nothing. Nothing to indicate anything; he'd gotten his mission, been seen off on the ship that carried him, there was nothing out of the ordinary from any other Chosen mission that he himself had seen off.

"There's nothing," she murmured, opening her eyes. "But then... why?" She stared down at him, a puzzle appearing, and she did not like the many sides it had. "Why are you here? Why are you travelling with these people? What is your objective?" She waited, but he was staring at the ground, eyes blank. She growled and grabbed his collar, lifting him up to snarl in his face, "Answer me!"

"... I was sent here because of necromancy. I travelled with them, because they were after the same thing I was. I'm here, because they sent me here."

"Who gave you this mission? What were their words exactly?!"

"... The Council." She resisted the urge to spit on the ground. "Our seers have foreseen great darkness in Brinia. You are to go investigate, and end the spread before it stamps out the Light."

"That's it? Those were their exact words?"

"... The exact words I was given."

She dropped him, "Ooph!" and spun around.

"What the hell is going on?" she asked herself, bewildered. "The Premise is straightforward, predictable, their arrogance of late is cause of this. A many-layered plan is beyond their current state, so what has changed?"

"That isn't true!" he snapped, leaping to his feet and glaring at her, hands starting to spark. "They wouldn't use someone as bait like that! It's immoral, evil!"

"Just like telling them you can only heal the faithful, and telling you to ignore the pain and suffering of others around them." She tossed back over her shoulder. "Oh boy, reality is not going to be kind to you."

They were so invested in their argument and their own thoughts that they didn't notice Valour twitching.

"There has to be another reason," he insisted.

"Boy, your Council is made up of the elders and, of note, people of the Premise. Tacticians, warriors, the wise and the brave." She screwed up her face as she complimented them. "They would not miss a detail as obvious as me. Especially not me."

"Then maybe—" he paused as the wind shifted. He spun around and stared in shock, even Cereza had to blink and take it in. "Uh, Valour? Not to sound... anything but joyous, but how are you standing up right now?"

"Don't sugar-coat it, kid. Blood loss, shock, the pain alone should have her still..." She caught the look in her eye. "Out. Oh, this will be interesting," she grinned.

"What's that supposed to mean?!" he snapped at her.

"It means our presence here, both at the same time, has triggered her instincts."

He frowned, "Wait what?"

"Unconscious and in pain, she has two very powerful sources of energy surrounding her, both hostile to each other. Her blood's kicking in."

"You noticed that?!"

"How could I not? I have eyes, and I can see into hers. Little suggestion, don't move if you don't want to die. I still have use for you." She hid her arm from Valour's sight and rotated her wrist.

***

Valour groaned in agony. She could feel her body moving, but it was like she was just a passenger in a wagon. She could only watch and fight a losing battle for the reins. Her body twitched and her vision locked on Anthony as he shuffled his feet.

He was repositioning himself, getting ready to lunge. 'Wait, no he's not.' She frowned, watching him edge backwards. 'He's nervous, and why did I think that?'

She heard a low growl and suddenly her body moved, her arm snatching a wrist just before the claws could reach her eyes. Her head snapped forwards and smashed into Plato's nose, before she kicked him away.

She looked around. The new woman was sitting down comfortably a few metres away from the battlefield, looking quite amused. Anthony was slowly edging forwards, his hands held up in a clear-cut attack position.

'Wait! That's surrender, not attack!'

A blur slammed into her ribs; so the Light Chosen was a distraction then. 'I don't have a clear argument, but that is not true!' Why else would he be coming towards her like that, occupying her attention so she didn't see the attack coming?

'Oh, I don't know, probably because you keep coming up with reasons to murder the poor sod!?'

She landed and rolled, her momentum keeping her away from the snarling lunges. His arms swung wide and she ducked under him, kicking his legs out and punching the back of his head.

Deeming him neutralised, she turned to the other threats on the field. 'Threat! Singular!'

"Uh, Valour? We um, kind of need him alive?"

Showing pity for an enemy. Clearly he is biding time for his ally to regain himself. 'Clearly, instincts don't work too well without logic or common sense!'

She dashed forwards, lightly surprised when he managed to put up a shield, but she punched through it easily and grabbed his shirt, pulling him close. She struck his rib with her knee and then let go to punch him in the face. A smaller shield appeared and she broke through it, but her fist whistled past his ear.

A blow crashed against the back of her head and she whirled around. 'Ow! Oh, why is everything spinning?' She put up an arm and blocked a wild swing, but his other arm slammed into her stomach, forcing her up off the ground.

She growled and directed her magic towards the back of her throat. 'Wait, what are you doing? How are you doing?!'

She breathed in deep, then forced the air back out. Something clicked in her throat and a great gush of fire spewed out. Plato howled in pain as his body was set alight and he hit the ground a few feet away, rolling around.

"... Since when the hell could you do that?!"

'... Since when indeed.' She wondered, incredulous, stopping her struggle to regain control in order to stare.

She felt the air leave her lungs, felt it change somehow when it passed her throat, and felt something ignite it. She also felt the skin of her mouth blister and crack, flesh peeling away as it burned. And then she felt new skin regrow, immune to the blistering heat, a feeling washing over her she remembered from her arm, but familiar. Safe.

The fire sputtered out and her body reached up to tear the charred skin that used to be her lips, revealing the fresh new skin beneath. 'Oh my god, I'm a salamander!'

"Her power is coming out." The woman strode over with a small smirk. "Your own magics triggered it when you healed her. Our presence here amplified it. You should run along, kid; I want this one."

"Wait, did you know this would happen when you told me how to heal her?!"

"Probably would have, if I cared enough to put thought into it. Plus, you can't blame me, I didn't know the woman had ancient blood in her."

'What blood now?'

"I won't say it again. Run along; I want this one." She smirked again and her body tensed up. There was something really dangerous about this woman. It was like being one step away from the jaws of a terrifying beast.

And then she was literally one step away as the woman blurred and she grabbed a slow punch, but another rocked her jaw. She took a single step back, then swung a leg, but her shin was caught and she was pulled off her feet and slammed into the ground.

Her throat clicked and fire spewed out into the woman's face. Valour heard a yelp and winced in apology, then gaped in awe as purple light shone through. Her face was singed, a little pink around the everywhere, a purple hexagon spinning in front of her.

"That was close!" she congratulated, then smiled. "Too bad you've lost yourself; this could've been interesting."

She tightened her grip around Valour's leg and then pulled whilst twisting herself to launch a kick at her face. Valour grabbed her by the ankle and leaned her head forwards. She slowed the impact, but still whimpered when it connected painfully with her forehead. She opened her mouth and lunged forwards, biting through her trousers into her leg.

"Ahh you little!" She jumped back, swinging her leg around like crazy, dislodging Valour and letting the woman get to her feet as she rolled her trouser leg up. "Are you crazy?! What kind of silly! Who *bites* someone?!"

'Yeah, fear the jaws! I'm actually getting into this one!'

She lunged forwards and lashed out, hitting Cereza's flat palm, but the woman winced as red bloomed across her skin from impact.

She kicked out and Valour skidded away. "… Not bad." She waved her hand through the air, grimacing as she blew on it. "You know, I think I'm starting to like you. Probably like you even better if you talked to me. Cereza by the way, and you are?"

'Hi, I'm Valour!'

"… Not a talker, huh? Not surprised, 'specially when you're like that."

'But I just—! Oh, wait. Never mind.'

"This has been a nice warm-up and all, but I need to get going. I have a plan in the works, and I need to get back to planning it out. Sorry, but lights out for now."

She waved her hands forwards and small flashes of light congregated in her palms. A small whisper she couldn't hear later and they shot out. She twisted her body and the lights flashed past. She crouched and prepared to lunge, but was thrown off by her smile.

'I get a bad feeling every time she does that. I sincerely doubt it's due to joy—'

The lights smacked into her back and the back of her head, and everything went blank.

32. In the Dark

Vivian had a bad feeling. It only got worse as they approached the treeline. Raven tensed and then started running. "What's happening?" she asked Bastian, who was going pale.

"That's... that is not good," he murmured, quickening his own pace.

Vivian burst into a sprint. There was only one thing that could have them both worried like that. She ignored Bastian's warnings and exited the forest in time to see Valour struck by light and fall limply to the ground.

Raven charged forwards with a yell, drawing the newcomer's attention away from her, but Vivian was stuck. She couldn't move. She couldn't speak. She couldn't breathe. She just saw Valour falling on replay, over and over, paling as she saw her state and almost crying out when she couldn't see her left arm.

"W-what?"

Bastian gasped behind her and then hurried over. He checked her pulse, checked her breathing and when he sighed in relief, Vivian felt her body relax. He moved the cloth of her shirt carefully away from the wound and recoiled when small sparks flew off the healed skin.

"This is light..." He straightened up and stared as Anthony shuffled over to him.

"Is she alright?" he asked nervously. "I, I managed to do her arm, but Malachite hit her with something that knocked her out. Is, is she alright?"

Something in Bastian's gaze softened. "Yes, I believe so. But, where is the limb? If we get it back, we can still reattach it!"

Anthony winced. "The werewolf... was lost in his animalistic side. He treated it like a stick."

Her knuckles cracked as her fists clenched.

"I... I see. That is unfortunate." He ran a hand over her forehead. "All physical damage is going to heal perfectly fine."

"Physical," Anthony noted quizzically.

"Her arm was taken in an act of savagery. I will say no more, but we must move her to somewhere safe. What is happening over there?"

Her head twitched.

"Cereza Malachite. She saved Valour from anything further, but I don't trust her. And I don't think Raven's going to let up any time soon."

Vivian stood up and ran for the fight.

The woman, Cereza, was matching Raven blow for blow, a serious grimace on her face. The two clashed, arms locked together as they pushed. "Enough!" She slammed into them both, knocking them off their feet with undignified yelps.

"Raven! Valour needs us! This is no time to be fighting her!"

Raven rolled to his feet, crouched and glared at Cereza. "Kid, I know you don't know who this is, but trust me when I say we really shouldn't turn our backs on her."

Cereza got up more smoothly, taking her time and leaning back in a casual way, even as she eyed him. "The kid is correct. I have no wish to fight here. I realised my time was wasted the second I laid eyes on the boy. I will take my leave. Have the Light Chosen confirm my departure."

She walked backwards slowly, until she was a good distance away, then spun around on her foot and blurred away, faint violet trails disappearing quickly behind her.

Raven waited a few seconds, then turned and they jogged over to Valour. "Damn it," he whispered, carefully picking her up and holding her against his chest. "We make for the hills, make camp and see what more we can do."

***

"First time I've ever seen you defeated," Bastian commented, groaning as he sat down. "Damn these bones," he grumbled. "Looks like I'm retiring sooner rather than later."

"This was my fault," he muttered, unable to take his eyes off the two of them. Valour was lying down on the grass, resting her head on a pillow of shirts. "This has happened before, but it's the first time it's hit this hard."

"Because she's a child," Bastian murmured. "Because you care for her, and are close to her. We both are, me more so, obviously. I have time on you and you're relatively new. But she's been injured more in the past few weeks than she has in all her previous years."

Raven frowned. "I understand the arm, but clearly she's had to have been knocked around a bit before."

Bastian stared at him weirdly. "I beg your pardon?"

"I remember my own training, wasn't *that* far off of soldier training, and I went to bed every night covered in bruises, broken bones in some cases."

"Well, yes, but that's training to be a soldier, a warrior."

Raven returned the weird look and then had a thought. A terrifying thought. He gulped down his sudden nervousness. "Bastian, how much combat training has Valour had?"

Bastian looked at him, confused. "None. Why do you ask?" His heart dropped. "Well, she chopped down and collected trees for the carpenters in the village, so she had a bit of physical conditioning." He felt like he'd been dropped in icy water.

"You're telling me I brought a civilian into a battlefield, more than one battlefield actually, and then left her alone with an incompetent telling her to only act in self-defence against someone we knew was a violent man with a history of attacking her?"

"I did think that was a bit strange, yes."

"And why," he paused to take a breath, "did you not tell me this?"

"Well, I thought it was obvious at first. Also, I don't know if you noticed, but I didn't like talking to you in general to start with." He rolled his shoulders and grimaced, "Still don't, if I'm honest."

"Oh my gods, I've made a terrible mistake."

"How bad?"

"I saw her enhanced strength and speed, assumed magic and believed she must've been trained. I saw her performance against the transformed werewolf and *complimented* whoever taught her."

"Well, in a roundabout way, you complimented her. She is self-taught after all."

"Oh my gods, I've made a terrible mistake."

"It's not as bad as you think."

"I recklessly endangered the life of a 16-year-old *child*. I brought her to fights that I didn't know she couldn't handle and let her go off with two others because I believed that their training could make up for their lack of experience."

Bastian frowned at him. "Now hold on. She is capable. She can switch her mindset to her instincts and hold her own against multiple foes."

"But that's a problem as well, isn't it?" Anthony said, collapsing in a heap beside them. "She attacked me, because she instinctively labelled me as a threat. If Cereza weren't there, I'd have died." He blankly stared at Raven. "I heard you call me incompetent by the way. You're right, but screw you for saying it out loud."

They watched him groan in pain and roll himself over, away from their conversation and trying to find a somewhat decent place to sleep.

"Something happened. He's broke," Bastian murmured in worry.

"Yeah. One problem at a time though." He buried his face in his hands and groaned, and then threw his head back. "Oh gods, why is this hitting me so hard?!"

Bastian sighed, shaking his head. "I've already told you. I'm not repeating myself. Our only problem is what are we going to do now?"

***

Nothing is wrong.

'Shut up.'

You are worrying over nothing.

'I said shut up.'

The Light cannot mislead you. It goes against its very core. Deception is of the Dark.

'And yet, it seems the Premise have no problems lying to me.'

You would believe your sworn enemy?

'I would believe the facts, when they are laid out in front of me so obviously.'

…

'… Figures.'

He stared at the sky, hoping to find some kind of peace, but no matter how beautiful they were, the stars just hurt his eyes. He closed them tight. Incompetent? Yeah, he hadn't really shown otherwise. He'd been uncaring, unsympathetic, tried to close himself off, but it didn't work.

'Have you ever known yourself to be nothing?'

…?

'Have you ever been just another face, someone wandering around day in, day out, just repeating the same thing, over and over? Someone with no purpose, just bored but waiting for that one moment when you can prove to yourself that your life had meaning, that you weren't just wasting everyone's time with your existence?'

…

'Of course not. You're just a voice in my head, and I was just another guy, waiting to die. Until that light. Until I was chosen. Suddenly, that moment was thrust upon me, and I could prove to not only myself, but everyone. And then, that one, *bloody* question came, and kept coming. What did you do, that was so momentous, that you were chosen by the Light? What great feat brought the eyes of the closest things to gods we have, on someone like you?'

I hear you.

'So desperate to prove myself, I threw aside everything I was. Even when I was nothing, I had something. My pride, my conduct, and I threw it away. And no one said, *anything.* Just looked at me as though they were surprised it didn't happen sooner. A few years of that, and then I get the opportunity of a lifetime.'

A mission. The youngest Chosen to be sent out of Premise lands, to purge the Dark from a valuable foothold.

'And like a desperate fool, I didn't question anything. And it only took other people noticing the obvious and slapping me in the face with it. Bait, huh? Is that all I'm worth? Is that all I'll ever amount to?'

No. You are a Chosen. All you need—

'Is a moment to prove myself? You've said that before. How many times I've forgotten. This was my chance, everyone said so, and look how it's turned out.'

... I'm sorry.

'Yeah?' He discretely reached up to brush away a single tear. 'Me too.'

***

The next morning, Raven couldn't do anything but stare. Valour was sitting up, pale faced and staring at her shoulder. Vivian was sitting behind, arms wrapped around her in a tight hug and whispering to her.

"I have led people into battles, that have resulted in worse wounds than this and not blinked an eye. I have caused wounds like these and never looked back."

"I'm aware," Bastian grunted. "One difference between then and now? You care. And it's only when we see the pain inflicted on someone we care about, that the true horrors are realised like knives in your heart."

"It was war."

"An inevitable one, yes. I still remember that day, you know? The day I started questioning everything."

"And the relevance?"

"None. I just want you to know, that you pretty much ruined my life and caused me to get banished from the only home I ever knew." Raven twitched and stared at him incredulously. "And I thank you for it."

"You're... welcome?"

"I never would have met Valour and Lydia, I never would have had a life outside the Premise, the pain and anguish. I have a library now. Granted, I was banished and forced into it, but it grew on me. It has its charms."

"Okay? What's the point of all this?" he gestured awkwardly at him.

"The point, is that life's greatest joys sometimes come from the unexpected. What seems like a branch from your path, sometimes becomes a road to something greater than you had ever hoped." Bastian clapped Raven's shoulder, smiled at him and walked over to Valour.

"... I knew he still hated me. Wasted however many minutes of my life, just to give me some advice for a completely different situation." He sighed. "But, it *did* help me focus. And decide."

***

Raven sat down in front of the gathered group. Anthony was on his left, looking like he was trying to hide how sad he currently was. Bastian was on his right, studying the boy like he was a particularly annoying puzzle.

And across from him, Valour and Vivian hadn't moved from their previous spot.

"We're heading back to Solitude," he announced, getting everyone's attention. "We are unprepared for what we will be facing. Our enemy has weapons we don't know about, both living and material. We, no, I jumped into this underestimating them, and overestimating us. For that, I am so sorry. I put you all at risk doing this, and I was... so wrong. I can't even find a comparison. I need to come up with a plan moving forwards, something that utilises everything we have." He hesitated and looked at Valour mournfully. "But, I need to know this. Are you all still willing to fight with me?"

"I am," Anthony immediately said, but his voice was subdued, as was his expression. Something about the grim way he set his mouth unsettled him.

"I began this journey, because I desired justice," Vivian said. "Only now do I realise that I had fallen for the ivory cloak that vengeance wears. I wish to continue, but I choose to do so now to protect what they seek to destroy." She smiled as he looked at her in confusion. "So long as I have strength enough to move, I will stand by this cause."

"I won't be good for a fight," Bastian grumbled, "and I may slow you down, but I'll keep you going as long as I can."

Raven nodded and looked to Valour. "... I want to keep going, but I need answers first. Answers and..."

"Time," Raven added. "You will have both, I swear. I'm sorry, that I still need you. I wish you will never have to raise your fists again, but this world won't allow that. Where there is life, there will always be conflict. But I can do my damned hardest to make sure you can give as good as you get."

***

It was four days later that they practically stumbled back home. Lydia greeted them with a smile, which quickly turned into a look of horror and a scream as she saw Valour's state. Vivian took Valour to her room as the woman started yelling at Bastian and Raven, who just stood there with bowed heads and arms crossed behind their backs.

She stormed out of the house, to the surprise of them both, and Raven followed after her but kept an obvious distance.

He followed her all the way to the edge of the village and had a strange thought that she was going to leave and track down Plato to finish him off. Raven scowled and took out his flask, rolling it around in his hands as he remembered planning to do just that himself.

It was Bastian who talked him out of it and he cursed himself because this would mean abandoning the kids he'd grown fond of. He chuckled and took the smallest sip from the flask. Because isn't that a kicker? Actually caring about someone and not because his life depended on their survival.

He watched as Lydia stopped at the border and she was joined by someone. He narrowed his eyes but couldn't make out any details, just blonde hair and a lot of green. They spoke for maybe a few seconds and then the blonde sprinted back the way she came, into the woods.

A few seconds later, a green blur as large as a house broke through the canopy and soared away through the sky.

"Close your mouth, you'll catch flies," Lydia scorned him as she strode past, giving him an angry look.

"You know one of *them*?" he muttered, following after her loosely.

"Obviously. How do you think I was able to take care of Valour?"

"Honestly, that one did make me scratch my head for a bit, but then I stopped caring. Bigger issues and all that."

"Sorry, but if you're hoping for an exposé, there's a line," she drawled sarcastically.

"Of course," he murmured, fully understanding. He scratched at the flask with a fingernail, tossing a look over his shoulder.

"Don't worry, she's not breaking the Treaty. She's an enforcer. She just comes along for updates to pass along." Lydia glanced down at the flask and grimaced at the smell. "I'm an accomplished alcoholic, and I've never smelled anything like that. What is it?"

He stuttered, "O-oh, sorry," and quickly screwed the lid back on. "I helped someone out a few years back. At that point, I was just carrying this thing," he rattled the flask, "without anything in it. He told me bluntly that it was pretty pathetic, and that as a reward for helping, he'd give me some 'home-brewed whisky.'" He smirked. "A day later, I took my first sip, and blacked out instantly."

Lydia whistled. "Lightweight, or?"

He laughed. "Nah. Turns out the guy I helped was Oélthrinír. And not just that, but the supplier for the Day Court itself. That sip knocked me out, and when I woke up, I was shirtless and shoeless in a field, holding this thing and clutching a sword I'd never seen before in my life. There was also a goat statue, and uh…" he actually blushed as he admitted, "there was also a bell. From a church tower."

"Ha!" She slapped her knee and cackled. "The thing that's twice the size of ya?! How in the hell!"

"Trust me, if I knew, I'd tell ya," he grimaced. "Gods, the fines I got almost made me want to fake my own death again. But, it did teach me moderation, so all's well if it ends well, I guess."

Lydia chuckled and then locked up. Raven flinched but relaxed when he saw she was just in the throes of another vision. She sagged a few seconds later, rubbing her head with a pained grimace, and scowled.

"The same again? What the hell is happening?"

Raven shrugged. "Couldn't tell you. When we were there, nothing special was happening, and the only thing abnormal about the place was the tower. Nothing that would explain anything."

"Hmm." She shook it off, the feeling that it was important wasn't going away, but they had more important things to worry about.

***

"I want to apologise."

Bastian glanced at Anthony over his shoulder, hearing his words and feeling doubt, but the look on the kid's face was tragic. If anything but the truth was being spoken, it was hidden to him.

"I see." He turned to place a book from his pile onto the shelf. He checked the name of the next one and moved to place it a few shelves down. "What for, may I ask?"

With a clenched fist, Anthony pulled a book from the pile and placed it on another shelf. "Everything, I guess." Rubbing the back of his neck, he glanced away with shame and embarrassment. "For the way I talked to you, for the way I acted, for everything. I'm sorry."

"As you should," he said back. "You were arrogant, condescending, unempathetic and acted in a way that disgraced all the tenants taught by the Premise. Well, while I was there at least." He didn't look back, not needing to see the look on his face to know his words struck like a physical blow. "But I understand."

"W-wait, what?" he asked, baffled, turning around to fully face his back.

"I understand, though I do not condone it, obviously. I know what it's like to feel as though you were not enough. To feel like you are just a piece on the board to be used and tossed aside on a whim. I was a healer, forced to fight on the frontlines. No combat training or anything, and when I got home, I confided in who I thought was a friend, and they turned me in. I was brought before the Council, reprimanded and banished. Lost my home, my purpose, and all of my friends in one fell swoop."

"What was it that was so bad? I mean no offense, but a punishment that great surely befits a crime on the scale of... well, it had to have been big," he finished lamely.

"... On my first and final mission, after the bombardment destroyed the tower and killed the Dark Lord, I almost died as well. I'll save you the gruesome details, but I was able to keep my organs and blood in place through obscene amounts of healing magic, and the exhaustion nearly finished me off. But then, I saw someone coming through the dust, climbing over the wreckage. I knew it wasn't one of my squad, they'd died already, so I thought that was it. I'd just wasted my magic and I was going to die exhausted and tired."

"That's pretty morbid."

"Don't interrupt me kid. I control how hard your job is while you're here. Where was I? Ah yes, he came through the smoke and I thought I was dead. He saved my life, dragged me out to the bailey and told me he saved my life. I thought that was obvious and he'd taken a blow to the head, but then he invoked a life debt."

He pushed up the sleeves of his shirt and pointed to extremely faint lines on his forearm. Too intricate and specific to be veins, they coiled around like they were trying to be a picture. "He looked me dead in the eye, and ordered me to tell all who asked that the people died when the fortress fell. He told me to identify no one, to keep their identities close. He put it more detailed than that, but you get the gist.

"I was unable to tell my friend the cause of my doubt, but I asked her whether the Ring could have good people in it. If, in the armies of darkness, there could be a few rays of light. She called me a heretic, slapped me, and accused me of turning my back on everything we fought for. She stormed out, but I naively thought it was just a fight, and we'd make up and go back to being friends again the next day. Obviously, that didn't happen."

Anthony nodded slowly. "If there was a life debt, how are you saying any of this now?"

"I met the guy a while back. He saw the pitiful position I was in, and released me from it. Said all debts were more than paid, and what's done is done."

"I see," he murmured. "Is it really that easy to forgive someone? I mean, I understand he saved your life, but then using that to force you into something that got you banished, it's just... hard for me to imagine."

"First of all, his actions didn't get me banished. It was my reaction to a situation I found implausible. My decision to tell someone that was clearly more loyal to the Premise than to me. Sure, I like to guilt him a lot, but that's mostly because it's hilarious. Do I forgive him? I did, yes. I may not like him for it, but I do understand it. He was ensuring the safety and protection of all those who survived the explosion. I can hardly fault him for that."

"How did they survive? I know about that weapon, and I've seen the ruined fortress it left behind. How many survived? And how did they survive?"

Bastian shrugged blithely, "Who knows. Far as I'm aware, everything and everyone was buried in the rubble." He smirked with a mischievous twinkle in his eyes.

33. What Am I?

When they entered the house, Lydia walked straight over to Valour and Vivian. She spoke quietly and Raven didn't even try listening in. He leaned against the wall and rolled his flask around in his hands, not for the first time wishing he wasn't in a potentially dangerous situation.

He'd already bent that rule once and regretted it, though as he watched Lydia and Valour move upstairs, he bit back a smile and found he didn't wish for all of it to have never happened. He watched Vivian, smiling reassuringly at Valour until they both left her sight, and her face fell.

He watched her shuffle about, looking up at the ceiling not longingly and with a curiosity he knew well. She eyed him with surprise as he sat down next to her with a huff and uncapped his flask. He didn't take a drink but, when she smelled it, her eyes flashed and he held back a small smile.

"Oélthrinír whisky," he supplied, and then recapped it. "An old friend gave it to me after I helped him out of a spot. I learned quite a bit about his species that day. Mannerisms, peculiarities, the instincts, all of them very different from humans. Of course, you couldn't spot an Oélthrinír, their disguises are perfect." He glanced at her out of the corner of his eye. "Except for when they're under the night sky."

"So you know," she murmured. She was surprised at her own indifference. It was supposed to be a great secret but, right now, she didn't really care. Maybe it was the situation, maybe it was the company, who knows.

"Yup. Had you pegged the first time I saw you. That glow, leftover Oélthrinír magic. Recognised it instantly."

She sighed deeply. "Then perhaps you can gift me another perspective."

He shrugged, "I'll try my best, kid."

"When I transform, everything changes. I become something, more inclined to violence." Raven twitched and put his flask on the table, turning to her fully with wide eyes. "When we met an assassin back in Senway, my other self punished him. He not only kidnapped Valour, but he insulted my appearance. When 'I' came back, I saw the state he was in, but I could not do anything about him. Something wasn't letting me."

"A curse?" Raven murmured. "If your magic was used to do so, then it stands to reason that your magic was against the idea of helping someone who necessitated something like that."

"And when that golem attacked us at the tower, I cursed it after it attacked Valour and made her bleed. Then I sent it somewhere, though I don't really know where."

"... I see. Tell me, what do you know about the Oélthrinír?"

She shrugged and a bitter expression crossed her face. "Little to nothing. Only fairy tales, anything else was deemed too dangerous for me to know."

He nodded. "I can understand their hesitance, but there are some things both safe, and necessary. Let's start with the Day Court. Made up of the Väéthrinír, the spirits that rule the day. Led by their queen, they are... neutral, is the best way to put it. They don't act on violent urges, and they have a unique kind of magic. It's something more powerful, closer to the gods than any other. Think, along the lines of powerful Chosen."

"That's terrifying," she deadpanned.

"Oh yeah, you don't know the half of it, kid. You don't need to know much, the Väéthrinír have pretty much secluded themselves, finding their own land and ordeals more interesting than the human realm."

"Okay, but what does that have to do with me?"

"... Pretty much everything. Whose blood runs in your veins?"

"Alysiia, the enchantress of the Day Court."

Raven winced. "Okay, that actually explains everything. Your mother, is the reason the Day Court was able to secure a forceful ceasefire with their counterparts."

"Wait, what?" She looked at him, confused. "Ceasefire? Counterparts? I know nothing of either."

He looked away, quietly cursing. "Of course you don't," he sighed. "Then let me tell you, about the Aélthrinír. They don't have a court, per se, they have a queen. They have soldiers, and she has a palace. As a people, they are passionate, driven, loyal to their own. And they are easily influenced by their emotions. Anger, jealousy, love and joy. Trample on their pride, and retribution will be swift."

"So what makes them different, is their emotions?" she murmured in confusion.

"Sort of. It's the fact they're so close to them, that is the problem. When the Day Court was reached out to by Uru Almesh, remember the city with the tower on the cliff? Well, when the Night Court didn't receive a message as well, they felt slighted and cast the curse, which led to the tower being built to counter it. The Day were keener to interact with species outside their own, whereas the Night were more guarded. Can't speak for them now, the Day didn't really talk about them."

"I see," she said, contemplating the words in her head. "So the Night are not evil, just prone to losing themselves to their emotions?"

He smiled faintly at her hopeful tone, "They're not evil, they don't conform to human views of good and bad. See, a curse like that, one that made those people ill? It would have been a humorous prank for one of them. Immortal beings that don't get sick or age, it would have just made them some kind of loopy."

"So they didn't know it would actually kill them?"

"No, I don't believe so."

Vivian frowned, "So they put a curse on a land not knowing the effects it would have on them. Isn't that a form of neglect? Just because you don't understand the situation, doesn't mean you are without fault if you carry out careless and uninformed actions. You should wait and do research or, better yet, do nothing at all. Leave it lie, and someone wishes to make friends that aren't you? Don't allow yourself to fall to jealousy."

Raven blinked and then slowly nodded. "I agree. Neglect, huh? Sounds like you're doing a bit of parroting there."

She blushed and looked away. "I am. Valour spoke with me about... an issue. I was trying to comfort her and, for some reason, she took it to be the most appropriate time to speak on it. Her words were... enlightening, to say the least. It gave me a new perspective, and I need to talk with my father, to have an overdue conversation."

She grimaced, not looking forwards to it. "Alright, just go easy on the guy. I've seen him looking at the two of you, and whatever mistake he made, I'm sure it was only out of fear and wanting what was best for you. That tends to blind someone to the faults in their thinking and, when you break it to him, do it gently."

"I will. But back to the courts, what is this about a ceasefire? Shouldn't the emotions of the Night cause them to doubt the Day, or even scorn them?"

Raven chuckled. "It was quite the lucky stroke, actually. See, when the plan was proposed, the Night didn't want to accept. The queen insulted the Day, and informed them that, should a single denizen of the night be willing, the Treaty would hold. She, and almost every other Aélthrinír, believed that none of them were willing to coexist. And then, Alysiia stepped forwards. She declared her desire for peace, and upheld the terms of the Treaty. The queen was distraught and betrayed, and sent her away to the Day Court."

"So what were the terms? The fighting between Day and Night would stop, and they wouldn't interfere with the humans?"

"Not quite. The fighting would stop, yes, but they were allowed to fight in self-defence. They can interact with the human realm, but they lost interest a while ago."

"But if they did that, then how am I here?" she asked, confused.

"I don't know, kid. That's a question for your parents." His gaze softened as her shoulders slumped down, a look of sadness in her eyes. "I'm sorry. But know that you're Alysiia's daughter. She was able to control her impulses and gained peace between two warring realms. You can do the same."

He grinned, then faltered, "Gain control, I mean. Well, I don't doubt you could do the peace thing as well, but I don't really want to put you in the kind of situation where you'd have to, you know?"

She nodded with a small smile and then turned back to him curiously. "How do you even know about all of this? The Oélthrinír, Day and Night, the ceasefire, I highly doubt it is all common knowledge."

"Let's just say I have a few connections, and I've had more than one adventure with the Day Court. The guy I helped recommended me, and you can't really refuse a request from Queen Bellatone herself."

"But that doesn't explain your knowledge of the Night Court. Like you said, the Day doesn't speak of them, so how did you know?"

He sighed, rolling his eyes as he cursed Vivian's accurate point. Of all the times for a teenager to be willing to listen to a somewhat boring story, it had to be one of the few times when he contradicted himself.

"That's, entirely fair. Look, when I was younger, I gained access to a library with quite a few lost texts." He stared blankly at a wall, eyes fogging over as he thought back. "I was taken in after an incident, by a seemingly nice person. He was a collector of sorts, and he requested I read a few specific tomes as part of my home education."

She was about to ask more, but, looking at him, she didn't think her line of questioning would be welcomed right now. He looked in pain and was rubbing at his chest like there was a physical wound. So she bowed her head and stowed her curiosity, willing to wait for a better time.

***

As Valour followed Lydia up the stairs, her mind was whirring. Her feet felt heavier, she felt that thing in the back of her throat like a tiny pebble beneath her skin. It was part of her, thanks to whatever had happened during the last fight, but also it was so shockingly new that it disturbed her.

When her grandmother came up to her and told her it was time for answers, she'd entered into something almost like a trance. She had so many imagined scenarios of how this could go, so many ideas and theories, not all of them good.

And yet, none of her imaginings began like this.

They entered Valour's room and Valour sat on her bed. Then, Lydia walked up to the wall above her headboard and pulled a section of it away, revealing a glass bottle.

"Uh, granny?" The woman hummed as she checked the label. "Why is there alcohol hidden in my wall?"

"Had to figure out a way around that nose somehow, didn't I? I gave up, of course, just ended up getting rid of everything alcoholic in the house. Little you sniffed out this stuff like a bloodhound. Actually forgot about this thing 'til I cleaned the place out after we moved in."

"Okay, but we've never lived in this house before, so why would you put it here?"

"Come now, dear, why do you think we moved to this house specifically?"

"Because everyone moved away from us because they were scared and superstitious, and no one would say anything if we did end up moving in here?"

"Good point, and yes kind of, but also no. I had a feeling we might've been attacked one day, so I stocked up a few of the spare houses as decoys, and then built a bunker outside the village border. This is one of the more habitable decoys."

"You have a *bunker*?! Where, why, how did you build it? Did you have a vision about needing it?!"

"Nope, and that actually ties in with what we need to talk about." She unscrewed the lid and took a sip. "Wow, actually awful. I'll admit, didn't expect that." She put the lid back on, tossed it back in the wall and shut the partition.

"I'm sorry, I'm still stuck on the bunker part. What in the hell?!"

"Some 18 or so years ago," she began, completely ignoring Valour's question, "I took a walk in the woods. I had a vision that something out there would be important. And it was in the shrubbery, almost perfectly camouflaged, that I found a woman. She was injured, so I took her home and fixed her up."

"Why didn't you take her to a healer?" Valour asked.

Lydia scowled at her, but the effect was ruined by the embarrassed flush and grimace. "I was a bit... arrogant, back then. I thought that, if I didn't have a vision of her dying on my table, then everything was gonna be fine. I fixed her up and, when she woke up, we got to talking. Well, after she tried to kill me and failed, pulling all her stitches and nearly bleeding out on my floor. But we talked and eventually became friends. She visited me often over the next 2 years, until that moment 16 years ago. She showed up at my doorstep, terrified out of her mind. I knew she was pregnant, see, but she was so happy she told me she forgot the ramifications. Half-breeds aren't looked upon favourably here."

"I'm half human," Valour acknowledged.

"Yes. And not just here. Her species is vain and prideful, even your mother to some extent, though she and her group are more tempered and caring of 'outsiders' than the rest. See, if one of them knew you existed, it wouldn't be long before hell was thrown onto you. They'd kill your mother for 'the betrayal' and would take you back where they'd raise you, but it wouldn't be nice or a happy life. So she begged me to take you in, and then left the country to grow strong enough to where, when she did claim you as hers, no one would dare try and harm a hair on your head."

"I see. So I'm half human. But what else? You keep dancing around the name, even that Malachite lady did it. Why?"

"Because when you know what you are, it has an effect on you. It changes your magic, sends up a flare, many times more than now. You are safe here. I promise I will tell you, after Raven trains you."

Valour nodded. "Okay then. Is that it?"

Lydia frowned, "It? Don't you have more questions?"

"Not any you can answer, but honestly? Right now, I'm just tired. My arm itches," she winced and Lydia flinched. "My head hurts. I've been feeling aches and pains for a while now, and I just want to sleep." She lay back dejected and saddened.

"I see. I'm sorry I can't tell you more, but it isn't my place." Lydia bowed her head, grimacing.

"It's fine." She gave her a wobbly smile, "Really. Just adds a few more questions to the list."

Her grandmother got up and headed for the door, but paused before she left. "I want you to know," she murmured softly, "that taking you in, raising you, loving you. That was the first decision I'd ever made on my own. No vision told me it would make me happy or live longer. I didn't care where it would lead me. I held you in my arms that day, and knew I would love you until the end."

Valour looked over her shoulder shyly and gave her the biggest smile she could.

***

Vivian jumped up when Lydia walked into the room and sat down with a huff. "Go on," she muttered, "she'll probably want an ear that isn't us." Vivian sprinted for the stairs and took them two at a time.

"Everything go alright?"

Lydia huffed. "Better than I imagined," she murmured, still in shock and disbelief. "Thought for sure she'd throw a few choice words my way, but she took it... well, more maturely than *I* would've at least. She's alright with waiting."

"She's smart, and grown up for a kid," he smirked. Then the humour slipped away as he asked, "Anything different about the visions?"

She shook her head. "No. Same thing, over and over. I force visions 'til I can't handle any more, but they're all the same. I'm lost on what it could mean, but that's because I don't want to consider the alternative."

Raven grimaced as she turned to him and let him see just how scared she was. "The Final Moment. Something's happened, something's triggered it. The apocalypse, the end of it all. I just wish Seren didn't cause it. Gods, it would annoy the hell out of me if he did."

"So what do we do?"

"The first plan failed. We couldn't kill Seren. We tried to kill Plato, but he's slippery, escaped everything we tried to throw at him."

"Oh, don't worry about him for now." Raven paused and looked at her questioningly, but she just smiled.

"Okay... we don't know how many golems Seren has made, we know about the teleporting cat thing he has, but not what it's for other than getting him out of danger. I know about Barney, or 'Savage' as he calls himself, but not where he is or what he's doing. We don't know their plans, save the end, when they destroy everything."

Lydia's grimace grew worse as he went on, and, when he finally stopped, she chuckled bitterly. "That's a lot of potential. Are you sure you can take a break here?"

"Don't have a lot of choice. I'm waiting for everyone to heal, then I'm giving them a few crash courses. We have Rosalina and the Senway coven looking for them, so I'm going to leave it to them for now. I don't like this, stopping before we've really accomplished anything, but sometimes that's how it goes. We run out of steam and we have to stop with nothing to show for it."

"Well," Lydia smirked, folding her arms and leaning back. "I wouldn't say we have nothing."

34. Epilogue – The Bar

Plato snarled angrily as he slammed a dagger through the painfully accurate drawing, pinning it to the wall. He let go of the handle with an anguished roar, his skin sticking to the leather, and cursed her name again, glaring at the charcoal girl.

A week. It took him a whole blasted week to get back, even with all the power at his disposal. He entered the city without issue, entered his bar without issue, locked it all up and placed the 'CLOSED' sign out front and finally collapsed in searing agony.

The fire not only hurt him, but it was stopping him from healing as quickly as usual. So he was stuck feeling every moment of hurt. He crawled over to the bar and grabbed a bottle from behind the counter, and slumped against it to numb the pain.

He sniffed, grinning when the sour scent blocked out that faint smell of smoke he'd been irritated by for a few minutes now. He took a swig and sighed as he relaxed.

The handle turned and he flinched as the lock broke. The door swung wide open and in came the methodical steps, an iron thunk with a feather-soft tap. The swirl of ash sent across the room by the floor-length dark-blue duster coat tickled his nose, and, with a sneeze, he growled and pushed himself up.

"Didn't you see the sign? We're clo—" his throat bulged as he choked on the words he forced himself to swallow.

The woman glanced at him once and then sauntered over to the wall. *Thunk, tap, thunk, tap* She reached out to the picture on the wall and caressed the image with a soft look in her red eyes. She pulled the knife free of the wood, catching the picture before it could fall.

She walked over to Plato, stopping a few feet away, and held the paper to her chest, right over her heart. To him, that was a clear sign. She folded it gently and placed it in the pocket of her coat.

"Sh-she's yours?! P-please, I-I didn't know! I'd never have messed with her!" *Thunk* He fell to the floor screaming, blood spraying from his shoulder, his severed arm hitting the ground.

She turned in disgust, walking towards the door and then half turned, flinging her arm out. She smirked and spat on the floor, leaving the building behind, its owner pinned to the bar by the long knife lodged in his eye.

***

The street was on fire.

She pulled the picture out of her pocket and stared down at it blankly, but, against her will, a small smile curled her lip and she felt a warmth in her chest she hadn't felt in 16 years.

"Boss." She nodded but didn't look up. "Area's secure. Rathi's holding back the vampires, but the big one's kicking up a fuss. Got about thirty seconds before she breaks through the shield." Despite the urgency of his words, the jade-haired man looked amused.

"We move. They are my daughter's allies. We shan't move on them."

"Allies? Vampires?" A blue-haired man laughed as he jumped down from the rooftop. "Damn, kid's a riot! I'm actually proud of the little tyke, long way from a lumberjack!"

"Of course," jade-haired man snaps back, straightening himself with a proud smile. "She's one of ours, of course she's a prodigy!"

A green-haired woman appeared next to the blue-haired man with an eager smile on her face. "Are we talking about her? She's had a fair few adventures over the past weeks, and she's proven herself a great warrior and! An excellent diplomat as well. She is part of a group with two trained wizards, a Light Chosen *and* a daughter of the Night!"

"She'll learn a lot from them. But she'll truly come into her own when she stops relying on her instincts and learns to use her magic."

"She works with what she has," green-haired woman snaps back. "And it'll work for now. The black-haired man apparently believed her to have advanced training already, so he will be teaching her."

"Already believed?" the blue-haired man grinned, "Hell yeah, hatchling's a badass!" he crowed.

"Excuse me." They all paused as Lady Rosalina glided towards them, her dress lifted up so as not to trail in the ash.

"Oh crap, we got so caught up praising the kid we forgot to get out of here," the jade-haired man deadpanned.

"Sacrifices must be made and the priorities will always be clear!" the blue-haired man hissed, raising his fist in some kind of gesture.

"You have attacked this city. Unfortunately, it happens to be the one that resides above my territory. What intentions do you have here?"

"Do not worry, coven elder," the jade-haired man rumbled. "Our business here is done. The owner of that establishment grievously injured one of our own. We were paying back the favour."

"I see. And whom did he injure? To my knowledge, you all look fine."

"My daughter," the woman in the blue coat spoke up.

Rosalina rolled her eyes, "And where would this daughter be—" She paused, eyes widening as she took her in. "Valour?"

"No," she deadpanned.

"Obviously not," blue-haired man muttered, "One's a child. This one clearly isn't."

"I am Valcien. I am Valour's mother. He took my hatchling's arm, so I took his life." She turned back to the bar and took in a deep breath. Flames poured out of her mouth and she watched in satisfaction as the front wall was knocked inwards, the wood caught alight and, a few seconds later, it all collapsed.

"Let this be a warning to you, Queen of the Damned." Rosalina tensed up but didn't dare move as slitted crimson eyes burned towards her. "I shall not tolerate fatal aggression towards what is *mine*. I know of your nature, and now you shall know mine."

Her body erupted, a great explosion of fire and magic, and the power twisted and coalesced in the air. A great red dragon stretched her wings, knocking houses down either side as she loomed three times greater than the average building. Her mouth opened and a gush of steam rushed out, her eyes blazed red and she roared.

The end

Printed in Great Britain
by Amazon